RECOVERING RITA

A TUPER MYSTERY

TERESA BURRELL

SILENT THUNDER PUBLISHING

COPYRIGHT

This book is a work of fiction. References to real people, events, establishments, organizations, or locales are intended only to provide a sense of authenticity and are used fictitiously. All other characters and all incidents and dialogue are drawn from the author's imagination and are not to be construed as real.

Dedicated to Clarice Preece

You have suffered so much and had so many losses in your life. You didn't deserve another. Covid has been so destructive. I'm deeply sorry it took Ron away from you. May he rest in peace, and your memories of him be only good ones. And I hope you can find solace in your family and friends—all of us who love you so very much.

Acknowledgments

A special thanks to those who made this book possible.

Pat Cox
Clarice Preece

Thank you, **Karen Parrish Baker**, for suggesting the title of this book.

Thank You to My Amazing Beta Readers:

Beth Sisel Agejew
Melissa Ammons
Linda Athridge-Langille
Vickie Barrier
Meli White Cardullo
Janie Greene-Livingston
Crystal Kamada
Sheila Krueger
Rodger Peabody
MaryAnn Schaefer
Colleen Scott
Uma Van Roosenbeek
Brad Williams
Nikki Tomlin
Denise Zendel

OTHER MYSTERIES BY TERESA BURRELL

THE TUPER MYSTERY SERIES

THE ADVOCATE SERIES

CHAPTER 1

Monday morning

Lana looked up from her computer, startled. She turned to Tuper. "Hey, Pops, why is there a horse and buggy outside?"

Tuper stood up from the table and stared out the window. "What in thunder is he doing here?" A man in his early seventies, Tuper wore jeans, a plaid cotton shirt, western boots, a black cowboy hat, and a holster on his belt.

Lana shook her head. "This is the twenty-first century. Isn't the better question: Why is he using a horse and buggy?"

"Good point," Tuper said. "Why *does* he have the buggy?"

Lana watched outside as a bearded old man dressed in plain black and gray clothes and a wide-brimmed hat made his way to the front door. A younger man, dressed similarly but without a beard, remained in the buggy. As a millennial, Lana knew her fashion sense was questionable, but at least she was in this century.

"*Willkommen, Brüderlein,*" Tuper said as he greeted the man.

The familiar German tongue sounded pleasant to Lana's

ears. It reminded her of her grandma who'd never really mastered the English language, or at least not the American accent. Clarice, the woman who owned this home, reminded her a bit of her grandmother, but she was much younger. She was more like an aunt to her—a favorite aunt. Lana listened intently as the men continued to speak in some form of German dialect, understanding most of it.

Tuper switched to English. "Come in. I was just having a cup of tea. Join me."

The man followed Tuper to the table. "Lana, this is Jacob. We go way back."

"Nice to meet you," Jacob said.

"You too."

"Have a seat," Tuper gestured. "The teapot is on."

Lana tried not to stare at Jacob. He looked so different. She'd seen many pictures of Amish people but had never met any. She had so many questions, but she didn't want to embarrass the man. He looked so stoic and almost sad.

Tuper set cups of tea on the table, then sat down. "It's nice to see you, Jacob, but I know you didn't just seek me out for a social call. What's up?"

Jacob glanced at Lana.

"She's okay." Tuper nodded. "Lana's a big help with my work, but if you'd rather talk privately, we can step outside."

"If you trust her, I trust her." Jacob wrapped both hands around the tea mug, holding on tightly. "It is my granddaughter, Rita, Tobias' youngest daughter. She left the *Bruderhof*."

"On her own?"

"I don't think so, but I cannot be certain. She's a rebellious girl and her head is filled with adventurous thoughts. Even as a small child, she wandered away and explored. She always wanted to go to town or wherever anyone was going away from the colony. Unfortunately, she was allowed to go more than she should. Her father hoped it would fulfill her needs, but she only seemed to develop a greater thirst."

"How long has she been gone?"

"Since the night before last, but we do not know where she is, and we are afraid she might be in danger. That is why I am here to get your help. Will you look for her?"

"Of course," Tuper said. "I'll need more information."

Lana opened a document on her computer and started to take notes.

"What's her full name?" Tuper asked.

"Margarete Pullman."

"And her physical description?"

Before Jacob could answer, Lana cut in. "Don't you have a photo of her? That would be best. We can tell a lot from a photo."

Tuper glowered at Lana. "They don't believe in taking photos."

"What's to be—? Never mind. Sorry."

"It is okay," Jacob said. "She is five-four, with long blonde hair, almond-shaped blue eyes, and pale skin. She is way too beautiful for her own good." He paused. "I just mean that she can be a little vain and men stare at her when she goes out in public. It must be hard for her to be humble."

Lana flinched, but kept her comments to herself.

"When exactly did you notice she was missing?" Tuper asked.

"She was there for supper, but she did not return to their room after kitchen chores. Annie P. said Rita took out some trash from the kitchen and that was the last time she saw her. The same with other girls who were working in the kitchen. They did not really notice until they got back to their room and she did not show up. No one seems to know anything else."

"And what if I find her? Do you want me to bring her home?"

"She turned eighteen two days ago. I cannot legally make her come home."

"Didn't ask you that," Tuper said.

Jacob sat in silence.

"If you want me to bring her home, I will. Just tell me what you want."

Lana glared at Tuper, but neither man seemed to notice.

"When you find her, let me know." Jacob closed his eyes. "We will decide then."

The late autumn sun was bright and felt good on Tuper's face as he walked Jacob out. He greeted the young man in the buggy, then turned back to his old friend. "Try not to worry. If it's all right, I'll go to the colony now and ask a few questions."

"I have to stop and take care of something, and then I will be there. I will call my wife and tell her you are coming."

"You have a phone at the house now?"

"Yes. Ever since that problem you had with your friend, Ron, we got a second phone. I carry one with me and one stays at the house. I had to teach Mary how to use it. She does not like it much, but I think she feels a little safer."

"Does anyone else use it?"

"No one is allowed except with permission."

"Tell Mary I'll be there shortly." Tuper started toward the house, then stopped. "Can Joseph run your errand? You'll get home a lot quicker if you ride back with me in Ringo's car."

Tuper called it that because Ringo, his last dog, had torn up the seats when he was a puppy. "My car is in pretty bad shape, but it can't be as bad as riding all that way in that buggy."

"Are you okay with that?" Jacob asked the young man.

"I can handle it, *Opa*."

"And you do not mind making the drive by yourself?"

"I know the way. I'll be fine." He held back a smile.

"Okay then."

"Let me get my keys and my jacket," Tuper said.

"I'll wait here." Jacob stepped toward the buggy. "I want to go over a few things with Joseph. Take your time."

Tuper turned and went inside.

"That was strange," Lana said, still at the table.

"I'm sure he thought the same about you."

"Is he Amish or something?"

"Hutterite."

Lana was typing almost before Tuper finished the word. He waited for a few seconds, hoping she wouldn't come at him with a lot of questions.

She launched into a summary of her search. "The Hutterites are anabaptists like the Mennonites and the Amish. The Mennonites formed first to avoid religious persecution, and the Amish are an offshoot of them. But the Hutterites formed on their own out of Austria, following a man named Jacob Hutter. They all believe that you shouldn't be baptized until you're an adult and can make your own choice. The biggest difference is that the Hutterites live communally." She paused for a breath. "I wonder what that's like. I don't think I'd like it. I like my own space. Have you ever been to their colony?" Before Tuper could answer, she continued. "And he talks without using any contractions. That's a little odd. Do they all talk like that?" She scowled at

Tuper. "Why would he think I'm strange? He did look at me like I was the odd one."

Tuper tipped his head to the side and gave her a look, hoping she was finished jabbering. "Really? He's a man who lives a plain, simple life. You have bright red hair that sticks up like you just put your finger in an electric socket. You're wearing combat boots and banging away on a machine that I'm sure looks as foreign to him as a UFO."

"Good point. By the way, I found out why they don't take photos. They believe the Bible's second commandment—*Thou shalt not make unto thee any graven image*—prohibits them from taking photographs. Although, in some colonies they allow it as long as the pictures are candid shots. They believe posing for them is the actual sin."

"Agony, I know full well what the Hutterites believe."

"So, how do we find this girl? And what if she doesn't want our help? What if she left because she wanted her own life? It sounds like it wouldn't be much fun living the way they do. I can't blame her for running away." Lana's expression tightened. "Although, maybe she didn't run away. Maybe someone snatched her up. We'd better help. What can we do?"

"*We* don't do anything. I'm gonna go to Little Boulder Colony to see what else I can find out. We don't really have much to go on."

"Did they call the police?"

"I'm sure they didn't. They're not much for outside government help. They prefer to police themselves."

"But they asked for *your* help. Jacob must really trust you." But Lana knew if anyone could find Rita, Tuper could. He seemed to know everyone in the state of Montana, and most of them owed him a favor. He'd even saved her once from being accosted by a drunk cowboy. She hadn't asked for his

6

help, but she was grateful for it, even though she would never admit it to him.

"We go way back."

"How far back? How do you know him?"

Tuper retrieved his jacket from the back of the chair and headed for the door. "I need to go ask some questions."

"Can I go with you?"

"No. You stay here and learn what you can about the Hutterites on that machine. It might help us later."

Tuper opened the door.

"Hey, you didn't answer my question. How do you know Jacob?"

"You're right, I didn't." Tuper walked out.

CHAPTER 2

Monday morning

Twenty minutes later, Tuper and Jacob were headed down Highway 15 outside of Helena in Tuper's beat-up Mazda. "I'm glad you decided to ride with me," Tuper said. "You must be exhausted from the trip this morning." Tuper paused. "Wait a minute. You couldn't have driven that buggy all the way from Great Falls. Even riding hard on a horse woulda took you a day and a half."

"We had the pickup, but it broke down. A farmer loaned us the horse and buggy. Right up ahead is where we stopped."

"And your truck is there?"

"Yes. It would not go any further. I do not know much about fixing vehicles. Benjamin usually does that."

"And the guy just loaned you a horse and buggy?"

"He didn't offer until I told him I was headed to see you and that you would help me find my granddaughter."

"Where's this place exactly?"

"Next right, and then a quick left." Jacob pointed to a farmhouse. "You can see it from here."

Tuper made the turn. "That's Denver's place. Good guy."

Tuper pulled into the yard and parked alongside an old flatbed pickup with a handmade railing. The colony had owned the pickup for twenty years, and it was ancient when they got it. They had no sooner stepped out of the car when the door of the farmhouse opened. A gray-haired, short, stocky man with muscled arms and a farmer's tan greeted them. "Well I'll be, if it isn't the man himself." Denver extended his hand as he walked over. He gave Tuper a vigorous handshake and nodded at Jacob.

"Nice to see you." Tuper grinned.

"You're lookin' good, Toop." Denver patted himself on the stomach. "Not like me. I'm gettin' a bit of a paunch. Poor eatin' habits, I guess. I suppose the couple of extra Bud Lights I've added to my daily routine dudn't help much either."

Tuper glanced at the flatbed. "Thanks for helping Jacob."

"As soon as he said he was headed to see you, I knew he could be trusted. Of course, I would've taken it out of your hide if he'd done me wrong." Denver patted Tuper on the back. "Sure is nice to have some company." His voice softened. "It's mighty lonely around here without my Catherine. It's been over a year, but it dudn't get much easier."

"She was a good woman."

Denver smiled sadly. "She was indeed."

"Hey, do you still have that old buffalo?"

"Yep. Sally's fifteen now and still going strong."

"You're one crazy son-of-a-gun."

"So, I've been told. Are you here to get the pickup?" Denver looked at Jacob. "Where's my horse and buggy?"

"Jacob's grandson is bringing it back, and we're headed to

9

Great Falls to find his granddaughter," Tuper said. "I'll send Squirrely over to have a look at the truck. He's not a bad mechanic. I'd do it myself, but I don't have the time right now."

"No need," Denver said. "I already fixed her. I have a few old junk vehicles here that I was able to scrounge parts from. She's good as new."

"Can we give you a few bucks for your trouble and for the loan of the buggy?" Tuper asked.

"Don't you go insultin' me now. It was the neighborly thing to do and that's what I did."

"Thank you," Jacob said. "Joseph will pick up the truck. Your generosity is much appreciated."

"We'd better go," Tuper said. "Time's wastin'."

"Come back and visit when you can." Denver waved. "If you don't want to see me, at least come visit Sally. She misses you."

Once inside the car, Tuper said, "How are you going to reach Joseph?"

"I left my phone with him. Can I use yours to call him?"

"Of course." Tuper handed over his flip phone.

"Oh, good. I was afraid you might have gotten one of those fancy phones that I do not know how to work."

They spent the rest of the ninety-minute trip mostly talking about Rita and the circumstances around her disappearance. Tuper hoped to learn as much as he could about the girl to help him retrace her steps. He couldn't tell from Jacob's comments whether he believed she had run away or been kidnapped.

CHAPTER 3

Monday morning

The stark, clean buildings in Little Boulder Colony were in a rectangular pattern divided into three rows with a large barn off to the right. Each row was one single building divided into separate apartments. Jacob's living quarters were at the end of the first. His home consisted of one bedroom, a small living room, and a small kitchen/dining area. Next to his room was his office. There were several other rooms that served as storage rooms. The second and third rows were longer buildings than the first. The second row had the dining area and the church, which also served as the school. The building also had a large kitchen, showers, and a craft area, as well as two dormitories for school-age children. The last row was housing for couples with very young children and elders who lived alone or with their spouses. On each end were two dormitories for the teenagers, one for the boys and one for the girls. Tuper felt at home here, but then he had spent part of his youth right here in this colony.

When Tuper and Jacob walked into the *Haushalter's* house, Jacob's wife, Mary, smiled, but her eyes were red and swollen.

"I'm so sorry," Tuper said.

"I'm glad you're here. I know God will take care of Margarete, but He may need your help."

"You know I'll do whatever I can."

"Please have a seat." She gestured to a long wooden table in the small kitchen/dining area. "Can I get you anything?"

"Just some information." Tuper sat down. "Jacob told me what he knows, but I understand you were the last adult to see her."

"That's correct." Mary hovered for a moment, then sat across from him. Jacob excused himself and went to his office.

"Who was in the kitchen with Margarete when she left?"

"All the girls from her dorm—Mary J., Mary B., Helen, Annie P., Magdalena J., Ursula, and Elisabeth J. They were performing their cleanup duties the night before last."

"Did you see them there yourself?"

"Yes. I checked on them after I finished eating. Everyone was gone from the dining area. Mary J. and Magdalena J. finished their duties and left when I did."

"So, that left six girls, including Margarete, who were there when she took the trash outside."

"Yes."

"Could I speak to each of them?"

She got up. "I'll bring them here one at a time."

After Mary left, Tuper stood and paced in the small room. He didn't like to sit much. He thought about stepping outside, but the door opened and Mary walked in with a slightly over-weight young girl of about seventeen.

"This is Annie P.," Mary said. "You remember Tuper?"

"Yes." The girl smiled politely, and her dimples came to life.

"He has some questions for you about Margarete." Mary gestured for the girl to sit, then plopped down next to her.

Tuper worried the girl wouldn't be as open with Mary there, but he didn't ask her to leave. He knew their customs, and if Mary felt she should be present, he wasn't going to oppose her. He didn't bother with any small talk and started right off with questions. "Did you see Margarete leave with the trash?"

"Yes. I was right by the sink putting the last dishes away. Helen helped her gather it up."

"Did Helen go outside with her?"

"No. She offered, but Rita, I mean Margarete, said she didn't need any help."

"You call her Rita?"

"All the girls do."

"Do the adults call her that too?"

"Not so much." Annie P. glanced at Mary, then back at Tuper. "But they're okay with nicknames as long as they're close to the name, nothing *auslandish*. But we're not supposed to use them with the *Welt Leut*. You know, the worldly people, like you." Annie P. smiled again. This time, it appeared more genuine and a little apologetic. "Some of the girls call me 'Smiley' because I smile a lot. It just feels right. But they only do that in our room. We have other nicknames we use for each other sometimes, but only in our dorm."

"Nothin' wrong with that," Tuper said. Mary nodded in agreement. He knew what *Welt Leut* meant, but he didn't think of himself as an outsider, even though he really was. He pushed on. "Did anyone go outside with Rita?" He turned to Mary. "Would you prefer I call her Margarete?"

"No," Mary said. "Jacob and I call her Rita as well. It seems to fit her. And you're,"—she paused—"one of us."

Tuper had a momentary flashback to his childhood, playing with Jacob and his brother, Peter. The memory had faded over the years, but parts of it were etched in his mind like it was yesterday. Annie P.'s voice snapped him out of it.

"No one went outside with her. We were all busy trying to get our chores done so we could get out of the kitchen. It's like that every night."

"You were doing dishes, and Helen was helping with the trash. What were the other girls doing?"

"Elisabeth J. was sweeping the floor."

"What about the other two?"

"Mary B. and Ursula had already left. There were just Helen, Elisabeth J., Rita, and me."

Tuper was glad the group had narrowed. When he finished questioning Annie P., he asked Mary to bring in one of the other two girls. She returned with Elisabeth J., who was about the same age as Annie P., but more solemn. The tall girl was almost statuesque in the way she carried herself.

Mary introduced them and, once again, remained in the room. "Tuper is going to ask you some questions."

"Okay."

"When did you last see Rita?" Tuper asked.

"I don't know. We were all working. I saw her gathering up trash, but I didn't actually see her leave the building. I was sweeping, so I wasn't really watching what the others were doing."

"Who were the last to leave the kitchen?"

"Besides me, there were just Helen and Annie P. When we were done, Margarete had not returned. We waited for a few minutes, then Helen went out to check on her. But she couldn't find her. We figured she had gone straight back to the dorm."

"Is that normal?"

"Sort of. We usually all walk together, but not always, and it was still daylight."

"What did you do then?"

"Annie P. and I went back to the dorm. Helen said she would check again for Margarete, then she went out the back door."

"Was there anything unusual about that?"

"No. Helen and Margarete are best friends."

Tuper found it interesting that the girl continued to call her friend Margarete even though Mary had referred to her as Rita. He wondered if that was because she adhered to the rules more strictly than the others or if it was based on something else. He decided to use the more formal name too. "Has Margarete ever done anything like this before?"

"Not that I know of."

"What did you do when you got back to your dorm?"

"We got ready for evening church services."

"Did Helen come back to the dorm?"

"No. She went straight to the schoolhouse for the service."

"Without Margarete?"

"Yes."

"When was she reported missing?"

"After church. We all talked and decided we'd better tell someone. If the others didn't, I was going to anyway. That's when I went to the *Haushalter*."

"Jacob?"

"Yes. The men all went looking for Margarete, but they couldn't find her."

"What do you think happened?"

"I don't know, but I think Margarete was too interested in the *Welt Leut* world."

"Thank you." Tuper released her.

A few minutes later, Mary returned with Helen, a freckle-faced girl with bushy red hair that struggled to stay under her scarf. At sixteen, she was the youngest of the group, but she could have passed for twelve or thirteen. She appeared more nervous than the others but gave the same account of events.

"You seem a little jittery. Are you okay?"

"I'm worried about Rita. She's my best friend."

"Then it's important that you tell me everything you know."

"I heard Brother Jacob say that if anyone could find her, you could. Can you?"

"I hope so, but I really need your help. Is there anything you're not telling me?"

"No."

Tuper thought he saw her eyes move toward Mary. "You knew her better than anyone," he noted. "Did she have any contact with the *Welt Leut?*"

Helen's freckles blurred as she silently shook her head.

"Why didn't you report her missing before the church service?"

"I went looking for her, but I thought she had just wandered off somewhere. Rita did that sometimes, but she never went very far. She called it her *adventures.*" Helen glanced down at her hands. "By the time I got back, I was almost late for the service. I hoped no one would notice she was missing and that she would be back before church was over. But she wasn't. I didn't want to get Rita in trouble, but Elisabeth J. started asking questions, then reported her missing."

Tuper felt like the girl was holding something back, but he couldn't be certain. He *was* certain that she wouldn't confide in him with Mary in the room. He would have to find another way to get her to talk.

CHAPTER 4

Monday afternoon

After Mary and the girls left, Jacob came into the room.

"Are you sure no one else besides the girls saw Margarete after dinner last night?" Tuper asked.

"We had a meeting, and I asked everyone to come forward if they knew anything. No one saw her take out the trash." Jacob looked stressed. "It is not likely that they would because no one had any reason to be in that area."

"When was the last time she was off the property?"

"She went to Smith's Supermarket with her father last Saturday."

"Can I talk to him?"

"Of course. I will get him."

Jacob returned momentarily with a tall, lanky man in his mid-forties, accompanied by a slender woman with deep-set eyes and full lips. Tuper wondered if their daughter had turned out to be as attractive as her mother. In the colonies, that could be a real hindrance. And he'd forgotten how much Tobias resembled his father.

"You know Tobias," Jacob said. "Do you remember his wife Frieda?"

"Of course," Tuper said. "I'm sorry to hear about Margarete."

"I'm glad you're here." Tobias was visibly shaken, although he held his chin up.

Tuper admired his attempt to be strong. "I'll do whatever I can to help."

"I know you will," Tobias said. "I brought Frieda with me because she thinks Rita has been acting different lately."

"How is that?"

Tobias turned to his wife. "Tell him what you told me."

"I'm not sure it's anything," Frieda said. "But it seems like something has been bothering Rita for the last month. I tried to get her to talk to me, but she wouldn't. She just kept saying everything was fine. Rita is different than our other children. She's so adventurous."

She was the second person to use that word to describe her, Tuper thought. He hoped it didn't mean Rita took risks that might put her in danger. "What specific behavior was different than usual?"

"She would go from really happy to sullen," Frieda explained. "I would catch her crying sometimes, but she always played it off and said nothing was wrong. Other times, she would be singing and dancing around. She came to me once and asked how I knew Tobias was the man for me. I questioned her about it to see if she was interested in someone, but I couldn't imagine who it could be since we haven't been around any other colonies for a while. She said there was no one, that she was just curious about what life would bring her."

"How long ago did she ask about your marriage?"

"About three weeks."

"I understand Margarete went to the grocery store with you on Saturday." Tuper turned to Tobias. "Is that right?"

"Yes. She loves to go to town. I guess I shouldn't have indulged her, but it makes her so happy."

"Did she talk to anyone?"

"Not while she was with me, but she waited in the van for a while. It's possible she talked to someone then."

Tuper got the details about when and where they were parked. He hoped it would lead him somewhere.

Tuper stopped at Smith's Supermarket and asked to speak to the manager. The middle-aged man knew Tobias but hadn't been working Saturday so couldn't be helpful. Just as the manager walked away, Tuper heard a familiar voice. "They'll let just anybody in this store these days." He turned to see a short, brown-haired woman wearing a huge smile. "Tuper! What are you doing in my neck of the woods?"

"Rhonda Brugman! I forgot you worked here. You just might be able to help me."

"Thirteen years and counting. I was just about to take my break. Come on." She gestured toward the side of the store. "I'll buy you a soda or a cup of tea, whatever you're drinking these days, and you can tell me what you need."

"Tea sounds good."

"Hot or cold?"

"Hot, of course."

They walked over to a small table in the deli section, and Tuper sat down. Rhonda returned shortly with his tea and a soda for herself. They caught up quickly on the current events in their lives.

"So, what can I do for you?" Rhonda asked.

"You know Jacob, the *Haushalter* from the Hutterite colony?"

"Yes. Good guy."

"His granddaughter is missing."

"Oh no! How old is she?"

"She just turned eighteen."

Rhonda tipped her head and raised her eyebrows.

"I know. She might have just decided to leave the *Bruderhof* on her own." Tuper shrugged. "But if that's the case, she could've just told them. They wouldn't keep her prisoner. Any adult can leave if they choose. They just take the clothes on their back and they go."

"But maybe she didn't have the nerve to tell them she wanted to leave. I've seen that before."

"Possibly. But until we know, I'm looking to find her."

"So, how can I help?"

"Were you working last Saturday morning?"

"I came in early, around six, and worked until one."

"Did you see anyone from the colony?"

"I think the man's name is Tobias. He usually comes to pick up their orders. He had a young blonde girl with him. I've seen her before, and I assume she's his daughter." Rhonda's eyes widened. "Was that the girl?"

"Yes. Her name is Rita."

"She is a beautiful young woman. Men are always gaping at her."

"Did she come inside?"

"For a few minutes, but then she asked if she could wait outside." Rhonda sipped her soda. "Her father walked her out, then came back in."

"Did you see Rita after that?"

"I took a cart of groceries to the truck, and she was sitting in the cab. She smiled and said hello and told me to have a nice day."

"Did you see anyone else around?"

"No," Rhonda said, then changed her mind. "Wait. Yes, I did. There was a young man parked in the car next to her, sitting in the driver's seat. I remember because he was smoking a cigarette, and I walked right into the smoke as he blew it out the window." She made a face. "I hate cigarette smoke. You know how reformed smokers are."

"Did he say anything?"

"No. And I don't know if they had been talking. Neither said anything to the other while I was there. He was probably just a random person waiting for someone to come out of the store."

"Did you see anyone else?"

"Just people coming and going to their cars. I went back inside and brought out another load of groceries. The guy was still there, but he drove off just as Tobias came out."

"Was anyone with him in the car at that point?"

Rhonda thought for a second. "I don't believe there was."

"Can you describe him?"

"I didn't see him very well, but he seemed a little scruffy. Not a bad-looking guy though. Early twenties. Oh, and he had a big spider web tattoo on his left upper arm and a lizard on his forearm, like the lizard was watching the spider. It was kind of creepy, but I'm not big on tattoos, so that might just be me."

CHAPTER 5

Monday afternoon

"Who are you?" Lana stared at the blond man standing outside. He'd knocked moments ago and interrupted her research.

"My name is Ron. Is Clarice here?"

"No."

"I'm a friend of Tuper's. Is he here?"

"No." Lana started to close the door.

"Excuse me. Do you know if Tuper is coming by here today?"

"Probably."

"It's a beautiful day. Sunny and clear skies."

"What are you, a weatherman?"

"I just wondered if it's always nice this time of year. The last time I was here, it was snowing like crazy."

Just then Clarice, an attractive woman in her mid-fifties with naturally silver hair, drove up and got out of her car. She stood about five-foot-four and maintained a shapely, healthy body. Ron hurried toward her, so Lana closed the door. From the window, she watched as Clarice and Ron hugged, looking happy to see each other. But Clarice was like that. She'd taken Lana in six months earlier and had treated her like family. A few minutes later, they both came inside.

"Lana, this is Ron Brown," Clarice said.

"Yeah, we met."

"We didn't exactly, since you didn't tell me your name." He held out his hand.

Lana wasn't comfortable around strangers. She never knew when one would show up looking for her, and he was the second unexpected visitor she'd had to deal with today. She wasn't too concerned about the Hutterite, but this guy was far more suspect. She was particularly bothered by his speech patterns. She would bet he was from California, and she didn't need that.

"You heard Clarice," she said. "It's Lana."

"Pretty name." Ron smiled.

Lana didn't smile back.

"Ron is an old friend of Tuper's," Clarice said.

"That's nice." Lana didn't even try to sound friendly.

"I have a dog in the car," Ron announced. "I need to walk him for a bit, and then I'd like to bring him inside, if that's all right."

"Of course." Clarice nodded. "All dogs are welcome here. You know that."

After Ron left, Lana shook her head. "What's with all the people coming and going today?"

"Who else was here?" Clarice asked.

"Jacob, the—"

Clarice cut her off. "The Hutterite?"

"Yes, that's the one."

"What did he want?"

Lana explained what she knew about the missing girl.

"Tuper must be very concerned."

"Why? It's not *his* granddaughter."

"No, but they go way back."

"That's just what Pops said. How far back do they go?"

"To childhood."

"What's the thing with them?"

"You'll have to ask Tuper."

"I did, but he didn't answer. So, what's the deal?"

"It's not my place to tell."

The door opened, and Ron came in with a beautiful, black and white border collie. "This is Dually."

Lana and Clarice both knelt down to pet him. Dually wagged his tail and sucked it all in. "He's so pretty," Lana exclaimed.

"He's a sweetheart too." Ron caught Lana's eye. "I guess I should've sent Dually to the door. I may have gotten a better reception."

"Dogs are nicer than people. They can be trusted."

"True enough."

Clarice stood, but Lana continued to pet the dog for a moment. When she got up, he followed her to the dining table. When she sat down at her laptop, Dually placed his head on her lap and stayed by her side.

"He sure has taken a shine to you," Ron said.

"Smart dog," Lana responded.

Clarice offered Ron a soda, and he followed her to the kitchen on the other side of the counter.

"Do you know if Tuper will be coming by?" Ron asked.

"He usually manages to happen in around dinnertime," Clarice said. "But I'm not too sure. He went to Great Falls to help Jacob find his granddaughter Rita. Seems she left the colony last night. They don't know if she left of her own volition or if something is wrong."

"Rita is the little blonde with the wild spirit, right?"

"You remember her?"

"She was a pistol even a few years ago. Rita was so curious about the outside world and asked Sabre tons of questions when we were there." Ron glanced at Lana as he talked. "Several of the girls were inquisitive, but none quite like Rita. She wanted to know what things looked like, smelled like, tasted like. She needed every detail."

Lana started to relax a little. *Ron knew Sabre, JP's girlfriend, and Tuper trusted JP implicitly.* She had recently helped JP with a case he and Sabre were working. Then it hit Lana again. They were all from San Diego, and that was risky. Ron could have been sent to find her. But that meant he had found her, and it was already too late. Lana took a deep breath and exhaled. She was being paranoid. If they already knew where she was, he wouldn't have just waltzed in here and said hello. She would have been taken out or snatched up by now. She decided to play it out and keep her eyes and ears open.

CHAPTER 6

Monday evening

While catching up with Clarice, Ron occasionally tried to engage Lana, but she gave only curt, almost polite responses. Forty minutes later, Tuper walked in.

"It's sure nice to see you," Tuper said. "But what in thunder are you doing here, boy?"

"I came to take a horseback ride with you. You told me I could stop by any time."

"Long way to travel to ride a horse."

"Actually, I have to deliver some ashes to Glacier National Park. Our Aunt Goldie died." Ron stopped and looked at Lana. "That's right. You helped us find information about her. I really appreciate that. We may never have discovered what we did without your help."

"It was nothing," Lana said.

"Anyway, the park is one of the places she wanted to be scattered."

"One of the places? There are more?" Tuper took off his cowboy hat, set it on a stool, and took a seat at the table.

"Three others. San Diego, Bakersfield, and Sarasota, Florida."

"Why?"

"Goldie just said they had special meaning." Ron sat across from Tuper. "I can understand San Diego because she lived there, and Bakersfield is where her son is buried. But Glacier Park and Sarasota are beyond me. Sabre is still going through a lot of Goldie's paperwork, so we may find out, but for now I'm just following instructions."

"That's odd," Clarice commented.

"You have no idea. Aunt Goldie lived an interesting, but strange life. I'll tell you about it when we have more time."

Dually finally left Lana's side and wandered over to Tuper, who reached down and rubbed the dog's head. "Who are you?"

"That's Dually."

Tuper's eyes watered as he petted the dog. The room went quiet for a few seconds.

"I'm so sorry about Ringo," Ron said.

"It's been hard losing him, especially since it wasn't necessary. It's hard to believe someone could be so cold as to hit an animal and leave him to suffer by the side of the road."

No one knew what to say. Finally, Clarice broke the silence. "I'm about to fix supper. You'll stay won't you, Ron?"

"I'd like that."

"You're welcome to stay here tonight as well. Beds and sofa are all taken, but we have floor space."

"Thank you, but I have a room at the Residence Inn. Aunt Goldie left a hefty expense account to cover this job."

"Good," Tuper said. "I'll join you for breakfast tomorrow morning. I haven't been there in a while."

"Tell me what's going on with Jacob and Rita. Clarice filled me in a little, but did you learn anything else today?"

"Not enough. They've checked every inch of the property, and she definitely isn't there, which I guess is a good thing. At least they didn't find her body somewhere." Tuper grimaced. "I questioned her roommates, the last people to see her, but I didn't get much. I think a few might know more than they admitted, but they're not going to tell me, at least not in front of Jacob or his wife."

"Of course not," Lana piped in. "All teenagers have secrets they don't want authority figures to know. Why didn't you question them alone?"

"Because it wouldn't be proper."

Lana rolled her eyes.

"I'll find another way."

"I could go undercover. You could plant me in their room, and I bet I'd get all kinds of information."

Tuper tipped his head. "Really? You look young, but seventeen? I don't think so. Not to mention your hair and those combat boots. And how would you survive without your laptop? You couldn't have that in the colony. It would never work."

"Maybe it would," Ron said. "Lana could put a rinse on her hair and wear a scarf. She'd wear their clothes, so all she would need is different shoes. And she does look pretty young. I would have guessed twelve." He actually thought she was quite attractive and womanly, but he loved to tease, and she was obviously easy to goad.

Lana rolled her eyes at Ron.

"She acts twelve, but …" Tuper grinned.

"Guys, I'm right here. I can talk for myself." Lana paused, then said, "Ron's right."

"What's that?" Ron asked. "I didn't hear you."

"I said, you're right. I could do all those things. The hardest part would be not having my laptop. Maybe I could stash it somewhere and check in once in a while."

"Naw. I don't think Jacob would go for it," Tuper countered. "Rita went to Smith's Supermarket on Saturday with her father, so I went there to ask questions. I ran into someone I know—"

"Of course you did," Ron and Lana said in unison.

"You know a guy, right?" Lana said.

"Actually, she's a gal, but yes. She saw a man sitting in his car next to Jacob's truck while Rita was waiting for him. I need to find out who the guy is, but I don't have much to go on." Tuper shared what he knew about the man, including his tattoos, then looked at Lana. "Do you think you could find anything on him?"

"That's not much to go on, but I'll see what I can do."

"Supper's ready," Clarice announced, carrying in a big casserole. Ron saw her and offered to help, but she declined.

They ate their meal, then Ron and Tuper went out to the front porch. Dually followed them outside. The dog ran off for a few seconds and peed, then returned to Tuper's side.

"I think he likes me," Tuper said.

Ron shared the update about JP and Sabre living as a family and raising JP's niece and nephew, then briefly explained his Aunt Goldie's final wishes and how he would be running her charity trust.

"A desk job?" Tuper asked. "That doesn't sound like you."

"Actually, I'll be out and about a lot, dealing with people and making decisions that help others. I'll be free to travel and make my own hours. I think it'll work."

After a little more chatting, Ron changed the subject. "What's the deal with Lana?"

"What do you mean?"

"I don't think she likes me much."

"She's skeptical about strangers, and I don't know why. Not really any of my business, so I don't ask."

"She sure doesn't talk much."

Tuper laughed. "Wait until you get to know her. I'm just glad you're here because it gives me a break from her non-stop chatter. You can't shut that woman up once she gets rollin'."

"You know, she just might be able to pass for one of them. She does look pretty young."

Tuper stared at him for a second. "How long do you plan to stay?"

"A few days, but I'm not on a schedule. I can stay longer if you think I could be of help finding Rita."

"Maybe you could."

"What do you have in mind?"

"Would you mind spending a little time at the *Bruderhof*? I would do it, but I think you might get more information out of the young men there. They still have that loft in the barn, and you could keep a lookout from there if you needed to. And if Lana went, you could hold on to her computer in case she needed it."

"That just might work."

Lana flung the front door open and approached Tuper. "I could do this. I can pass for seventeen and get information from those teenagers. I've been reading about the Hutterites online, and I know I can do this. I'll know all their customs by morning and be ready to go." She paced the porch, sounding excited. "I'll change the color of my hair and borrow some shoes from Clarice. I want to help, but there's not much I can do from my computer. That poor girl is out there in a world she knows nothing about. Maybe there's a guy she's infatuated with. I could find out from the girls. You said Helen was her best friend. She must know something. Teenage girls confide in their best friend. Of course, there are cultural differences, but all teenagers have hormones, and it's a time in their life when the world opens up and they're curious. Rita is even more curious than others so she's more susceptible. Their bodies are developing and so are their personalities. It's not any different in this colony." Lana stopped and sucked in a quick breath. "Well, maybe a bit different because of Rita's background, but teenagers are impulsive. They don't understand their emotions, and they take risks and make dangerous choices. They think, feel, and behave differently than adults. That's biology." She spun toward Tuper, still talking. "Did you know they studied teenagers in the sixties and the same group again fifty years later and discovered a correlation to dementia. Calm, mature, and energetic teenagers were less likely to have dementia."

"Agony! What's your point?"

"My point is that I'd like to know if you were calm, mature, and energetic when you were a teen. I'm guessing you weren't. You're still not calm or mature. I need to be aware if you're about to get dementia."

Tuper shook his head. "What does this have to do with Rita?"

"Nothing, Pops. It's just something I came across when I

was researching. The thing is, I know I can help you get information about Rita, and you don't have a lot of choices. You're already at a dead end, and you just got started. Other than a random guy in a car with a tattoo, you've got nothing."

Lana stopped pacing and stared at Tuper.

"Okay."

CHAPTER 7

Tuesday morning

On the trip from Helena to Great Falls, Ron drove his black, 2014 Chevy Impala. Tuper didn't argue when Ron offered to drive. He was fine with someone else at the wheel, and it was far more comfortable than Ringo's car. Tuper sat in the passenger seat; Lana and Dually were in the back. They discussed some of the colony's rituals, most of which Lana had already discovered online. From experience, Tuper explained which customs were more localized because some things varied from colony to colony.

They were nearing Great Falls when Lana asked, "Is there a Walmart in this town?"

"Yes. Why?" Tuper wasn't in the mood to stop and shop.

"I need to buy some panties."

"You forgot your underwear?" Tuper turned and stared at Lana open-mouthed.

"No. But I don't think mine are appropriate. From what I've read, there likely won't be much privacy at the colony. I wasn't thinking when I packed. I just grabbed a few pairs, but now I don't believe it's a good idea to go in with what I have. I know they'll have clothes for me, but I'm not wearing someone else's underwear. That's going a little too far. So, can we stop?"

"I don't want to waste any more time than we need to," Tuper grumbled. "How bad can they be?"

Ron chuckled.

"What are you smirkin' about?" Tuper asked. "Underwear is underwear."

Lana reached in her bag and pulled out a pair of bright-red thongs and held them up. Ron glanced in the rearview mirror and laughed out loud.

"Holy cow, woman," Tuper said. "That's more like dental floss."

"So, will you guys stop? You two don't even have to go in. I'll run in there and grab some old-lady panties and be out in a jiff. How hard can they be to find? I expect there'll be plenty to choose from. I'll get white since I'm sure that's what they would wear. Besides, I'm the one who has to wear the silly things. I haven't worn underwear like that since I was a kid. I hope they're not too uncomfortable."

"All right. Quit the chatter, Agony," Tuper said. "We'll stop."

An hour later, they all sat in Jacob's office with Dually at Tuper's feet. The wooden desk and chairs were all handmade but finely finished. Jacob seemed to accept Ron's presence with ease. Ron had visited the colony with Tuper a few years back, and most of the members knew Ron and liked him.

Lana, on the other hand, was a harder sell, even though she'd changed her hair color and shoes.

"I know Helen, and maybe the other girls, aren't giving me the whole picture," Tuper pressed his point.

"I will speak to them again," Jacob said.

"They'll be even less likely to open up to you. They need to talk to another female, someone closer in age who won't judge them. I'm not saying any of the girls are lying to you, but I believe they know more than they're telling. They may not even realize they know it or that it pertains to Rita's disappearance. And Lana will only be here for a few days."

"So, what will I tell them?"

"Say that she's a young sinner who lost her way. That's the truth." Lana scowled at him, but Tuper continued. "Tell them Ron is escorting her home, but they need a place to stay for a night or so. All true."

"Tuper, you heathen." Jacob looked distressed. "You bend the truth to match your life. The Lord said, '*Keep your tongue from evil and your lips from speaking deceit.*' Psalm 34:13."

Tuper knew a counterpoint. "He also said, '*But whoever causes one of these little ones who believe in me to sin, it would be better to have a great millstone fastened around his neck and to be drowned in the depth of the sea.*' Matthew 18:6." Tuper saw Ron and Lana exchange puzzled glances, but he ignored them and focused on Jacob. "We need to find Rita. If someone has taken her, the guy needs to be punished." He hesitated. "And other girls may be at risk."

Jacob gave him a condescending smile. "Do what you need to do. I will say as little as possible."

"What about your wife?" Ron asked. "Or anyone else. I need to know who's privy to our real objective."

"I will tell Mary to trust me and not ask. She will obey. I

will not lie to her, and I will not implicate her in a lie. No one else will be told. You can volunteer to help search for Rita if you wish. Everyone at the colony knows you and would expect you to offer to help. You can decide what would make them more forthcoming." Jacob stood to leave. "I will make arrangements for Lana to sleep in the girls' dorm. But first, I will ask Mary to bring some appropriate clothes. Ron, as requested, can stay in the loft."

After Jacob left, Lana asked, "Why does Ron have to stay? It's not like I'm in danger or anything. And even if I were, I can handle myself." She glanced at Ron. "Probably better than he can."

"You heard Jacob," Tuper said. "This is hard enough for him. Besides, Ron can keep your laptop with him, and if you need it, you'll have access."

"No," Lana snapped. "He doesn't need to have my laptop. I want it with me."

"That won't work," Tuper argued. "You can keep your phone as long as you shut it off. It's small enough to conceal, but you won't have your own space in the dorm."

Ron stared at Lana. "Why are you so paranoid? It's not like I'll use your laptop."

Tuper knew Lana was afraid of someone in her past and was always looking over her shoulder. He didn't know who it was, and he didn't ask. He didn't really understand how her machine worked, but the way she guarded it, she obviously didn't want anyone else getting into it.

"Look, Lana," Tuper said, "I know you don't want anyone using your computer. But you can trust Ron. I've known him a long time. Still, I brought along a tool chest and a padlock. You can put your laptop in there and keep the key."

"I guess that'll have to do. I just don't like strangers

touching my things," Lana said. She glanced from Ron back to Tuper. "What story am I supposed to tell? Can I just make it up as I go? I think I should say that I left a colony up north, one far enough away that they wouldn't likely know the people. But I changed my mind and want to go back. It's best if I've lived among the *Welt Leut* because it will explain some of my actions. That way I don't have to be as careful about making mistakes." She got up and paced as she talked. "I also think that'll make them more curious, which will give me an opening to ask about Rita. I studied the Hutterite way of life and even learned a few prayers. Thanks to my grandmother, I also have a working knowledge of the German language."

Tuper stared at her, open-mouthed.

Lana laughed. "You can't be any more surprised than I was to hear you speak it too. But that wasn't as shocking as you quoting a Bible verse. Where did that come from?"

"The Bible. Learned it when I was a kid."

"But how? When?"

"Just told ya."

A knock on the door made Dually's ears perk up. Mary entered with clothes for Lana. "Come with me, dear."

As she followed Mary out, Lana glanced back at Tuper, who stood to leave.

"You're right," Ron said, getting up. "That girl can talk, but what is her problem with me?"

"I don't know for certain, but she's runnin' from something. Not sure what, but she's good people. And she's been a great help to me."

"Where did she come from anyway?"

Tuper headed for the door. "She was in Nickels Bar and some cowboy hit on her. She told him, in no uncertain terms, that she wasn't interested. He waited for her outside and tried to grab her, so I stepped in." Tuper shrugged to downplay his part. "She didn't show much appreciation at the time, but I knew she was grateful. Since she had nowhere to go, Clarice took her home for the night. Lana's been there ever since. That was a good six months ago."

They stepped outside, and the dog whimpered a little.

"She sure is touchy about her laptop."

"She's a whiz on that thing—a chopper, or dicer, or something."

"A hacker?"

"Yeah, that's it. It ain't legal. I know that much. Lana's probably afraid you might figure out what she's doing. Or that you might be the law."

Ron chuckled. "So, what do we do now?"

"Visit Green Valley Colony. It's only about twenty miles from here. Maybe someone there knows something."

CHAPTER 8

Tuesday afternoon

Lana followed Mary across the commons. All she had was a bag that held her toothbrush, toothpaste, hairbrush, a towel, and her new underwear. Mary had given her privacy when she'd changed into her new clothes—an ankle-length, plaid gathered skirt, white blouse, flowered vest, and a black kerchief with white polka dots. And underneath, of course, her granny panties.

They reached the dorm and stepped inside. Lana glanced around the foyer, which contained a table with four straight-backed chairs and a small wall cupboard. To the left, a wash-basin sat on a small stand. On the right, stairs led to a second floor. Most remarkable was what it lacked—no pictures, no knick-knacks, and nothing out of place.

Beyond the entrance was the dorm itself. It had four double beds, each adorned by a simple but exquisite quilt, a large dresser, a small closet, and a door that Lana assumed led to a bathroom. She knew eight girls were assigned to the room, which meant they slept two in a bed. She hadn't even considered that. Lana took a deep breath. *There would be a lot more than that to deal with.*

Despite all she'd read, Lana hadn't realized what a culture shock it would be. Living it was different. They had all agreed that she would use the age of twenty even though it was a little older than the other girls. Her thoughts were interrupted by Mary. "The girls are in school, but they will be out shortly. You will use Rita's place for now. I expect you'll be gone when Rita returns."

Lana looked at Mary with admiration. *This woman was no dummy.* "Why do you say that?"

"I know my husband, and I know Tuper. It's no coincidence you and Ron happened here today. When we entered the room, the look on your face confirmed it. You have never been in a Hutterite dorm before." Mary pointed to the northeast corner of the room. "That's Rita's bed. She shares with Helen. I hope you're okay with that."

"I'll be fine."

"Now make yourself comfortable. In a couple of minutes, the room will be overrun by teenage girls who will bombard you with questions. Some are more astute than you might think, especially Elisabeth J. Be careful what you say to her. She's a stickler for rules and might not appreciate the ruse." Mary smiled. "If you need anything, let me know."

"Thank you."

As soon as Mary left, Lana opened the interior door, but discovered it was a small storage area. Still looking for a bathroom, she tried the stairs in the foyer, but they led to an attic that contained tools and seasonal clothes, all stored in an orderly fashion.

Back downstairs, seven chattering girls filled the dorm.

Word must've gotten around because no one seemed surprised to see her. When they introduced themselves, she tried to relate their names to something about the person to help her remember them. Usually, she focused on clothing or hair color, but the girls were all dressed similarly and wore scarves. Lana tried to associate each with a physical characteristic. Annie P. was short, a little overweight, and had deep dimples. That one would be easy. Helen's freckled face and red hair at the edge of her scarf made her easily identifiable. Elisabeth J. was taller than the rest, and Ursula had bushy eyebrows. That was all Lana could master. The others looked too much alike for a quick association.

"Welcome to our room," said Annie P. "We don't get a lot of visitors, so it's nice to have you here."

Before Lana could comment, Elisabeth J. cut in. "We heard you were here, but no one said why." The girl looked stern. "Why are you here?"

"I'm on my way back to my colony."

"Which one?"

"It's north of here, almost to the Canadian border." Lana had done her homework and, so far, felt confident.

"Gilford Colony?"

"Yes."

"That's where my sister is now," Ursula added. "She married a Gilford man and lives there now. I've never been, but she writes letters. It's not much different than here except they are *Dariusleut*." Ursula plopped on a bed, seeming wistful. "Their clothes are a little different, and they're not quite as strict in some of their practices. But church and school are pretty much the same."

Lana had read about the *Dariusleut* and knew they weren't quite as conservative as this colony. She wasn't concerned there would be any meaningful contact between Ursula and her sister in the next few days. Without phones, they wouldn't be chatting on Instagram, so that meant snail mail. She'd be long gone before letters could be exchanged.

"Mary said you had room because someone was gone for a while. Where is she?"

"Rita is missing," Ursula said.

"What do you mean *missing*?"

Ursula kept her face stoic. "She took the trash out night before last and didn't return."

"Do you mean someone kidnapped her?" Lana glanced around, pretending to be worried. "Is it unsafe here?"

"She might have just wandered off." Ursula pressed her lips together. "But I think someone took her."

Elisabeth J. stepped between them. "We shouldn't jump to conclusions until we know." She turned the questioning back on Lana. "Where have you been recently?"

"I left my colony and went out on my own."

That got everyone's attention, and they all gathered around her. Lana felt silly in the clothes she was wearing, but she tried to remember her high school acting days. She took drama and was quite good at it. She had an excellent memory so the lines were easy, but the part she liked most was getting lost in the character. She liked being someone other than herself. It also went a long way to bring her out of her shyness. When she got into an uncomfortable position, she would pretend she was on stage.

"Where did you go?" Helen asked.

"I made my way to Helena and tried to get a job, but it wasn't easy."

"How did you get by? Where did you sleep?" Helen seemed the most curious, or at least was the quickest with questions.

Lana thought that was a sign that she was thinking about Rita. She decided to not make the outside world sound too glorious, hoping Helen would be concerned enough to share whatever information she had.

"I walked most of the way to Helena and slept on the ground. I found a farmhouse along the way, and the people gave me a blanket and food and drove me the rest of the way. If I hadn't found them, I probably would've frozen to death. It was a few months ago, but it was still pretty cold."

"What did you do when you got to Helena?" Elisabeth J. asked.

"I found a cheap motel that let me stay there if I cleaned the rooms. But I had a lot of problems I'd rather not talk about."

The customs of the *Bruderhof* were frustrating for Lana, especially the ones that didn't align with her women-are-equal-to-men view. Here, women were definitely a step lower than men on the social ladder. That was evident throughout the colony. Women were not mistreated, rather they were revered for their positions, but were also limited by the social norms. Everyone had jobs and they all did them without complaint, and Lana soon discovered that decisions were made as a group. She glanced around. "What time is dinner? I'm hungry."

"We have to leave here in about ten minutes to help in the kitchen."

"Come," Helen said. "I can make room in my drawer for your stuff. Rita's things are still in her drawers."

"Thanks, but I'll just leave them in my bag. I'll only be staying a few days." Lana was relieved the questions had stopped. She would try to get more information after dinner.

CHAPTER 9

Tuesday late afternoon

About thirty minutes later, Tuper stepped out of the car and glanced around Green Valley Colony. It looked much like Jacob's complex. The classroom, dining hall, dorms, and barn all had the same layout. Ron and his dog climbed out too, and they walked to the door of the *Haushalter*. A tall, bearded man who looked a lot like Jacob greeted them. He smiled and shook Tuper's hand. "*Willkommen, Brüderlein.*"

"*Danke*, Peter," Tuper said. "You remember my friend Ron from a few years back?"

"Of course." Peter looked down at Dually. "And who is this? I'm glad to see you got another dog. He's beautiful."

"That's Dually, Ron's dog."

"He's welcome as well. Come on in. It is so good to see you."

They all stepped inside and were greeted by Peter's wife, Magdalena.

"Please sit," Peter said. "Magdalena, will you get these men something to drink?"

"Water will be fine," Tuper said. "And some for Dually too, please."

"Of course," Magdalena said. "I'm glad you're here, Tuper. I feel better now."

Peter's face turned solemn. "I was thinking about calling on you for help. Something terrible has happened."

Concern squeezed Tuper's chest. "What's going on?"

"One of the girls has disappeared. Gertrude is eighteen but not old enough to leave on her own. I don't believe she's a *Weglaufen*. Can you help find her?"

Tuper hadn't heard the term in a while, but he knew it meant runaway; more specifically, it referred to someone who'd left to join the *Welt Leuts*.

"When did she go missing?"

"Sunday night. She didn't show up for the evening church service, but I didn't know she was gone until after it was over. We've been scouring the grounds and checking in town but have found no sign of her."

Magdalena brought them all glasses of water and set a bowl down for Dually.

"Have you talked to Jacob in the last two days?" Tuper asked.

"No. Why?" Peter's eyes widened. "Do you think Gertrude's there?"

"Jacob's granddaughter Rita is also missing."

"Oh, no." Peter sighed and looked pensive. "Do you think the girls might be together?"

"It's possible. Do they know each other well?"

"Our colonies are close, and we do a lot of trading and

social gatherings together, but I don't know if those two girls are close."

"Have you questioned her friends and family?"

"None of them know anything about her whereabouts, and no one saw her leave. And no one saw anyone who didn't belong here."

Ron stepped forward. "All girls that age have another girl they confide in," he said. "If we can speak with her, maybe we can at least find out how close Gertrude was to Rita."

Peter glanced at his wife. "Please bring Rebekka." Magdalena left without comment.

Tuper needed more information. "Does Gertrude ever go to Smith's in Great Falls when someone goes for supplies?"

"A few times. And she went last Saturday. We've been tracing her steps and looking for any outside influences, but so far have not discovered anything."

"I don't expect you have any photos?"

"Of course not."

"Then tell me what she looks like."

Magdalena walked in with a nervous teenager. With her hands clasped tightly, the girl answered Tuper's question.

"She's short, with brown, curly hair and a dimple in her right cheek. She's quite pretty, although she doesn't know it."

"Thank you," Tuper said. Magdalena left the room again.

"Rebekka," Peter said, his voice soothing. "Tuper will ask you some more questions, and you must tell him the truth."

"I don't really know anything," she muttered.

"You may know something that doesn't seem important but could help us," Tuper said. "Are you and Gertrude close?"

"We're best friends."

"Do you know Rita T. from Little Boulder?"

Rebekka nodded.

"Do you know her well?"

"Not really. She's older than me and very pretty. I know her friend Helen better."

"Are Gertrude and Rita close?"

"They don't spend much time together at gatherings, if that's what you mean. But—" She paused.

"What were you going to say?" Tuper kept his tone soft.

"Trudi, er, Gertrude saw Rita last Saturday in Great Falls."

"Did she talk to her?"

"Just to say hello. She said Rita came in the store with her father, but when he walked her out, a young man followed them. Gertrude watched out the store's window and said the boy approached Rita in the truck after her father went back inside."

"Did Gertrude say anything else?"

"That's all she saw because she had to help with their order."

"Did she say what the guy looked like?"

"Just that he was handsome and blond. Gertrude thinks they may have been interested in each other, but she likes love stories, and it may have been all in her imagination."

"Thank you, Rebekka. You've been a big help."

When they started out the door, Dually followed alongside Tuper.

"That dog stays mighty close to you, Tuper. Are you sure he isn't yours?"

"Nope. He belongs to Ron."

"Does the dog know that?" Peter asked.

"Don't know for sure." Tuper opened the door, and despite his trying to lighten the mood, he was more worried than ever. *Was a charming predator preying on young Hutterite girls?*

CHAPTER 10

Tuesday evening

After dinner, Lana hurried through her chores, hoping to get some time alone with Helen. But when Ursula headed outside with the trash, Lana volunteered to go with her so she could see exactly where Rita had been before she disappeared.

"Does it scare you to be out here now?" Lana asked.

"Not really. It's no different than before."

"Do you think Rita went off on her own?"

"Maybe. She is ... different."

"How so?"

"She isn't afraid of anything. When she was small, she would take walks in the woods by herself. She never seemed to understand danger from man or beast."

Lana looked around. There was no place to hide, except around the corner of the dining hall. If someone had approached, Rita could have probably made it back inside before he got to her—unless she'd interacted with him. But since Rita wasn't afraid of strangers, it still could've been someone she didn't know.

When they went back inside, Lana grabbed a dishtowel and headed for Helen, who was doing dishes. "Can I help?"

"Sure."

They chatted a little, but Lana didn't bring up Rita. When the other girls were done, Lana stalled, and Helen waited for her. As they walked back to the dorm, Lana commented, "I heard you are Rita's best friend. What do you think happened to her?"

"I don't think she'd run off, but Rita sure wanted to see the outside world."

"Was she in contact with anyone in the *Welt Leut*?"

The color rose in Helen's cheeks.

"I only ask because that's what got me to do it," Lana said. "I started talking to people outside the colony, and it all sounded so exciting. But it wasn't what I thought. The idea of being free to do as you please sounds good until you realize how many responsibilities go with it. I was a dreamer."

"That's the way Rita is." Helen spoke softly so the girls a few steps ahead couldn't hear. "She loves adventure, and she always thinks the *Welt Leuts* have so much fun. I tried to tell her that they didn't have it so easy, that it wasn't all fun. But Rita has a forbidden Hollywood magazine, and everything is so colorful and pretty. I told her I didn't think the world was like that. She would say, 'We live in a black-and-white world. I want my world to be in color, like the magazine.'"

They reached the dorm, and the other girls went inside.

"Do we have church services now?" Lana asked. Mary had already given her a rundown of the schedule, but Lana wanted to let Helen know she was familiar with the program.

"At six-thirty."

"So, we have about fifteen minutes. Can you show me where the showers are? I've noticed that, although this colony has the same structures, they're laid out a little differently."

"I thought Ursula said they were the same."

"Almost, but there are a few differences."

"The showers are over there." Helen pointed and led her toward the end of the building.

Lana chatted about the other colony, then circled back. "You said Rita was talking to a *Welt Leut*. Do you know who?"

"Some guy at Smith's Supermarket."

"Does he work there?"

"Part time. They met by accident the first time, but afterward, they arranged to meet again. Her father goes to town every Saturday, and Rita always tries to go along. If the guy wasn't working, he would show up anyway in hopes of seeing her."

They were getting close to the dorms, so Lana stopped. She wanted to get as much information as she could while she had Helen alone. "How long ago did she meet him?"

"About four months, but she's only seen him seven times."

"Did he ever come here?"

"No."

"Could he have been here, and you not know it?"

"I'm sure he wasn't. Rita would've told me. She was always anxious to talk about him. If she didn't have me to talk to, I don't know what she would've done."

"Did she tell you his name?" Lana thought it was too much to hope for, but it couldn't hurt to ask.

"It's Finn."

"Did she give you a last name?"

"No. Why do you ask so many questions?"

"I just had such a horrible time when I was out there. I feel bad for her."

"I'm really scared for her too, but there's nothing we can do."

Ron and Tuper returned to the barn after the church services. Tuper sent for Lana, who joined them for a briefing. Dually greeted her with his usual exuberance. She scratched his head and, without greeting Ron, asked, "Where's my laptop?"

"Hello to you too," Ron said. "It's in the loft. I'll get it."

Before Ron could say any more, Lana scurried up the ladder to the loft and returned with her laptop. She found a plug not far from the ladder and sat down on a bale of hay. Within minutes, she had her hotspot from her phone set up, and she was connected to the internet. She started searching for Finn. Ten minutes later, Jacob came in, and Tuper told him about the other missing girl.

"What do you make of it?" Jacob asked, visibly distressed.

"It now seems less likely that Rita left of her own accord," Tuper said. "Unless the girls planned something and ran off together. Based on what I heard about Gertrude, that seems unlikely. She isn't as adventurous as Rita."

"What now?" Jacob asked.

"Why don't you see what you can learn from the other colonies, especially if anyone else has gone missing. Then call me."

"Good idea. I need your phone number though. I do not have it, or I would have called you instead of hunting you down."

Lana reached out her hand. "Give me your phone."

Jacob pulled his phone from his pocket and gave it to her. Lana quickly keyed in her and Tuper's contact info, then looked at Ron. "What's your number?"

"I thought you'd never ask," he joked, then blushed.

Lana scowled. *Was he flirting with her?*

As Ron recited the digits, she entered them in Jacob's phone, then handed it back to him. "Now you have all three of our numbers in case you need them."

"If you learn anything from your calls," Tuper said to Jacob, "we can stop at other colonies on our way home."

"I have new information," Lana said. "For the past four months, Rita has been talking to a young man at Smith's named Finn. I looked at the payroll records for Smith's and found a Finn Nelson. He's eighteen years old, lives at home with his mother, and has worked there for six months." She glanced at Jacob to see how he was handling the news. He was clearly surprised, but stoic. Lana continued. "I also found Finn's Facebook, Twitter, and Snapchat accounts. He's blond, about six feet tall, and doesn't seem to have anything radical on his social media accounts. He isn't on Parler or anything other than the popular ones. I didn't look too deep, so it's possible he's on some underground sites. I'll check that later if I need to."

"You saw photos of him?" Ron asked.

"Yes. He looks pretty clean cut."

"No tattoos?"

"Nothing that shows, and he's shirtless in a couple of photos, so nothing on his arms or upper body."

"Then he's not the guy in the car who parked next to Rita," Tuper said.

"Nope. Not that guy."

"And you have a home address for him?" Tuper asked.

"Sure do, Pops."

"Before we leave town tomorrow, we'll stop at Smith's. If he's not there, we'll go to his house."

CHAPTER 11

Wednesday early morning

After coffee with Jacob, Tuper stood and glanced at Ron and Lana. "Let's get on the road." The dog jumped up, and as soon as the car door was opened, he jumped in. Lana climbed into the backseat with Dually, then asked, "When can I get out of these prairie clothes?"

"Soon enough," Tuper said from the front passenger side. "I didn't want you changing until we left the colony. Those clothes may come in useful."

"What's the plan, Pops?" Lana asked as they drove away from the colony. "Are we going to interrogate Finn? If he's not at the grocery store, we can't go to his house yet. We could if he lived alone or with other kids his age, but he lives with his mother. She probably won't be happy if you bang on her door this early."

Tuper glanced at Ron and rolled his eyes. "I told you. She never shuts up, except when she's on her machine." He glanced back at Lana. "Isn't there something you can do on that contraption to keep you quiet?"

"How far is it to town?"

"About ten more minutes."

"I don't want to get started and get interrupted. I'll wait until we leave Great Falls. It'll give me something to do on the way home."

"Well, that's somethin' to look forward to," Tuper mumbled.

At Smith's Supermarket, they all headed inside, and Tuper went looking for Rhonda. He spotted her carrying a box to the back room. Lana and Ron hung back as Tuper walked toward her.

Rhonda looked up. "Good morning, Toop. Nice to see you again."

"Say, there's a guy who works here by the name of Finn. Can you tell me what he's like?"

"He's a good kid, very personable, works hard and puts in a lot of shifts. He's real good about coming in when he's needed, even when he's not scheduled." Rhonda gave Tuper a curious look. "If this is about that missing girl at the Hutterite colony, I can't imagine Finn would be mixed up in something like that."

"His name came up. You ever see him talking to Rita?"

"Not that I recall. I see girls giggling over Finn all the time, my niece included, but he seems kind of shy around them."

"Is he here today?"

"Yes, in the produce section."

"Thanks."

As they walked over, Lana said, "Why don't you let me talk to Finn? I'm wearing the prairie stuff, and he might be open with me if he thinks I'm Rita's friend."

"Okay, but Ron and I will stick close in case he decides to run."

"What would you do if he does, Pops?" Lana laughed. "You'd better make sure Ron is close."

"You'll get old someday, Agony—unless you keep mouthin' off, then maybe not."

"I think that's him," Lana said, nodding at a young man pushing a cart with produce boxes. She hurried toward the almost-empty lettuce shelf.

Tuper and Ron stopped near the stacked tomatoes, where they hoped to see and hear the interaction.

Ten feet away, Lana positioned herself and turned her back to Finn.

"What's she doin'?" Tuper asked.

"I think she's letting him find her."

"She's a smart one." Tuper glared at Ron. "Don't you dare tell her I said that. She gloats enough."

"Rita!" Finn called out as he approached Lana.

She didn't respond but turned around slowly.

"I'm not Rita."

His shoulders drooped, and he swallowed hard with disappointment.

"Sorry. I thought you might be someone else." He turned and started to stock the lettuce shelf.

"Are you Finn?" Lana asked.

"Yes." He looked up. "Do I know you?"

"We've never met, but Rita told me about you. I'm her best friend, Helen."

"She told me about you too." He glanced around as if looking for someone. "Is Rita with you?"

"No. We stopped here on our way to another colony." He looked disappointed. "When did you last see Rita?"

"She came with her father last Saturday. I didn't get to speak to her very long because we were pretty busy. I went out to her truck, but my department manager was out there, so I held back until she left."

"And you didn't see Rita after that?"

"No. Why do you ask?"

"She disappeared on Sunday."

"What?" He seemed genuinely concerned. Either that, or he was a very good actor. "Did someone kidnap her?"

"We don't know. That's what we're trying to find out."

"You've got to find her. She wouldn't run away without me."

"Was she planning to run away *with* you?"

"We were making plans to be together someday. Rita talked about going to college next year, and that way we could see each other."

Lana glanced at Tuper and nodded, signaling he should come over. Finn removed more lettuce heads from a box and stacked them on the shelf, his hands shaking.

Lana introduced everyone and tried to put Finn at ease. "They're good friends with Rita's grandfather, and they're trying to find her. You need to tell them everything you know." She turned to Tuper. "Finn doesn't think Rita would run away without him. They were planning a future together."

Tuper asked questions about the time they'd spent together, but he didn't learn anything new. According to Finn, their relationship was all very innocent, just two kids from different worlds falling for each other.

"You talked to her last Saturday, right?" Tuper asked.

"Yes. Very briefly in the store and a few minutes at her truck."

"Did you see a man sitting in a car next to her?"

"He was staring at Rita when I walked up. That's not unusual. All the men stare at her because she's so beautiful." Finn's eyes sparked with emotion. "I didn't want to leave her there with him because he seemed like a creep, but I saw Rhonda, and I knew Rita's father would be there soon. I told her I didn't want to leave, but she said she'd be okay."

"Did you get a good look at him?"

"Not really. I saw tattoos all along his arm, but I didn't look at his face except for a quick glance. He was smoking and blew smoke at me. I think he was trying to get me to react. I just ignored him."

"Can you give me any description?"

"A little older than me, but not more than twenty-five. He had brown hair and needed a shave. That's about all I can tell you. I didn't want to stare. I was afraid it would make things worse."

"Make what worse?"

"He was ragging on me. Calling me a kid. And when I started to leave, he called me other names and said, 'She needs a real man, not a punk-ass kid like you.' I didn't want to leave Rita, but I didn't want Rhonda to see me. So, I stood back and watched. Then Rita's father came out, and the guy drove off."

"Did you notice what kind of car he was driving?" Ron asked.

"A twilight blue metallic 1970 Oldsmobile Cutlass Supreme convertible. It would be worth something if it wasn't so beat up. The paint looked original, as if it had been garaged for most of its life. But the back window on the passenger side had cardboard taped over it, and the vinyl top had tears." Finn paused as if digging deep for more detail. "And the whole passenger side was dented and scratched like it had recently been in an accident, maybe even rolled." He snapped his fingers. "Oh, and there was a sticker on the windshield in the corner on the driver's side."

"That's quite a description," Tuper said. "I thought you didn't get a good look."

"Not at him, but I'm into old cars, and his was unusual."

Tuper and Ron exchanged glances. "You didn't happen to get the license plate number, did you?" Ron asked.

Finn shook his head. "But I did notice the plate had a bucking bronco."

"Wyoming," Tuper said.

CHAPTER 12

Wednesday afternoon

On the drive back to Helena, Lana buried herself in research. She was determined to find the man with the tattoos. She had a lot more to go on now with the car's description. How many 1970 Oldsmobile Cutlass Supremes could be registered in Wyoming? She was struggling to hack into the state's vehicle-licensing department when Tuper's phone rang. She realized it was Jacob and stopped to listen.

"When?" Tuper said into his cell. "We'll let you know what we find out." He hung up. "A girl is missing from Wild Grass Colony too. She's been gone since Monday."

Lana quickly googled the colony. "The turnoff is coming up. Are we headed there?"

"You okay with that, Ron?" Tuper asked.

"You bet. I'm in no hurry."

"Do you want directions?" Lana asked.

"Nope," Tuper said. "I know the way."

Lana shut down her laptop and put it away. She would try again when they got back on the road.

Fifteen minutes later, they reached the colony. "Who will you to talk to?" Lana asked, as they got out of the car.

"I know a guy," Tuper said.

"Of course, you do."

Lana was surprised to see that the buildings were set up exactly like the last colony's. She wondered if she'd screwed up when she told Helen the colony up north was different. It didn't seem to matter, because Helen had told her Rita's secrets.

They approached the home of the *Haushalter,* and a bearded man who looked about sixty answered the door.

"Hello, Eli," Tuper said.

"Welcome, Tuper. Jacob said you would be coming by. We sure appreciate it." He gestured for them to come inside, then stopped. "Would you like to visit my father first? He'll be glad to see you."

"Yes, thank you."

"You know where to find him."

Tuper introduced Ron and Lana, then they walked to a nearby cabin. Tuper knocked, and a tall, thin man with a long, gray beard came to the door.

"*Kleiner Bruder.*" He reached out and hugged Tuper. "*Schön dich zu sehen. Wie geht es dir?*" He must have noticed Lana and Ron because he added in English, "I'm sorry to be rude. I'm Joseph."

"This is my friend Ron," Tuper said. "And this is Lana."

Joseph glanced down at the dog.

"This is Dually," Tuper added.

"Come in," Joseph said.

"We have little time. I need to talk to Eli about the missing girl." Tuper gestured with his head toward Eli's home. "Come with us."

"I'm pretty slow these days. You go ahead, and I'll meet you there."

A few minutes later, Eli invited them all inside and offered tea and coffee. They all declined and sat down at the kitchen table.

"I understand Sarah went missing on Monday," Tuper said. "Is that right?"

"Right after services. She never made it from the church back to her dorm."

"And no one saw anyone around?"

"No. I've spoken to all the girls, and they don't think she ran away. Sarah was pretty devoted and had little interest in the *Welt Leut*."

"And you've checked the property?"

"Every inch. She's not on our land."

The door opened, and Joseph walked in.

"*Hallo, lieber Vater*," Eli said.

Joseph nodded to everyone, and Eli brought him a chair.

"*Danke, mein Sohn*," Joseph said, then looked at Tuper. "I can't stand too long anymore."

"We're all getting old," Tuper said with a smile. He noticed Lana nodding, scowled at her, then turned back to Eli. "Did Sarah ever go to Smith's Supermarket in Great Falls?"

"She went for the first time last Saturday. Sarah liked visiting people at other colonies, but she never asked to go to town." Eli looked puzzled. "How is that important?"

"The girls missing from the other colonies were in town that same day. I'm not sure if it matters, but it seems like a strange coincidence."

Tuper asked a few more questions and got a good description of Sarah. She was almost nineteen and had brown hair. Five-foot-five, thin, and very quiet.

They said their goodbyes, and Joseph walked them out. "I'm glad you're here to help, and that you're helping Jacob as well."

"You know I'll do whatever I can, but you may want to call the police on this one. Sarah doesn't sound like a runaway girl."

"That is not likely to happen, so you'd better get the job done, *mein kleiner Bruder*."

As they drove off, Lana asked, "Is Joseph your brother?"

"Why?"

"Because he called you his *kleiner Bruder*, which means *little brother*."

"Oh that." Tuper shrugged. "Let's get back to Helena."

CHAPTER 13

Wednesday afternoon

It was quiet in the Impala, with Ron and Tuper chatting only occasionally. Lana sat in the backseat, deep in research with the motor vehicle department in Wyoming. If she knew the first number on the license plate, it would have narrowed her search to the county, but with no details, she had to do a statewide search. She pulled up the form to request a title search, but she didn't have enough information even for that. It would take too long anyway. The easiest way was to hack into the Department of Transportation Motor Vehicle Services—which she did.

Lana found a total of ten 1970 Oldsmobile Cutlass Supremes in the state. That was more than she'd expected, but she could narrow down the lot. Four were not convertibles, leaving six. Four were blue, and only three of those were twilight blue metallic. *Finn really knew his cars.* Three of the sedans were presently on a car dealer's lot, waiting to be purchased. One was blue. She decided to concentrate on the other blue vehicles. One was in an auto museum in Gillette, Wyoming. She dug deeper into the last blue Cutlass. It was registered to Nellie and Virgil Dunn.

"I think I may have found the car, but I'm not sure how much good it will do us."

"Why's that?" Tuper asked, then mumbled to Ron, "I hope I don't regret askin'."

"The owner has lived at the same address in Cody for over fifty years. I looked at her house on Google Maps. It's small, but cute and well kept, and she has a garage. Her driver's license is still active, but I can't imagine she drives too far at her age." Lana scanned the summary she'd created. "Nellie was married to Virgil for sixty-two years, but he passed away two years ago. They had two children, a boy and a girl. Their son had a heart attack and died a few months before his father. He lived at home, was never married, and had no children."

"He must have been fairly young. Did he have a history of heart disease?" Ron asked, apparently caught up in her story.

"I don't know. I'll follow that later," Lana said. "The daughter, Leona, moved to Helena after attending college in Missoula. She married a man named Wylde and had two boys, Owen and Kingston. Mr. Wylde was killed in a car accident when the boys were still young. As adults, the boys went in different directions. Owen became a preacher; Kingston went to prison."

"And you think one of them is the guy with the tattoos." Tuper turned in his seat to look at her.

"Yes, I do."

"The preacher or the prisoner?"

"Come on, Pops."

"That's a pretty big leap," Tuper said.

"You got something better?"

"Nope, sure don't."

"Is he worth checking out?" Ron asked.

"She doesn't miss many," Tuper whispered to Ron.

"I heard that, Pops. Thanks."

"Don't let it go to yer head."

"What now?" Ron asked.

Lana knew the question was meant for Tuper, but she answered it anyway. "I have a home address for Leona and for her job at Daffy's Lucky Duck Casino. We should go by her house and see if the car is there. If it's not, we could knock on the door and ask some questions."

"That might make him run," Tuper said.

"We can stake out the place and follow him if he shows up," Ron added. "That might lead us to the girls."

"Or maybe we knock some sense into his head," Tuper said. "But this guy may not have anything to do with them."

"We don't have anything else to go on," Lana said. "I'll keep researching these guys and see where that leads. We can call Grandma Nellie and ask her about her car."

"Maybe it was stolen," Ron suggested.

"If so, it wasn't reported. I checked."

Ron took his eyes off the road, glanced back, and gave Lana a quizzical look.

Tuper grinned. "Like I said, she's good."

Lana went back to searching for information about Owen and Kingston Wylde. She found social media accounts for both, but with quite different results. While Kingston was being a delinquent in his young adult years, Owen was doing missionary work in Mexico. The preacher had a following, but most were his church members, and he was active daily on Facebook and Twitter.

But Kingston's Facebook posts were sporadic, and his

friends were of a different caliber. And there were periods when he was totally inactive. Lana checked his prison time and that coincided with his inactivity for eighteen months. Other times, she surmised, he had lacked internet access. She found only a few photos of Kingston from when he was much younger.

When they were nearly to Helena, Lana placed a call. "Is this Nellie Dunn?"

"Yes. Who's calling?"

"My name is Betty Smith, and I work at the Wyoming Classic Auto Museum. I heard you own a 1970 Oldsmobile Cutlass Supreme. Is that correct?"

"Yes."

"My boss is interested in purchasing the vehicle for our museum, assuming it's in good condition. Is that something you would consider?"

"It's in nearly perfect condition. The car belonged to my late husband, and I wouldn't want it to leave the family."

"He might be pleased to know it's in a museum, ma'am. Some men get pretty attached to their cars. Has it been kept in the garage all these years?"

"Yes. It's in very good shape, but my grandson is using it. He has always loved that car, and I know Virgil would want it to be driven."

"Do you think your grandson might want to sell it?"

"No. The car is still in my name, and I wouldn't allow that to happen."

"Thank you for your time, ma'am. You have a good day." Lana ended the call and looked at Tuper.

"Give us the directions to Leona Wylde's house."

CHAPTER 14

Wednesday late afternoon

The Wylde residence was a small house in a rough neighborhood. The garage door was open, revealing a packed space with no car. An older-looking, gray Toyota sat in the driveway. Nearby, a twenty-something man with short brown hair was putting a plastic bag into a trashcan. They watched from the car as he rolled the container out to the street and closed the garage door.

"That must be Owen," Lana said. "Because it sure doesn't fit the description of Kingston."

"Or neither," Tuper commented.

"It looks like Owen, the preacher." Lana turned her laptop toward Pops. "Look, that's him. Let's go ask if Kingston has the car."

"Not sure that's the best move," Tuper said. "We don't want to tip our hand. Just because those brothers are different doesn't mean they're not close."

"Like you and Joseph?" Lana asked. "You guys are different. Are you close?"

Tuper didn't answer. "He's getting into that green Infiniti parked on the street. Follow him."

The man stopped for gas at a mini-mart, then drove to a strip mall at the edge of town. He parked in front of a building with a sign that read: ALTERED LIFE ASSEMBLY CHURCH. The church sat between a donut shop and a vacant building that still had the sign on it indicating it was once a dry cleaner. The man got out of the car and walked inside.

"That must be Owen's church," Lana said. "Although it looks more like an accountant's office. I just checked online, and this is Owen's home address. There's an apartment upstairs, and that's probably where he lives. He's not married and has no kids. Maybe his brother lives there with him." She glanced around. "I don't see the Cutlass. According to the aerial view, there's parking in the back. Want me to walk around and check for the car?"

"We'll drive," Tuper said.

In the back, two cars were parked behind the donut shop and none behind the church or the dry cleaners.

"What now?" Ron asked.

"Do you have a home address for Kingston?" Tuper asked Lana.

"It's listed as his mother's home, but it's been that forever, so it might just mean he never formally changed it. We need to find that car. We know one of Nellie's grandsons has it, and it doesn't appear to be Owen."

"All that will tell us is that Kingston has his grandmother's Cutlass," Tuper said. "It doesn't mean he was at Smith's that day."

"It does if the car is beat up like Finn described," Lana countered.

Tuper turned to Ron. "What are your thoughts?"

"I wish we had something else to go on," Ron said. "This guy, even if he's the right one, may have just happened to be in the parking lot that day. We have no other reason to even suspect him. But Lana's right. If the car matches Finn's description, we will know we found the guy who was there, watching Rita." He looked back at Lana. "Did you find any photos of Kingston?"

"Nothing posted on social media since before his stint in prison. His profile pic is a spider web, like the tattoo Rhonda described." Lana visualized the poor missing girls, and a dark thought hit her. "I just realized something." She opened Google Maps to their area. "Saturday night, Rita went missing from Little Boulder. On Sunday, Gertrude disappeared from Green Valley, and Monday, Sarah vanished from Wild Grass." She turned her laptop toward the guys. "See the line he's following. That means he could hit close to Wild Grass next."

"But which way?" Ron sounded distressed too. "He could go to Cascade, or Milford, or drive up the 15 and hit Hillcrest Colony next. Maybe we should call Jacob and have him warn the others if he hasn't already."

"Or maybe I should go undercover at one of the colonies and see if we can smoke him out," Lana said.

"We need a better idea of where he's headed next, or it'll be a waste of time for you to act as bait," Tuper said. "Although, it would get you out of my hair for a few days."

"Thanks, Pops. But you're right. And the one thing we know for sure is that all three missing girls were at Smith's last Saturday, which may or may not have anything to do with it. But it is the one thing they have in common." Without pausing she went on, changing tactics. "Maybe we should try to track Kingston. If we could find that car and follow it, he might lead us to something. I wish there was more I could research, but we're kind of stuck here."

"Are you done jabberin'?" Tuper rolled his eyes. A moment later his phone rang, and he listened for a minute. "Thanks, Jacob." Tuper hung up.

"What?" Lana was eager to track a new lead.

"Hannah, a nineteen-year-old from Sandy Colony has been gone since Sunday, a week ago."

Lana checked the map. "That's still in line with the others, but at the opposite end, which makes sense. It started there and is moving this direction. But Hannah couldn't have been at Smith's on Saturday if she disappeared a week ago. We need to find out if she went the Saturday before. Where else do they go shopping? Great Falls is still the largest city closest to the colonies, but maybe some Hutterites go to a smaller town, something closer to them. What other supermarkets are in Montana? What about Walmart? Or maybe there's a Costco."

"Agony! Stop! We got the point. The Sandy colonists go to Great Falls to do their shopping."

"How do you know that? Did Jacob say so? Call him back and ask him."

"Agony, I know where they shop."

"Of course, you do." Lana raised her hands to make a grand gesture. "You know a guy there, right?"

"Know 'em all," Tuper grumbled.

"But if she's been gone a week, why wouldn't someone know about it?" Lana struggled to make sense of the new development. "Sandy Colony is not that far from Little Boulder or Green Valley. You'd think they would have shared the information. Don't they talk to each other? I don't get it."

"They have formal social meetings when they get together with other colonies," Tuper explained. "In between, there's not much communication unless they need something."

"But wouldn't they check to see if Hannah went to another colony? It seems that would be the first place they'd look."

Tuper rolled his eyes again. "If she was headed to another colony, she woulda told 'em. There'd be no need for secrecy. Besides, the Sandy *Haushalter* thought she left on her own. One of the girls claimed Hannah was smitten with some boy in town."

"Did she get his name? Or a description? Maybe Hannah didn't leave on her own. Maybe there was more to it. Do you want me to go undercover at Sandy? I learned stuff at Little Boulder that no one else did."

"I don't think the *Haushalter* will allow it." Tuper seemed resigned. "He's convinced that everyone is cooperating, and that Hannah left willingly."

CHAPTER 15

Wednesday evening

After dinner at Clarice's, Lana took out her laptop and began to work. Tuper picked up his hat and said, "I'm going out for a bit. Wanna come with me, Ron?"

"Sure." Ron got up from the table. "Where are we going?"

"I wanna see if we can find that Cutlass. And since you're comin' along, you might as well drive."

"Sure." Ron grabbed his keys off the counter. "Thanks for dinner, Clarice."

"You're welcome anytime."

Ron turned to Lana. "You did a great job at the colony." He smiled, started toward the door, and ran his hand through his hair. "I need to get me a cowboy hat if I'm going to stay here much longer. I feel out of place."

Tuper opened the door, and Dually darted to him.

"Is it okay if Dually goes? Because I think he's going with or without me."

"Yep."

"I'm beginning to think he likes you better than me," Ron said as he closed the door behind him.

As soon as they were gone, Clarice said, "I think Ron likes you. He's always checking you out. And you get a special kind of smile from him."

"Well, I don't like *him*. I mean, I like him okay, but I don't know if I trust him. He shows up here out of the blue, and he asks too many questions."

"That's called being friendly." Clarice stepped over and patted her shoulder. "Lana, you've been hanging out on your computer too long without socializing. I don't know what you're hiding from, but if it's a bad relationship, you need to let go at some point. Not every man is suspect. Certainly not Ron. He's one of the good guys. He's Sabre's brother and JP's best friend. If you knew them, you'd know Ron can be trusted."

"But I don't know them, and I don't really know him." Lana turned back to her laptop. "I'd better get to work. I have an idea."

"Something you can find on the web?"

"Yeah."

"It must be hard since the Hutterites don't do much with technology."

"But the *Welt Leuts*, as they call us, do. And if someone on the outside has some kind of ring going, they may be chatting about it."

"You mean like a Hutterite girl sex ring?"

"Why else would someone take them? There's a lot of weird men out there, and some have very strange sexual fantasies."

"And many people around here don't like the Hutterites."

"Why? They all seem so nice. It's just because they're

different, right? I get that. People look at me strangely all the time, and I'm just a *little* odd. They obviously have a hard time with anything that doesn't fit into their tiny, safe worlds."

"Then there are the rumors. People say the Hutterites can't be trusted and that they steal things. That's why the women wear those big skirts."

"What do you think?"

"I suppose some of it's true. I can't imagine everyone in the colonies follows all their teachings and rules, but mostly I think people are afraid because they're different."

"Rita had a Hollywood magazine that she looked at. Do you think she stole it?"

"She might have, or she could have bought it. They have access to some money, just not much. I know they like Harlequin romance novels. The elders know the women read them, but they don't do anything about it. But if they thought it led to something like these disappearances, they would stop it."

～

"Where to?" Ron asked.

"Let's go by Leona's first," Tuper said. "Remember the way?"

"I think so. It was only a few turns." But it was dark now, and Ron hoped he could find it again.

When they arrived, two of the lights on Leona's street were out, but they could tell the driveway was empty. The garage door was closed, but unless it had been cleaned out in the last couple of hours, there wasn't a car parked inside. The house was completely dark—no outside lights and no glow from inside.

Ron drove to the end of the street, then turned around and drove back. They both checked the cars for a block in each direction, but the Cutlass was not to be found.

"Just because Kingston uses this address doesn't mean he lives here," Ron said.

"I know. He probably only goes home to mama when he has nowhere else to go."

"Want to try the bar?"

"Yep."

"Do you know where Daffy's Lucky Duck Casino is?"

"Yep."

"Are there any bars or casinos in the area you don't know?"

"Nope."

Fifteen minutes later, Ron pulled into Daffy's parking lot. They cruised around looking for the Cutlass.

"There's the Toyota," Ron said, pointing. "That must be Leona's car."

Ron made a second trip around the lot, then asked, "Should we go in?"

"I don't want to talk to Leona," Tuper said. "Don't choose to tip our hand yet."

"But we can find out what she looks like in case we need to know later."

"Guess that wouldn't hurt."

Ron parked, cracked the window for Dually, and they got out. When they reached the door, a white-haired man staggered out. He stopped, swayed a little, and said, "Hi, Toop. I left a few for you, not many though." He zigzagged away.

"Do you think he's driving?" Ron asked.

"Naw. His son picks him up. He lost his license years ago."

They walked to the end of the bar counter, and a female bartender started toward them.

"Dang." Tuper spun around. "Let's go."

He hurried out and Ron followed.

Tuper stopped just outside the door, looking worried. "I didn't know it was *that* Leona."

Ron laughed. "How many Leonas do you know?"

"I guess I forgot her name. We had a thing going a while back. It didn't end well."

"The bartender?"

"Yep. You go back in and get a good look at her. I'll wait in the car."

Ron handed over his keys and went inside. He walked past the counter, but Leona moved swiftly to the other end. Ron kept going around the small casino, checking out the slot machines, then back toward the bar counter. This time, he got a good look at the woman. She had bleach-blonde hair, a slim figure, and a red-lipstick smile that welcomed each customer. She was only fifty-nine, but her face had more wrinkles than most women her age. Ron attributed it to smoking.

"That was quick," Tuper said when Ron climbed back in the car. "I thought you'd have a beer or something."

"I didn't want to keep you waiting, and I got a decent look at her. How bad is your relationship with her?"

"It's best I keep clear unless it's a last resort."

CHAPTER 16

Wednesday night

Lana searched social media sites for anything Hutterite connected, but found only a few comments made by individuals, mostly negative. She needed to go deeper into the dark web. She had to be careful. If she asked questions about Hutterites, and someone was watching, it would move them closer to her. The Hutterites covered a large part of Central Canada and had scattered colonies in Montana, North and South Dakota, Minnesota, and Washington. That narrowed her location. Along with another comment or two, and she could be pinpointed. She couldn't let that happen.

There was a better way to find information on the dark side. Ravic, her cyber friend. She trusted him, or her, she wasn't certain. But she had a hunch Ravic was a guy. They had never met, nor did they exchange information about themselves. It was all completely anonymous. As far as she kne, Ravic knew her only as Cricket.

She sent a message to his hacker account. He would check it right away unless he was offline. He got right back to her:

Cricket—*I need your help.*

Ravic—*Hi, Cricket. Nice to see you back. What can I do?*

Cricket—*Do you know of any underground sex rings?*

Ravic—*You looking to join one? (smiley face)*

Cricket—*They wouldn't want me. I'm looking for missing girls from a couple of colonies.*

Ravic—*What religion?*

Cricket—*Hutterites.*

Ravic—*That explains why you can't do it yourself, too localized. I'll look around.*

While waiting to hear back, Lana decided to check her old email, the one where the man from her past would contact her. She kept the account to keep tabs on him. She knew *he* couldn't resist emailing her once in a while, and she hoped he would tip his hand if he had learned anything about her. She opened the email, hoping to find nothing, and sighed. Just a bunch of junk mail. She took a deep breath, then wondered why she hadn't heard from him in a while.

She sat back and continued to wait for something from Ravic. Clarice had to open the bar in the morning, so she'd gone to bed. Lana thought about what Clarice had said about getting out more. She'd tried that with Brock, a fireman she'd met a few months back. She'd gone on one date, if you could call it that, but she'd been too afraid to do more. They had met for coffee, and although she'd enjoyed it, she'd felt uncomfortable sharing her past but hadn't wanted to lie either. It was too difficult to have a real relationship if she couldn't be truthful. And she still wasn't sure Brock hadn't been sent by someone to find her.

He'd continued to call her for about a month. At first, she'd made excuses not to see him. After a while, she stopped answering, so he quit calling. But if Brock was a plant, he knew enough about her to find her—and nothing had happened. *Maybe it was safe to see him,* she thought. *He sure was good-looking, and she'd enjoyed his company—in what little time they'd had.*

Her laptop dinged and startled her. Lana checked her email.

Ravic—*Found something. Not sure how helpful. Two girls missing from different Schmiedeleut colonies in North Dakota a few months ago. One body recovered.*

Cricket—*Oh no.*

Ravic—*You might check out a radical social media called Frinkers. Rumor says the name comes from "free thinkers."*

Cricket—*Never heard of them.*

Ravic—*They're new. Lots of different ones popping up. Some talk there that might be what you're looking for.*

Cricket—*Like what?*

Ravic—*Feelers put out for "Home grown obedient wife." From someone using the tag "Steller." His profile says "my name is Steller —because I am." Idiot!*

Cricket—*Maybe he means stealer. Either way he can't spell.*

Ravic—*Which wouldn't matter if he wasn't bragging about it. Not sure if it means anything. I'll keep looking.*

Cricket—*Thanks.*

It didn't take her long to find the Frinkers website and hack into it. It was only two months old and already had over ten thousand members. Ninety percent of them were men, and it only took a few minutes to determine that "free thinking" was about sexual exploration. The public posts were not explicit but were often personal. The private messages were a different story. Men telling other men what they were looking for, and guys responding with where to find those things.

Out of curiosity, Lana checked to see if the members were using their real names. She checked five and found they were all aliases. It didn't take long to find the real names for all of them. *Dummies.* They thought they were so clever.

Lana found the chat stream Ravic had referred to. The public post said, *I deserve a home grown obedient wife. Anyone?*

The private messaging follow-up read:

Steller—*I may be able to help with that. What exactly are you looking for?*

Bubba—*It's hard to find a woman who obeys her man in USA. I could get one from China, but I don't want a commie. Doesn't USA know how to raise a woman? And she must believe in God. None of them atheist heretics.*

Steller—*I might have something for you. How old?*

Bubba—*Young, virgin, but legal. If there is such a thing.*

Steller—*Give me a week or two. I'm working on some merchandise now.*

Lana followed Steller's private messages and found another exchange:

Jim Dandy—*Where do I find a nice virgin?*

Steller—*For marriage?*

Jim Dandy—*Hell no. I just want the experience. Never had it. Wife told me she was, but she lied. I've had lots of others since, but no virgins.*

Steller—*I'll see what I can do. Underage okay?*

Jim Dandy—*Don't matter as long as she's at least 14. I don't do no kids.*

"Like a fourteen-year-old is not a kid," Lana said out loud to an empty room. "Sickos."

CHAPTER 17

Wednesday night

"Who's a sicko?" Ron asked as he and Tuper walked in the door.

"Men," Lana said. "You're all a bunch of sickos."

"Hey, what did I do?" Ron looked hurt.

"Nothing." Lana took a breath and told them what she'd found. "It's a long shot, but I'll keep an eye on it."

"When did Bubba leave the message about the homegrown wife?" Ron asked, walking over to the counter and propping himself on a stool. He was positioned about three feet from Lana and facing her.

"Friday. So, it's only been a few days. And Steller said he needed a week or so to acquire the *merchandise*."

"What if he needs to cultivate it?" Ron grimaced. "If he meant one of these girls, how would he convince her to marry someone?"

"I don't know. Maybe show them a glimpse of a *better life*, or torture them until they give in."

"Either way would take some time," Ron said.

"True, and this conversation may not have anything to do with our missing girls."

"You're both gettin' off track." Tuper, still standing, gave Ron a look. "You gotta watch Agony. She can go down some pretty deep rabbit holes. Don't let her drag you down with her."

Lana ignored Tuper and told them about the two missing girls in North Dakota. "They were from different colonies, but both were *Schmiedeleut*."

"What's that?" Ron asked.

"You had to ask, didn't you?" Tuper mumbled.

Lana waved at Tuper in a dismissive gesture and shared her research. "The Hutterites trace their roots to the Radical Reformation of the early sixteenth century. Jacob Hutter, their founder, established the colonies in 1527. The first communes were formed in—"

"He don't need a history lesson," Tuper cut in. "Just tell him the differences in the branches."

"Okay. There are three, the *Lehrerleut*, the *Dariusleut*, and the *Schmiedeleut*. They have some distinct differences, including organizational structure and type of dress. Such as the scarves. The women all wear black scarves with white polka dots, but the dots for the *Schmiedeleut* are smaller." Tuper raised his eyebrows. "Anyway," Lana continued, "the *Lehrerleut* are the most conservative, then the *Dariusleut*, and the most liberal are the *Schmiedeleut*."

"Which group is Jacob's?"

"*Lehrerleut*. It's mostly *Lehrerleut* in and around Great Falls and Helena. There are a few *Dariusleut* colonies around Lewistown and Grass Range, but from what I've read, there aren't any *Schmiedeleut* in Montana. They're in North and South Dakota, Minnesota, and Canada, near Winnipeg."

"So, the most conservative groups are here?" Ron frowned. "That's curious."

"Why?"

"Because it seems like it would be easier to get inside the more liberal branches. Why infiltrate these strict colonies?"

"I suppose it depends on why they want the girls. Or maybe it's because whoever is taking them lives locally, and it's convenient. Or maybe it's part of a larger ring, and they have penetrated other colonies. We don't really know how much has happened." Lana stood and started to pace. "This could be happening all over Canada and in our northern states. We don't know because most of it wouldn't have been reported. The Hutterites won't call the police and create a record unless someone dies. This could've been going on for decades and is just now happening here. Or maybe girls have gone missing from local colonies before, and they just thought they left willingly."

"Agony! You're gettin' carried away again."

"What did you find, Pops? You do any better?"

"We saw Leona workin' at Daffy's, but we didn't talk to her. Didn't see the Cutlass."

"So, what now?" Ron asked.

"I'm leavin'," Tuper said. "See you first thing in the morning. We'll regroup."

"Off to see Louise?" Lana asked.

"None of yer business."

Dually followed Tuper to the door. Tuper scratched the dog's ears and patted his head before leaving.

Lana smiled at the sight, then became solemn. "Having Dually around has been good for Tuper. He sure misses Ringo and was pretty shaken up when he died. He was angry because he was hit by a car and left on the street. No one called him to let him know. I don't understand people. His phone number was on Ringo's collar."

"I'm glad Dually brings him some pleasure. I just hope it doesn't stir up too many memories of Ringo."

"I think it's good. He seems content having him around," Lana said. "Do you know what Tuper has planned for tomorrow?"

"No, but he probably *knows a guy* who can help."

"Right? That man knows more people than anyone I've ever met. He could do the Montana census all by himself. And they all seem to want to help him." Lana tilted her head. "I can't tell if they really like him, or if they all owe him something. He's kind of like a Cowboy Godfather, yet they aren't afraid of him. It's a weird kind of respect."

"I know what you mean. All he has to do is ask, and he gets answers or help. He does a lot for others though too. I know he's helped Jacob and Peter from the colonies." Ron walked to the refrigerator and took out a soda. "Would you like something to drink?"

"No, thanks," Lana said and continued her questioning. "Is Tuper Jacob's brother? Jacob kept calling him *Brüderlein*."

"Does that mean *brother* in German?" Ron asked, sitting back down at the counter.

"Yeah, and Joseph called him *kleiner Bruder*, which means *little brother*."

"Joseph, Jacob, and Peter are all brothers. Maybe Tuper is an honorary brother or something. Jacob and Peter claim Tuper saved their lives when they were young. I could never get more of the story, but I know it has something to do with that big scar Tuper has on his face."

"I asked him about the scar," Lana said. "He claimed he met up with a bear and didn't have a gun. When I asked him to tell me about it, he said"—Lana imitated Tuper's deep voice—"'I just did.' I tried once or twice after that, but I couldn't get any more information."

"That's Tuper. He doesn't share much about himself, but he has saved me a time or two. I wouldn't be around if it wasn't for him. That's all the more reason I want to help him find these girls—before it's too late."

"Me too."

CHAPTER 18

Thursday early morning

"Mornin'." Tuper walked in. "Clarice gone already?"

Lana sat at the table, laptop open, barely noticing when Tuper came in. When she realized he was talking to her, she said, "Sorry. She had to go in early."

Ron brought two cups of coffee from the kitchen and set one down for Lana. "You don't drink coffee, right, Toop?"

"Occasionally. Tea mostly."

"I've got the water on," Ron said. "I'll get you some tea. Are you hungry?"

"Already ate."

Lana and Ron exchanged glances and smiled, making Tuper scowl.

"So, how's Louise?" Lana asked.

"None of yer business. Are you two ready to work?"

"Always," Ron said. "What do you have in mind?"

"We need to find Kingston and figure out if he was at Smith's. If he wasn't, we can let him go and try somethin' else.

88

Don't know what, but somethin'. I'm hoping to hear back from Jacob or Peter. They're puttin' out feelers to all the colonies, locally, in other states, and even Canada."

"I take it that no one has heard from any of the girls," Lana said.

"Nope."

"We could drive by Leona's again and see if the Cutlass is there," Ron suggested.

"Already dunnit."

"Do you think there's a chance Kingston stays at his brother's?" Ron asked.

"Went by there too."

"Dang, Pops," Lana said. "What time did you get up?"

"In the mornin' like sensible people do. You miss the whole day if you sleep in like you do."

Lana waved off the insult. She was used to his remarks. "I worked late last night and discovered more about Kingston. I think I read every post on his Facebook account. He was on the site yesterday bragging about his new ride. He didn't say what it was or post a photo, so it may not be the Cutlass. Also, several of his contacts seem to be hot for him. Why wouldn't they be? The guy's a real catch, right?" Lana rolled her eyes. "Anyway, I think he may be hooking up with a woman here in East Helena and another one in Great Falls. I traced his local booty call to a house on York. She's a hairdresser named Babs Arragon." Lana gave them the street address.

"That's not far from here," Tuper said.

"Less than a mile." Lana nodded.

"Want me to have a look?" Ron asked.

"We'll both go," Tuper said. He headed for the door.

"Come back and get me if you decide to check out anything else," Lana called out.

Ron and Tuper climbed into Ron's car and drove the short distance to Babs' apartment. Ron had no trouble finding it, but there weren't many parking spaces. They drove around the complex twice, looking for the Cutlass, but didn't find it. They drove down a street that bordered the apartments and struck out again. They were almost a block away when Tuper spotted the dark blue sedan.

"Well, I'll be durned. Agony did it again."

"She's pretty sharp," Ron said.

"Don't ever tell her I said so. She's hard enough to put up with."

"She's feisty for sure," Ron said. "Do you want me to come back here and keep an eye on Kingston? I've done a lot of surveillance for JP. I'm almost good at it."

"The guy might lead us somewhere, but my bet is he won't be up for a few more hours. Let's go back to Clarice's and regroup."

The guys walked in, and Lana looked up from her laptop. They hadn't been gone long.

"Good lead," Ron said. "We found the Cutlass parked on the street near Babs' apartment."

"Why aren't you watching him?" Lana's voice had a shrill urgency. "We need to follow Kingston and see where he goes. It's all we really have, and he could lead us to the girls. The sooner we find them the better chance they have for survival."

Lana paused briefly as Ron walked past her into the kitchen, smiling.

"You'd better not let him get away. I'm frustrated because it's so difficult finding information about the victims." She squinted at Ron. "What are you doing?"

"Making sandwiches and filling my thermos with coffee. I may be gone a while, and I want to be prepared for a long day."

Lana followed him into the kitchen, took bread out of a drawer, and set it on the counter.

"Thanks," Ron said. "But I got this. I'm used to making my own lunches."

"I thought since you lived with your mother, she probably made your meals."

"Only when she's around and only because she likes to cook. I've been on my own for quite a while. I've learned to fend for myself."

"You're probably better at cooking than I am," Lana mumbled. Then she spoke up. "I just want you to get it done and get out of here before we lose our only suspect."

Ron made two sandwiches and filled his thermos. Lana retrieved a lunch sack and tossed in an apple and a Ziploc baggie of nuts when he wasn't looking. Ron loaded the sandwiches and thanked her.

"I'm off," he said. When he started for the door, the dog followed. "I don't think I should take Dually. He might bark when I need quiet. Although, he's awfully good most of the time."

"Leave him with me," Tuper said. "He should be all right anywhere I go."

"Keep me posted if anything new comes up," Ron said, looking directly at Lana.

Before she could respond, Tuper's phone rang. Ron waited by the door until Tuper finished his conversation.

"That was Jacob. Another girl is gone."

"Which colony?" Ron asked, alarmed.

"Diamond Valley." Tuper was even more tight-lipped than usual.

Lana googled the location. "It's just north of Great Falls." *What was happening to these poor girls?*

"When was she taken?" Ron asked.

"Last night around six."

Lana calculated the distance. "So, Kingston had plenty of time to snatch her, do whatever he does, and get back to Bab's place." Their one suspect was still in play.

CHAPTER 19

Thursday morning

"What else did Jacob say about the girl from Diamond Valley?" Lana asked, still sitting in front of her laptop at Clarice's kitchen table. "How old is she? Did you get her name? How about a description?"

"Do you ever wait for an answer before you ask ten more questions?" Tuper asked.

"Sometimes, but I have so many questions. I figure even an old guy like you can tackle more than one at a time."

"Her name is Tiffany."

"That's not a Hutterite name. What's the deal? I'm confused. I thought they only used Hutterite names. Why would they name her Tiffany?"

"Yer doin' it again. If yer done, I'll tell you what I know."

Lana made a motion to zip her lips.

"If only," Tuper muttered. "Most parents call their children solid Hutterite names. Family names mostly, but the last generation has reached out a bit, and you'll see a few that are different."

"That's good. There are so many Annies and Marys and Magdelenas that it's hard to keep track. I read that they use the initial of the first name of their father until they marry, then they take the initial from their husband. But without enough names to go around, you end up with lots of girls with the same name *and* initial. It's confusing. I know we use names that are sometimes unusual and hard to remember, but at least there's distinction. I like our way better."

"Your zipper's broken," Tuper said. Lana closed her lips tight, and Tuper continued. "The girl is eighteen, quite tall, with light brown hair and nice teeth."

"Nice teeth?"

"I'm just telling you what I know, and before you ask, yes, she was at Smith's on Saturday. The *Haushalter* has talked to all his girls, and they don't know much except that Tiffany was a lot like Rita and curious about the *Welt Leuts*." He paused. "By the way, she was engaged to be married in the spring."

"To who? Did you get his name? What colony is he from? Has anyone checked on him? Maybe they ran off together. Maybe they couldn't wait for the traditional group ceremony. You know they all get married together in one ceremony. They do that to save money, with only one social gathering instead of five or six." Lana took a breath and shook her head. "I don't blame them for that. Our traditions are horrible. Most couples go thousands of dollars into debt before the wedding. That's no way to start a marriage. We have enough problems without starting off in the hole financially."

"Agony, Agony, Agony. The *Haushalter* is checking on the

groom now. There's no phone in the boy's colony so they're driving over."

"How far—?"

Tuper held up his hand to stop her chatter. "It's about an hour drive. He'll let us know as soon as he can."

"What do we do? Maybe we should go to Diamond Valley. I may be able to get more information like I did at Little Boulder."

"They seem pretty sure the girls are telling all they know."

"But what if they're not? Maybe they're not asking the right questions. I know how young girls think. That's how I found out about Finn. Without his description of the car, we wouldn't have been able to track Kingston. I might pick up on little things that the adults wouldn't."

Lana's phone dinged, and she summarized Ron's text out loud. "Kingston just got in his car, and Ron's following him.

"Are we going to Diamond Valley? I have the clothes. Or I can go in as a *Welt Leut.* They may be even more open if they're curious about the outside world. The girls' questions at Little Boulder were more about what life was like out here than anything else."

Lana's phone dinged again. She read the text and responded.

Ron—*He's moving pretty slow, but I'm staying back.*

Lana—*Don't get spotted.*

Ron—*I think he's going to his brother's.*

Lana shared the info with Tuper.

"Is he texting while he drives?"

"His car has a navigation system that he hooks his phone into. He can do it all hands free. He just talks and the phone transcribes it."

"Robots will take over the world before long," Tuper mumbled.

Lana glanced at her phone again and texted back.

Ron—*I was right. He's pulling into the lot at the church.*

Lana—*Keep us posted.*

Ron—*He's going inside. I'll check his car. Maybe one of the girls left something.*

Lana—*Be careful.*

She summarized the text for Tuper again.

Tuper stood. "He's doing what?"

"Looking in Kingston's car."

"I know that, but no one is watching out for him." Tuper started pacing. "I should've gone with him."

"You always do that when you're nervous."

"Do what?"

"Pace back and forth."

"I'm not nervous."

"Ron's a big boy. He can take care of himself. I'm sure he'll be careful. Didn't you say Ron's done surveillance work with JP?"

"Yeah. I guess it's not his first rodeo."

"Then stop your pacing and sit down."

"Stop yer jabberin' and I will."

CHAPTER 20

Thursday morning

Ron watched as the church door closed behind Kingston. He rolled forward a few spaces, parked his car, and walked back to the Cutlass. The driver side window was rolled down, but it wouldn't have mattered. He knew several ways to get into a car if he wanted to. Ron scanned the inside. Empty Pepsi cans and fast-food wrappers littered the back floor. The front area was relatively clean, except for the ashtray filled with cigarette butts. He snapped some photos.

Ron glanced at the church door, then reached in and pulled the trunk latch. He walked around to the back and opened it. Beside the spare tire and jack, he spotted a pile of rags, some clean and some greasy. He shot a few more photos, then moved the rags, exposing automotive magazines, tools, and a roll of duct tape. He took more pictures.

Ron looked up and saw the church door open. Kingston and another man walked out. Ron quickly closed the trunk, pretty certain they hadn't seen him. He walked calmly to his car and positioned himself to get more photos. Both men headed toward the Cutlass. Ron started taking pictures. When the men reached the car, he zoomed in and got a good image of each. He assumed the second man was Owen Wylde but intended to check social media later. If that didn't work, Lana would surely figure it out.

The men stood by the car, talking, for a good five minutes. Ron took a couple more photos, then texted the best shots to Lana. The second man gave Kingston a quick hug and walked away. Kingston got into the Cutlass and drove off. Ron texted Lana to let her know they were on the move again.

Lana moved to the sofa with her laptop but kept the pressure on Tuper. "I still think we should go to Diamond Valley and maybe the other colonies as well." Lana said. "I know I could get information that the leaders can't. I know the girls are taught to tell the truth, but they have their share of secrets just like anyone else. Maybe if they've been told the truth about what's going on, they might be scared enough to not hold back, but otherwise, I doubt the elders learned everything. And like I said before, they may not be asking the right questions."

"Agony, I got your point."

"You mean I'm right?"

"Didn't say that. But we'll wait to see what they find out about Tiffany's betrothed. And if Ron hasn't gotten any closer on Kingston, we'll go." Tuper paced back and forth in the living room.

"Rita's already been gone five days, and those girls from

South Dakota have been missing for two months. If Kingston isn't the guy, then we have nothing."

"Ain't there somethin' you can do on that contraption?" Tuper pointed at her laptop.

"I'm trying, but there's nothing to trace on the victims. Unlike the rest of the world, these girls don't live their lives online, so I have no way to track them. How did the cops do this sort of thing before the internet?" She continued to explain. "Now everybody's life is out there for the whole world to see. People say and do things online that they would never do publicly. They don't realize that there is nothing more public than the internet." Frustrated, she closed her laptop lid. "That leaves Kingston. He's our only lead. I hate when we only have one road to follow because if it's wrong, we have nowhere to go."

Tuper stopped, shook his head, but didn't comment.

Lana had a new thought. "Maybe there are a few things I can do." She opened her laptop again.

Tuper looked up at the ceiling. "Thank God."

"Will you stop pacing? You're distracting me."

Tuper sat in the recliner, leaned back, and pulled his hat down over his eyes. Dually lay down by his side.

Lana double-checked Kingston's release date from prison: two months and four days earlier. Exactly three days before the first girl disappeared from the colony in South Dakota and five days before the second one. If he was involved, that meant he went straight from prison to snatching up girls.

Lana probed further into Kingston's past, looking for any kind of predatory behavior. He had a juvenile record for shoplifting at sixteen. At fourteen, he'd tried to steal a car, but didn't make it out of the lot because he couldn't release the parking brake. Apparently, that act was a warmup for later digressions. After a few drug possession charges, grand theft auto had landed him in prison.

Tuper's phone rang, jarring him out of a catnap. Lana looked up and listened to the conversation, which involved little from Tuper.

When he hung up, she asked, "Was that Jacob? What did he say? Did they talk to Tiffany's fiancé? Did he know anything?"

Tuper cocked his head and waited. "You done?"

"Tell me, Pops. What did you find out?"

"Tiffany's fiancé hasn't seen her and knows nothing about her disappearance."

"They're sure?"

"Yep. He's home and very worried."

"I think we should go to Diamond Valley. There's nothing more we can do here. Ron can do his thing. We're both getting antsy, so let's just do something."

"Check with Ron first."

Lana picked up her cell phone and called. Ron didn't answer. She waited a few minutes and sent a text: *Everything okay?*

No response.

"Dang," Tuper said. "I hope there's nothin' wrong. We shoulda had him check in more often."

"He's probably fine."

"But if he's in trouble, we don't even know where he is."

Lana noticed the dog at the door. "I think Dually wants out."

When Tuper took him outside, Lana brought up the tracker on her phone. The first night Ron had been there, he'd plugged his phone into the outlet in the dining area. Not trusting him yet, Lana had hacked into it and set up a tracker so she would know where he was.

She checked his path. He'd gone to Babs' apartment, then to the Altered Life Assembly Church, and now he was at a bar in downtown Helena. Maybe Tuper was right. They shouldn't leave town until they know Ron is okay.

As Lana got up and started toward the kitchen for another cup of coffee, Tuper returned with Dually. A moment later, her phone rang, and she quickly answered.

"You okay, Ron?" Lana pressed a button. "I have you on speaker so Tuper can hear too."

"Sorry I couldn't answer a few minutes ago. Kingston stopped at a bar downtown, and I followed him inside. But I had to be careful because it was pretty empty."

Lana heard traffic noises in the background.

"Did he talk to anyone?" Tuper asked.

"Some guy came in and sat down next to Kingston. They chatted, drank a beer, and left. They walked out together but then went in different directions. I took a couple of photos, but I'm not sure how good they are. Like I said, it was difficult being discreet, and I barely made it out of the bar in time to follow him, but we're rolling again. We just got on I-15 going north."

"That's toward Great Falls. We're headin' that way too," Tuper said. "Gonna see what we can learn at Diamond Valley."

"Can you bring Dually?"

"Sure will. He don't seem to want to leave my side."

"Thanks, Toop. Lana, I'll send more pics when I can."

CHAPTER 21

Thursday early afternoon

Tuper pulled into the Diamond Valley Colony just after noon. Lana and the dog jumped out of his cramped Mazda before he shut off the engine. Jacob had managed to set up their visit on short notice. Even though Tuper knew Benjamin, the *Haushalter*, fairly well, he wasn't on the same terms with him as with Jacob. But Benjamin trusted Jacob implicitly, and in turn Tuper as well. They had all decided not to bother with a ruse for Lana. They didn't have time. Benjamin led them to the dining hall, where Tuper ate with the men, and Lana ate with the young women.

During lunch, Lana met the girls from Tiffany's dorm and learned that the missing girl's closest friends were Magdalena T. and Judith. After their cleanup duties, they went back to the dorm.

She started the conversation by saying, "I want some information from you, and I need to learn about life here. So, you can ask anything you want about me, and I'll tell you the truth. I ask the same of you, and I expect the same honesty and openness. Is that a deal?"

"That's a deal." They all nodded and agreed.

At first, they seemed timid about asking what they really wanted to know, but once they got rolling, there was no stopping them. They asked things like, "Do you like choosing your own clothes? Do you go to church? Do you get up at the same time every morning? Do you drive?" Then they moved to more personal questions such as: "Why do you dress like that? Do you eat at McDonald's? Do you go out on dates?"

In turn, Lana had them explain what their lives were like, especially their interactions with boys or men. They told her about their dating customs and how they met boys from other colonies.

"We don't marry within our colony," Judith said. "We have social events with other colonies so we can meet and find a husband."

"Are any marriages arranged?" Lana knew the answer, but she wanted them to open up as much as possible.

That got a giggle from the group. "No. We choose our own mates," Annie A. said.

"I know Tiffany is engaged. How did she meet her fiancé? Do you call him that?"

"We call them boyfriends or our betrothed," Annie said.

Judith answered Lana's first question. "Tiffany met Abraham at the summer festival. They had seen each other before, but at the festival, he kept approaching her and talking to her until she finally broke down. He said he always had an eye for her even when they were young."

"And she fell for him as well?"

"Yes." Judith hesitated. "But not as much as he did."

Lana asked more questions of the group, then asked to speak to Judith alone. They went outside and sat on a bench.

"You and Tiffany are good friends?"

"Yes, the best."

"Are you worried that she's gone?"

"Sort of."

"But not like the other missing girls?"

"Her parents are very worried. They just want to hear from her."

"Have you heard from Tiffany since she left?"

"No, but she's only been gone for one day. She couldn't get a letter to me that quickly."

"Do you think she chose to leave the colony?"

"I don't know. Tiffany is curious, and she talked about leaving. Most of the girls don't want to leave. Benjamin has explained about the missing girls from the other colonies, and I'm afraid of what could happen to her if she didn't leave on her own. If it were me, I would be very scared." The girl twisted her hands in her lap. "But whenever Tiffany went to town, she would chat with anyone who made time. I told her to be more careful, but she was never afraid."

"Was there someone in particular she visited with in town?"

"There was a guy who worked at Smith's that she thought was really cute. I saw him once, and she was right. He is the most handsome boy I've ever seen. He's real tall and has blond hair and blue eyes."

"Do you know his name?"

"No. But he's not stuck up or judgmental like so many *Welt Leuts*." Her eyes widened. "No offense."

"None taken."

"He's very friendly. We have a nickname for him."

"Tell me."

"Prince Dreamy."

"Did Tiffany ever mention meeting anyone else at the store?"

"She talked to lots of people, men and women. They weren't always friendly. She couldn't understand why some people seemed afraid of her. She used to say, 'Do they think we have lice or something?' Then she would laugh. It never stopped her from trying again."

"Did she ever meet a man with tattoos on his arm?"

Judith made a face. "No."

"Why did you grimace?"

"Because tattoos are prohibited by God. *Ye shall not make any cuttings in your flesh for the dead, nor print any marks upon you.* I don't think Tiffany would be interested in anyone with tattoos."

Or just not tell anyone if she was.

CHAPTER 22

Thursday late afternoon

"I think we need to have another chat with Finn," Lana said on the way to the car. As they drove away, she told Tuper what little she'd learned, then added, "So, I think Prince Dreamy is probably Finn. Unless there's another tall, young, blond man working at Smith's."

As they pulled into the store parking lot a half hour later, Lana's phone started dinging, text after text. She showed Tuper the pictures Ron had sent. It was difficult to recognize the faces in the ones taken in the bar, so they couldn't tell who the man with Kingston was. Lana texted with Ron for an update.

Lana—*Where are you?*

Ron—*Great Falls, outside a house. Kingston went inside about five minutes ago.*

Lana—*What's going on there?*

Ron—*Not sure, but a young woman gave him a kiss before they went inside. I think it's an afternoon hookup.*

Lana—*Good for her.*

Ron—*I'll check the house number and text the address.*

Lana—*Thanks. I'll check it out as soon as I can.*

"What did he say?" Tuper asked. Lana handed him her phone, but when he touched it, the screen changed. "Dang it." He handed the phone back. "I don't know how to work this thing. Just tell me what he said."

"He's at a woman's house, and he thinks Kingston stopped to see another honey. He sounds like you, Pops—a woman in every town, or more in some."

"Humpf."

Lana's phone dinged again.

"What was that?" Tuper asked.

"Ron sent me the address he's surveilling."

They got out of the car and headed toward the store. Once inside, Tuper asked a clerk if Rhonda was working, but she wasn't. Lana spotted Finn pushing a cart with boxes and hurried over. She caught up with him on the canned vegetable aisle. "Excuse me," Lana said. "Can you help me?"

Finn turned. "What can I do for you?"

"Can you reach those black olives up there?"

"Sure." He stared at her. "Do I know you?"

"Don't think so. I'm not from around here."

Tuper rounded the corner, and Finn glanced at him, then back at Lana. "Are you Helen?"

"Not today," Lana said. "Have you heard from Rita?"

"You are Helen, or the girl who said she was Helen a couple of days ago."

"We'll talk about that later. Have you heard from Rita?"

"No. And I'm worried sick."

"Have you heard from Tiffany?"

"Who's Tiffany?"

"The other Hutterite girl you've been charming."

"What are you talking about? I don't know any other Hutterite girls."

"No one else, Prince Dreamy?"

"Why are you calling me that?" He looked upset now.

"Isn't that what the Hutterite girls call you?"

"Why would they?"

Lana made a gesture, indicating his whole package. "Because you're ... all that. The girls think you're dreamy."

He blushed. "I've said hello to a couple of Hutterite girls, just like I would to anyone. But I've never had a real conversation with any of them besides Rita."

He sounded sincere, but Lana still wasn't convinced. She decided to try another tack. "I believe you." She smiled to seem sincere. "It's just that we're worried, and we want to find Rita before something awful happens to her. You seem concerned about her too."

"I am, and there's nothing I can do. It's so frustrating."

"Why don't we exchange phone numbers, and you can call me if you hear anything. If we find her, I'll let you know."

"I'd appreciate that."

"Call me." Lana gave him her number. He called, and she texted back. "Now you have my number too. Save it in case you need it." She started to walk away.

"What name do I save it under?" Finn called after her.

"Helen."

"Are you really Rita's friend?"

"What did I say?" Lana turned and started to walk away.

"Hey! Why do you have a phone? Rita didn't have a phone."

"I have it to find Rita." She kept walking, with Tuper right behind her.

"Don't you think we should put pressure on him?" Tuper asked.

"I got what I wanted—his number."

"He's a little young for you, don't you think?"

"Come on, Pops. I don't have time for boy toys. Besides, he's not my type. But now I can find out who he's been in contact with."

"With just a phone number?"

"And the call he made to me. It'll take some work, but I can do it."

"How far away is Ron?" Tuper asked, as they exited the store.

"Let me check. I'll run the address." Before they reached the car, Lana had found it. "He's three point two miles from here. Are we going? If so, I'll text him and make sure he's still there. If Kingston is on a booty call, it could take a while."

"Or not," Tuper said. "See if Ron needs us to bring him anything to eat or drink."

Lana got in the car and sent a text to Ron. She set the map directions and put the phone on speaker so Tuper could hear if Ron or anyone else called. Ron declined rations but welcomed the company. They reached their destination in less than ten minutes and quickly located Ron's car. Tuper parked behind him, and they got out and climbed inside Ron's more comfortable vehicle. Dually stuck his head into the front seat, demanding attention from Ron.

"I missed you too." Ron petted the dog, then glanced back at Lana. "You as well. Surveillance is so boring."

"Yep, it is." Tuper looked around. "This place looks familiar."

"Maybe you have the same taste in women as Kingston."

Lana laughed. "Of course, she'd be a little young for you, or a lot old for Kingston. But maybe her mother lives here too, or her grandmother."

Tuper snorted. "Don't you have something to look up?"

Lana was already working her laptop, gathering information about the house. Tuper and Ron chatted as they watched for activity.

"By the way," Lana said, "I checked Kingston's prison release against the disappearances of those girls in South Dakota. The first one disappeared three days after he got out."

"That gave him time to get from Montana to South Dakota," Ron said.

"He sure didn't waste much time," Tuper added.

"I was thinking it was some kind of sex ring," Lana said. "But now that Kingston seems to be jumping from one woman to another, maybe he's getting them for his own sexual gratification. When he got out of prison, he was probably pretty libidinous."

"What the heck is libid-whatever?" Tuper grumbled.

"Concupiscent," Lana said.

"Huh?"

"Debauched."

"What the heck are you sayin', woman?"

"Horny," Ron interjected.

"Why didn't you just say that?" Tuper scowled at Lana.

"Because it's more fun to yank your chain."

Lana went back to work. While she waited for a site to load, she looked around. It was still daylight so they could easily see if anyone came and went from the house. But there was little movement in the neighborhood.

Tuper stared at her from the front seat. "Agony, do you know who owns this house?"

"Just got it. The guy's name is Henry Hawk, but he doesn't live here. It's rented to three flight attendants, which is pretty interesting. What if they're moving these girls through the house somehow? Maybe they have a way to fly them out of state. There could be a whole international ring going on. Well, at least national. How does a lowlife like Kingston get involved in something like that? He must be the grunt guy who nabs them. But if that's the case, he wouldn't have access to any of the important guys at the top. He's too big of a risk. But someone has to have that job," Lana continued. "And it's a more likely scenario than a hot flight attendant dating Kingston. He's like … a real creep. Have you seen him? Of course, you have," she said, looking at Ron. "You've been following him and taking photos." She turned to Tuper. "And you've seen the pictures."

"Are you done jabberin'?"

"Just thinking out loud."

"Try thinkin' to yerself, so's the rest of us can think too."

"I'm still looking for more information. But I've learned a little about the owner. No criminal record, and he's lived in Montana all his life. Grew up right in this area. In fact, he lived in this house for years. But he moved in with his daughter a couple of years ago, shortly after his wife died."

Tuper reached for his door handle. "I have a hunch. I'm gonna go check it out. I'll take Dually." He looked at Ron. "You keep Lana."

"What if Kingston comes out, and Ron has to follow him?" Lana asked.

"Then you'll go with him. Call me if you do. I'll check in before I drive back."

"Where are you going?" Lana asked.

"I may be able to get some information about this place."

"From who?"

"I know a guy."

Lana and Ron exchanged glances. Tuper frowned. Ron smiled.

CHAPTER 23

Thursday early evening

Tuper drove to a house on the north end of Great Falls. The area had changed quite a bit since he'd been there, but he found his way, thankful it wasn't dark yet. He parked on the street, walked to the front door, and knocked. A tall, weather-beaten man with rounded shoulders and messy white hair answered the door.

"Hello, Hawk," Tuper said.

"I know that voice. Is that really you, Toop?"

"It's me."

Hawk reached out a large, gnarled hand. Tuper took it and received a vigorous handshake.

"It's nice to see you, my friend," Hawk said. "That's a funny expression for a guy in my condition. The eyesight's almost gone. All I have left are shapes."

"I'm sorry."

"Ain't your fault macular degeneration got me. Let's not stand in the doorway jawing. Come on in."

Hawk walked slowly and deliberately, but without holding onto anything. He led Tuper to the living room, and they both sat down.

"I'm sorry I haven't been by here sooner. I've just been so darn busy."

"You going to apologize for the weather too?"

Tuper laughed. "I'll stop."

"I understand. There's just not enough time to do all the things we want. Life gets in the way of living sometimes."

"Don't you know it."

"I'm glad you're here now. Do you have enough time to visit before you tell me why you dropped in?"

"I do."

They caught up on their lives for the past few years, with Hawk doing most of the talking. He bragged about his grand-children and great-grandchildren and complained about his eyesight and the loneliness he felt with his wife gone. "For the most part, life is good. My daughter has been wonderful. I know I can be a burden on her, but she never lets on. And those little ones sure know how to brighten up a day. I have no real complaints about living here, and my daughter is a great cook."

"Do you still own your house?"

"Yeah, my granddaughter Willa lives there. She's a flight attendant, and she shares it with coworkers. She takes care of the place, collects rent from the others, and manages it for me. In turn, she gets free rent. She's a good girl, so I help her all I can."

"Is it all women living there?"

"I hear that stewards and pilots crash there sometimes, but only for a night or two. The regulars are all women." Hawk bragged about his granddaughter a little more, then asked, "What brings you to Great Falls?"

"Remember Jacob from Little Boulder Colony?"

"Of course. Is he all right?"

"He is, but his granddaughter Rita is missing. I'm trying to help find her."

"I assume she didn't just leave on her own." Hawk sounded skeptical.

"We don't think so, and she didn't say she was leaving. She just disappeared one evening."

"You think she was kidnapped?"

"Most likely. Girls are missin' from other colonies too. Same suspicious circumstances."

"Do you think it's a ring?"

"Possibly."

"Those poor girls." He blew out a breath that rattled his lips. "Bastards." He paused for a second. "Do you have any leads?"

"One guy who was seen hangin' around Rita at Smith's last Saturday. He's an ex-con from Helena. Only been out for a few months. He's at…"

"Spit it out, Tuper."

"He's at your old house right now."

"Are you sure?"

"I just left there. I have someone watching him. He's been there about an hour or so."

"Willa might be in danger," Hawk said. "I'm sure she isn't involved in anything like that. She's a good girl."

"Maybe somethin's going on that she doesn't know about."

"Maybe, but she's pretty astute."

"This whole thing is a long shot." Tuper shifted uncomfortably. "We don't even know for sure if Kingston is involved."

"Either way, I don't want some lowlife hanging around her house." Hawk reached in his pocket and took out a smart phone.

"Pretty impressive. You know how to use that thing?"

"Willa taught me. She set it up so I could just say who to call. I don't have to see anything."

"What's your plan?"

"Call Willa and see where she is, for starters. I won't say anything to her right now unless I think she's in danger."

Hawk made the call and put it on speaker. It rang three times before she answered.

"Hi, Grandpa. Is everything okay?"

"I'm fine, baby girl. We haven't talked in a few days, and I was missing you. Where are you?"

"I'm in Salt Lake City between flights. Just trying to get a bite to eat."

"Call me when you get back."

"My flight doesn't get in until eleven tonight. Can I call in the morning?"

"That would be fine."

"I love you, Grandpa."

"Love you too, baby."

Hawk hung up and looked at him.

Tuper stood. "I'm gonna get back to your house."

"Thanks for letting me know. I hope you find Jacob's granddaughter. And I'll let you know what I find out."

"Thanks, Hawk."

"Will you do me one more?"

"Of course."

Hawk reached in his pocket and pulled out a business card.

All it contained was *HAWK* and a phone number. "Please call and let me know when that man leaves Willa's house. Hopefully, it'll be before she gets home."

"I'll do that."

"I don't care what time it is. I won't sleep much tonight anyway."

Tuper slipped the card into his pocket. "I need to get me some of these."

"My grandson made them so I could just hand them out when I need to. You're getting the first one. Who'd a thought?"

Tuper walked to the door and Hawk followed. "You know I'll do whatever I can to help." Hawk put his hand on Tuper's shoulder. "Thanks for coming by. I've missed you, my friend."

CHAPTER 24

Thursday night

"Did you get the impression Tuper knows the guy who owns this place?" Lana had moved into the front seat so Ron didn't have to keep turning to talk to her.

"That was my guess."

Ron started to ask about her past life, but Lana cut him off. He was probably just making small talk, but she wasn't that comfortable with him yet. *Just because he's Sabre's brother and JP's friend doesn't mean he didn't sell out.* She had never even told Tuper the whole story, and she trusted him.

Ron seemed to get the message because he changed the subject. "Tuper said you got Finn's phone number and were going to check his contacts. Have you found anything yet?"

"Nothing worthwhile. He calls his mom a lot and a couple of what appear to be close friends, but no one we know. I'm still checking, but he looks more like a boy scout every time I check on him."

"Maybe he is."

"I'll see what else I can find out about Henry Hawk." Lana keyed his name into a hacked county database and soon had the names of his children and grandchildren.

"Look," Ron said. "Someone's coming out."

Lana glanced up and saw a woman who wore a light-blue blouse, navy pants, and a scarf with shades of blue and white lines. "She's from Alaska Airlines."

"You know that how?"

"That's their new uniform." Lana caught Ron's eye for a second longer than she intended. "The scarf is very distinctive."

The woman got into a car in the driveway and drove off. No one else came out, so they settled back in. Lana returned to her search, frustrated that she didn't have enough information to dive deeply into something. Then she remembered Finn and decided to look further into his phone history. She didn't get very far before her laptop dinged, indicating a message.

Ravic—*Found something else you might be interested in.*

Cricket—*Hit me.*

Ravic—*It's on Frinkers. Steller is at it again. Check out his PMs.*

Lana signed into Steller's account on the site and went straight to his private messages.

Steller had responded to a message from King Midas.

Steller—*How soon do you need them?*

King Midas—*Yesterday.*

Steller—*Will you settle for this Saturday?*

King Midas—*It'll have to do. Same deal?*

Steller—*Yes.*

King Midas—*How many?*

Steller—*Three.*

King Midas—*Is that the best you can do?*
Steller—*I'll try for more.*
King Midas—*Bonus if you can.*

"Disgusting," Lana said out loud.

"What?" Ron asked.

"Ever hear of a social site called Frinkers?"

"I don't think so."

"It's new and supposedly stands for Free Thinkers. I haven't had a chance to check out the owner or see his or her intentions, but the site is drawing perverts and possibly conducting sexual transactions."

"Wow. I didn't know such a thing existed."

"Then you have no idea what's out there, especially on the dark web."

"Is that where Frinkers is?"

"No. It's still a public site. When sites get too deviant or get caught, they go dark. Usually by then, they have a pretty large following."

A vehicle pulled up behind them, and the driver quickly shut off the lights. Lana turned, and Ron checked in the rearview mirror.

"It's Tuper," Ron said.

Tuper left Dually in his Mazda and walked up to Lana's window. He bent down so he wasn't visible from the house. "I've got some feelers out about what's going on in there."

"Do you think it's a sex ring?" Lana asked. "Did you talk to someone who's been inside? Is it time to get the cops involved? They won't give up their property easily. Do you know who the ringleader is?"

"Agony, I don't know anything about a sex ring. I'm still diggin'. I'll know more tomorrow."

"Do you want your seat? I can get in the back."

"No. I plan to stay at Jacob's colony tonight. I'm not up to drivin' back to Helena, and I want to see a guy here in the morning." He looked over at Ron. "Do you mind keeping Lana with you?"

"Why are you asking him and not me?" Lana blurted.

"Because he's the one I feel sorry for, havin' to put up with you. I was gonna ask you next."

Lana didn't answer.

"Do you mind stayin'?"

"It's fine. Ron's better company than you are."

Ron laughed, but neither Lana nor Tuper cracked a smile, keeping up their pretense. "That would work great for me," Ron said. "If it gets too late, we can take turns watching and sleeping."

"If you lose him or give up for some reason and don't want to drive home, feel free to come to the colony." Tuper stood up from his squat. "You can sleep in the barn with me. I'll let Jacob know that's a possibility so no one freaks out if you show up in the wee hours."

"Why don't you take Dually?" Ron suggested. "It'll be a whole lot better for him."

"I was hoping you'd say that." Tuper nodded. "And do me one more thing. Call if you leave this house. Don't matter how late it is."

"Will do," Lana said.

"And if Kingston leaves here and then returns, please stay with him. It's important."

CHAPTER 25

Thursday night

While they watched the house, Lana and Ron made awkward small talk, then started joking and laughing about Tuperisms. A noise caught Lana's attention, and she glanced over as the door opened and Kingston walked out. "He's on the move." She glanced at Ron, who already had his hands on the wheel.

Alone, their suspect walked to his car and drove away.

"We're heading out," Ron said.

Lana called Tuper and gave him the update.

A couple miles and several turns later, the Cutlass pulled into a parking lot in front of the Flying Monkey bar.

"Cool name for a bar," Lana commented. "Someone was a *Wizard of Oz* fan. Or they've been to Kuala Lumpur."

Ron wrinkled his brow. "Huh?"

"There's a semi-famous bar in the middle of the concrete jungle. And another one in Key West, Florida. It seems a little odd to have one here though, since this town isn't exactly what I would call exotic."

Kingston opened his door but didn't get out.

"If he goes in," Ron said, "we're going in too. No point in sitting out here. Maybe he'll lead us to someone else."

They sat, watching for Kingston to make a move. Five minutes passed and nothing. They could see that his vehicle door was still open, but not what he was doing.

"Do you think he's waiting for someone?" Lana asked. "Or maybe he's making phone calls. He could be lining up his next deal. He must be nabbing these girls. I can't imagine anyone going willingly with this guy, especially these women who have been so sheltered." Lana worked through her concerns out loud. "Yet there are no real signs of a struggle, and most of the girls have been interested in the *Welt Leut* world. Does he target Hutterites who are already looking for an adventure and then charm them into leaving? Eww and ick. How could that guy charm anyone? I don't get it."

A big grin crossed Ron's face.

"What are you smiling at?"

"You and the way your mind works. It goes faster than that computer of yours."

"I think that's why I like the internet. When things pop into my head, I can check them out quickly. I can get answers to the questions that race around in my brain with no place to go. But this case is hard because the information is so limited." A new thought hit her. "That's it."

"What?"

"Unless it's someone within the colonies, the information I need is still on the outside."

"You think they've been inside jobs?"

"Not at all. But the clues are out here, and that means I can trace them. We can follow them in the physical world and online."

"Okay," Ron sounded skeptical. "Wait. He's getting out."

"Who? Oh, yeah. So, we're going in?"

"Let's make sure he heads to the bar." Ron glanced at Lana and back at Kingston. "When we're inside, do you mind acting like a couple?"

"A couple of what?" She chuckled. "I think it would be fun. I've always wanted to play detective and go undercover." *That was a strange thing to say*, she thought. She'd been undercover for a long time now.

"Then detective it is. Let's go."

They followed Kingston into the bar. Inside, Ron put his arm around Lana's shoulder, and she shivered. It had been a long time since a man touched her. Although she knew it wasn't real, it felt good.

"You okay?" Ron asked.

"I'm fine. The gesture just surprised me." She looked over and spotted Kingston. "There he is."

The bar already had an evening crowd, but not enough people to get lost in. Kingston approached the counter and within seconds had a beer in his hand.

"He must be a regular," Lana said.

"Why?"

"Because the bartender brought his beer before he asked. Clarice taught me that. It brings in better tips when you know your customers and treat them like friends."

"Do you like bartending?"

"I do, but I don't get very many hours. Clarice tries to get me as many as she can, but I'm still just filling in when they need someone. I've been waiting for an opening at Nickels, but it's not looking very likely. I may have to find something else soon if I don't get hired there. I need to pay Clarice more rent. I feel like I'm freeloading. That bothers me."

Ron smiled and started toward the counter. "Do you want a drink? A beer? Whiskey?"

Lana raised her eyebrows. "Are you trying to ply me with liquor?"

"Just trying to fit in. And since I'm driving, I thought you could be the drinker. But if you want a soda or something, I'll get a beer. One isn't going to matter, and I don't have to drink it all."

"You don't have to drink any of it."

"Yeah, I do. I think it's alcohol abuse if you open a bottle and don't drink it."

Lana gave him a quizzical look, not used to his sense of humor yet. "I'll have an Affogato Martini."

"A what?"

She looked at the bartender and realized he wouldn't know either. "Never mind. Get me a Caesar."

"That's like a Bloody Mary, right?"

"Except with Clamato instead of tomato juice, plus a few other things if it's made right. Clarice turned me onto them. It's a specialty of hers."

A spot was open next to Kingston, and Ron offered the seat to Lana. She shook her head, he said, "Please," and she acquiesced. Ron stood behind her. Kingston didn't seem to notice them. His attention was on a brunette sitting next to him that he was hitting on. She was clearly not interested, but he persisted until she picked up her drink and left.

A few minutes later, two women walked up, and one asked, "Is this seat taken?"

"By all means, it's yours." Kingston stood and offered his seat to the second woman.

The bartender brought Ron and Lana's drinks, then took

an order from the women. Lana tasted her drink and made a face.

"Not so good?" Ron asked.

"Nothing like what Clarice makes."

Kingston stood behind the ladies, trying to make small talk. They were polite but obviously not interested. He kept leaning over and flirting. When their drinks came, they excused themselves and walked away. Kingston followed.

Lana got down off her stool.

"Where are you going?"

"Kingston is dogging those women."

"What are you going to do about it?"

"Give him a boot in the crotch if I need to."

"That's not the way to work undercover," Ron said.

But Lana was already headed across the room. She stopped when one of the women turned around and shouted over the clang of slot machines. "Leave us alone or I'm calling the bouncer!"

Kingston stopped, gulped down his drink, and started for the exit.

Lana spun around and hurried in the same direction. Ron met her at the door, they stepped out, and started toward their car. She glanced back and saw Kingston heading for the Cutlass. A minute later, they were ready to follow, but Kingston didn't move.

"What's he waiting for?" Ron gripped the wheel.

"He had several drinks and didn't look that sober when he went in." Lana had doubts but said it anyway. "Maybe he can't figure out how to start his car."

"Or maybe he's sleeping it off," Ron suggested.

"More likely, he's waiting for those women to come out."

CHAPTER 26

Thursday night, an hour earlier

Tuper pulled onto the dirt road leading to the colony. His phone rang just after he made the turn. He stopped and took Lana's call letting him know Kingston had left the house. Tuper called Hawk to pass on the word and promised to keep him updated. Hawk seemed relieved that the ex-con wouldn't be there when his granddaughter got home. Tuper hoped she wasn't involved in something illegal. That would break Hawk's heart, and Tuper didn't want to be the one to tell him.

Jacob was waiting when he arrived. Tuper told him everything he knew, but also reminded him that nothing was certain.

"I have to show you something." Jacob stopped him, then reached in his pocket and took out a letter. "It's from Rita. I will read it to you."

Dear Helen,

I'm finally on my adventure, my dream come true. It's not quite what I would expect, but exciting just the same. I know the Lord meant for me to do this.

Please don't tell anyone about this letter. I'll write more later when I have time and tell you all about it.

May the Lord, the prince, bless you.

Your best friend,

Margarete

Jacob folded the paper closed and sighed.

"Where is it postmarked?" Tuper had mixed feelings about the content. It seemed off somehow.

"Great Falls."

"So, she's close. Or whoever sent it is close. Do you believe it's from Rita?"

"It is written in her hand."

"Did Helen bring you the letter?"

"No. It came in the mail earlier today, but I did not see it until a little while ago. I did not call you because you were already on your way. I never expected to hear from her, or I would have looked at the mail sooner." Jacob's hand, still holding the letter, trembled a little. "When I saw the envelope was addressed to Helen, I checked the return address, and it just said Margarete. I heard it is against some federal law to open someone else's mail, but I do not heed that law. I read it. Do you not think it is from my granddaughter?"

"I think Rita wrote it, but I'm not sure she did it of her own free will."

"Why?"

"Rita knows the mail goes through you."

"Normally, I would not open someone else's mail. The young men and women receive mail all the time from other colonies, and I just pass it on to them."

"The tone doesn't seem right." Tuper finally realized the

problem. "If she took the time to send a letter to her friend, wouldn't she mention the exciting things that were happening? This is a note someone might send their folks to let them know she was okay, but not to a friend."

"You are correct. It does not sound like Rita. She loves to write and describes things like one might read in a book. She lives a life of prose." Jacob sighed again. "I hope this at least means she is still alive."

Tuper hoped the same, but the letter had taken at least a day to arrive, and so many things could have happened in the meantime.

"I think Rita would have written to her parents and not to her friend," Jacob continued. "She would know how worried they are; she is a thoughtful, sensitive girl."

"Do you know if any other colonies received letters from the missing girls?"

"I will call and ask," Jacob said.

"I'll call Peter." Tuper reached for his phone. "You can call the other two."

He walked outside so they wouldn't interrupt each other. The phone rang repeatedly before Peter finally answered.

"It's Tuper."

"Hello, *Bruder*. Do you have information for me?"

"I was hoping you had some for me. Have you received any letters from Gertrude?"

"Not that I'm aware of. Why do you ask?"

"I'm with Jacob, and one of the girls here got a note from Rita. At least, it says it's from Rita."

"My wife divides up the mail before I see it. I'll check with her. Let me call you back."

Tuper paced around for a minute, then finally went back inside. He heard Jacob say, "Thank you, Benjamin. Please let me know if you receive anything." Jacob hung up. "Neither have received anything, but they will let me know if they do."

"I'm waiting for Peter to call back."

Jacob stood. "I will make some tea."

"That sounds good." Tuper sat down. They were halfway through their tea when Peter finally called. "Rebekka didn't *want* to tell," Peter said, "but did when she was confronted."

"What did the letter say?"

"It's short. I'll read it to you."

Dear Rebekka,

I'm finally on my adventure, my dream. It's not quite what I would expect, but exciting just the same. I know the Lord meant for me to do this.

Please don't tell anyone about this letter. I'll write more later when I have time and tell you all about it.

May the Lord, the prince, bless you.

Your best friend,

Gertrude

Tuper's doubts were confirmed. "I want you to read it to Jacob now." He put his phone on speaker so Jacob could hear. "Open Rita's letter and listen to the one Peter has."

After a few seconds, Jacob said, "That is almost the exact same wording. Is it written in the hand of Gertrude?"

"It is."

CHAPTER 27

Thursday night

Ron watched the bar's front door as several people came and went. Kingston's car remained in its spot without moving. They stayed that way for nearly half an hour before the women from earlier came out.

"They're finally leaving," Ron said.

Lana looked up from her laptop. "I hope the tall one is driving because the other one seems pretty tipsy."

"She does." Ron saw them get into a gold Honda. "Good. She got in the passenger side." A moment later, Kingston's engine started, and his lights came on.

"Look at that," Lana said. "The creep is suddenly leaving too. He's going to follow them."

"And we'll follow him."

Lana abruptly flung open her door. "Be right back."

"Where are you—?"

Her door closed, and she moved quickly toward the Honda. He watched her walk behind it, pause, then slip in between other cars. She was back inside Ron's car before the women were out of their parking spot.

"What were you doing?"

Lana keyed something into her phone. "I got their license number, so I can find out who they are. Or at least who the car belongs to." Lana put down her phone and picked up her laptop. "Who knows what Kingston is up to? Maybe he's hoping they'll go to another bar and he'll get another shot at them. Or he might follow them home and break into their house. Or maybe assault them when they get to their destination."

While Lana was jabbering, the other cars left the parking lot.

Ron followed, smiling. "You sure have an imaginative mind."

"I like to think of every possible scenario, then figure out which one fits."

"You have an interesting way of doing it."

"I thought everyone processed like that. It just works better for me if I say it out loud."

"So, what do we do if one of those scenarios takes place?"

"If we're there, we'll stop him from hurting them."

"We?"

"You don't have to help if you don't want to. I'm pretty sure I can take Kingston. And if we lose them for some reason, you can report it."

"Why me? Why don't you report it?"

"I don't do that."

Lana started typing on her keyboard, and he assumed she was tracing the Honda's license plate. She glanced up occasionally to look around, then went right back to work. Ron kept a safe distance behind Kingston to keep from being spotted, but he noticed Kingston didn't do the same.

"He's probably too drunk to realize what he's doing," Ron said.

The Honda made several right turns into a residential neighborhood, then headed back to the main street. "I think she's caught on to him," Ron said.

"Then this ought to be good. Don't get too close."

"Why not?"

"Because the Honda is registered to a cop. Probably the driver's husband."

A mile later, Ron saw red lights flashing behind them. He dropped back and pulled over for the police car to pass, then got back on the road, keeping his distance. It took another mile for the flashing lights to register for Kingston. He pulled into a strip mall, and the cop followed him.

Ron made a right turn and entered the lot from the other side. He eased forward until they could see the action, then parked and shut off his lights. The only business open in the mall was a McDonald's at the opposite end.

They weren't close enough to hear anything, but they had a good visual. Ron grabbed his Nikon camera and zoomed in so he could get close-up photos.

After a few minutes, the cops made Kingston do a field sobriety test.

"I guess he picked the wrong woman to follow tonight," Lana said. "Serves him right."

It wasn't long before he was in the backseat of the squad car being carted away.

"What do we do now?" Lana asked.

"We can wait at the police station and see if he gets released."

"They won't release him tonight. Even if they don't book him for harassing a cop's wife, they'll keep him as long as they can. As for when he gets released, I can check that on my laptop."

Ron glanced at his phone. "It's eleven thirty. Do you want to head for the colony or back to Helena?"

"If we stay in the area, we can follow Kingston when he gets out tomorrow or see who picks him up. Maybe check on his car and see what happens to it." She finally looked up from her computer. "I don't mind driving back to Helena, but we'll just have to come right back here in the morning. If Kingston gets stuck in a holding cell, then we can go home. Or Tuper might have something else we can do." She stopped talking and stared at him. "Why are you smiling?"

"I find you refreshing." Ron started the car. "The colony it is."

CHAPTER 28

Friday morning

Lana woke and checked the time: *4:58 a.m.* It was still dark. She sat up, clicked on her phone's flashlight, and looked around the barn. Ron was asleep on some hay about ten feet from her, and a bedroll beyond him was empty. Tuper was probably having tea with Jacob.

Mary had left out plenty of blankets, and they'd kept Lana warm until she got up. Now, she was cold and considered crawling back into her makeshift bed. But she wanted to check on Kingston. With her laptop bag and a blanket over her shoulder, she climbed the ladder into the loft, where she'd discovered an outlet on her last visit. The space also had a good view when the sun came up and quiet privacy. She knew someone would soon come in to milk the cows.

She wrapped the blanket around her shoulders and started to work. It didn't take long to hack into the Great Falls Police Department. She'd done it before, and their security hadn't changed since. Within minutes, she found Kingston's records.

"Is he out of jail?"

Lana jumped at the sound of Ron's voice. She turned and saw his head and shoulders sticking up into the loft from the ladder. "You startled me."

"Sorry." Ron climbed the last few rungs and stepped in next to her. "Are you checking on Kingston?"

"Yes. I'm almost there."

He walked over to the window and looked out. "The sky is just starting to lighten. I heard Tuper leave the barn about an hour ago. That man doesn't sleep much."

Lana just kept scanning the file she'd loaded. A minute later, she looked up at Ron. "Kingston's still in the holding cell. They could have a video arraignment and let him go this morning. In that case, we should probably follow him again. Or they could hold him over and set bail, then we can see who rescues him. Either way, it will hopefully lead us to something. The bail thing might be better because we could find another player, unless it's his mother or brother."

"You'll be able to tell who bailed him out?"

"Yeah," she said cautiously.

"You're amazing."

A tingle ran up the back of her neck and across her cheeks. She was glad it wasn't full daylight, so Ron couldn't see her red face. Why was she blushing anyway? She didn't blush. "It's no big thing. Many hackers are better at this than I am." Not wanting to continue the conversation, she turned back to her computer.

They heard Tuper call out from below.

Ron went over to the ladder opening. "We're up here. Lana's checking on Kingston."

Tuper climbed up and into the loft. "Is he still in the joint?"

"His blood alcohol level was point-one-six, which is twice

the legal limit," Lana said. "So, they hit him with an enhancement. He has an arraignment scheduled for Monday morning."

"No stalking endorsement?" Tuper asked.

"No. But they could've arraigned him this morning. Instead, they opted for the full seventy-two hours."

"Do the cops decide that?" Ron asked.

"The prosecutor does, but officers have some influence in the decision. And when a cop's family is threatened, you can bet they're not going easy on him."

"Why wouldn't they charge him with stalking?" Ron asked.

"Maybe the women didn't want to testify, but I'm sure the cops will make it clear to Kingston to stay away."

"I'm glad the creep is in jail, but we don't have any other leads." Lana looked at Tuper. "I hope you have something, Pops."

"We have the letters I told you about last night."

"What good will they do? From what you said, there wasn't anything that would give us a lead. All we know is that Rita and Gertrude were abducted by the same person." She flipped her hand in the air. "Heck, we don't even know that for sure. Maybe they ran off together. Why would their abductor make them write letters at all? To throw us off so we think they ran away on their own? At least we know there's a connection, but if they weren't abducted, they could've written the letters together. We need something else."

"Agony, Agony, Agony. You're answering your own questions again." Tuper removed the letter from his pocket and handed it to her. "Have a look for yourself and see if you get something we didn't spot."

The room was brighter now with the sun almost up, but

Lana still took the letter to the window. She gestured for Ron to join her, hoping he would have some insight.

"You're sure the handwriting is Rita's?" Ron asked, looking over at Tuper.

"Her parents, her friend Helen, and Mary all say it is. So, either it's a good forgery, or she wrote it. The same with the letter from Gertrude."

Lana studied the letter carefully, as did Ron.

"I don't see anything that would help us." Ron shrugged. "It's pretty generic, as I think they meant it to be."

Lana read it over and over.

"Do you see somethin'?" Tuper asked.

"Not really, except ..." She looked at it again. "How did Gertrude sign her letter?"

"With a pen, I imagine," Tuper said.

"I mean, did she sign it Gertrude or Trudi?"

Tuper thought for a second. "Gertrude, I believe. Why?"

"If I was writing to my BFF, I wouldn't use my formal name, especially if my friends called me something else. Why aren't the letters signed Rita and Trudi? Unless that's a signal to let people know something is wrong. But we already know something is wrong. Maybe they're trying to say, 'I left on my own, but now I'm in trouble.' Or maybe it doesn't mean anything at all. That's all I got. Anyone else?"

"Yeah, what's a BFF?" Tuper asked.

"Best friends forever. I'm sure you have one of those, don't you? Like Jacob, or Peter maybe. Oh wait, those are brothers, right?"

"Sorry I asked," Tuper said, then changed the subject. "I'm going to meet Hawk at a coffee shop near the rental house this morning. Willa, his granddaughter, is joining us."

"Do you think she's involved in the sex ring? If she is, she's certainly not going to tell you anything. Maybe we should watch her a while and see what she does. I mean, instead of tipping your hand."

"Agony, we don't know that there's a sex ring. Hawk doesn't think she's involved in anything."

"Of course not, Pops; she's his granddaughter. He wants to believe her, and she won't say anything that makes her look bad."

"And that's why I'm meeting with her. Even if Hawk is right, she may have seen something going down that she doesn't realize is important."

"I should go with you. Maybe I can get some information that I can research."

"Okay. But I'm askin' the questions. When I'm done, you can fill in what you need," Tuper said. "Ron, what are you gonna do?"

"I thought I'd see if Kingston's car is still in that parking lot. I'll check in and see if you need me for anything later."

CHAPTER 29

Friday morning

Tuper walked into the coffee shop, with Lana right behind. Hawk and his granddaughter were already inside at a booth in the back.

When they approached the table, Hawk said, "This is my granddaughter Willa."

"Nice to meet you, Mr. Tuper." In her late twenties, she had long dark hair and a nice smile.

"Just Tuper. And it's my pleasure." He nodded, trying not to think about how pretty Willa was. "This is Agon—." He caught himself. "I mean Lana."

They sat down, and Willa offered to get them something to drink. But they both declined.

"I haven't told Willa much," Hawk said. "But she swears she doesn't know anyone named Kingston." He looked lovingly at his granddaughter. "You can ask her anything. She'll be truthful. Right?"

Willa nodded. "Absolutely."

"Did you show her the photo?"

"Not yet." Hawk took out his phone and it handed it to Willa. "Check my text messages. Lana sent me a photo of Kingston." He gave her time to look, then asked, "Do you know that guy?"

Willa shook her head. "No."

"You've never seen him before?" Tuper asked.

"No."

Lana started to ask a question, but Tuper scowled at her.

"Do you know why he might have visited your house?" Tuper pressed.

"I have an idea." She sighed. "He was probably there to see Sloopy."

"Who is Sloopy?" Lana blurted. Tuper rolled his eyes.

"One of my roommates brought her home, claiming Sloopy was an out-of-work flight attendant. She seemed nice at first, but she was desperate. I explained that she could only stay a night or two because we needed room for people who were flying. We couldn't let her take up a permanent room." A flash of guilt and frustration. "It's a four-bedroom house, and Gillian and I each have a room. The other rooms are open to a list of paying guests on a first come, first serve basis. Sloopy said she would take the sofa if the room was needed, but no one feels comfortable ousting her from her bed, so that never happens. But I don't want the pilots sleeping on the sofa. They need a good night's rest."

"You said she was nice at first," Lana cut in. "Other than overstaying her welcome, what's the problem?"

"That's an understatement. It's been three weeks. Now she's putting more and more personal stuff in the room and hasn't paid a penny. I know she doesn't have a job, but we're losing rental income."

"Why haven't you asked her to leave?" Hawk sounded frustrated.

"I have, Grandpa. She keeps saying she will, but she doesn't go."

"We'll see about that," Hawk grumbled.

"I should have come to you before now, Grandpa, but I thought I could handle it on my own." Willa's voice tightened with stress. "I didn't realize she was bringing men home until I heard scuttlebutt around the lounge. The house rule is that guests can't invite sexual partners. Too many people come and go, and we don't want it to be like a frat house. We've only had to ban one person."

"You haven't seen any of her visitors?" Lana asked.

"Sloopy knows mine and Gillian's schedules, so she doesn't have anyone over when we're home. But the other residents have been joking about how she has men coming in one door and going out the other. I don't mean to judge her. If a man was doing it, everyone would think it was great, or at least funny."

Lana nodded in agreement, giving Tuper a knowing look.

"I just don't want it happening in my house, man or woman," Willa added.

"I don't either," Hawk said.

"Willa," Tuper said gently, "I don't want to alarm you, but the man who was there last night has served time, and we think he might have recently abducted some women."

"Oh, no!" She gasped and turned to her grandfather. "Don't worry. I'll go right home and tell her she has to leave."

"You don't need to do a thing, sweetheart. It's my name on the title. I'll get her out."

"You keep calling her Sloopy." Lana leaned forward. "Do you know her real name?"

"I think I do now. Yesterday, we got a letter in the mail, and I didn't recognize the name on the envelope. But I bet it's for her. Our mailbox is locked and only Gillian and I have keys. Sloopy's been lurking around when I pick up the mail, and I saw her shuffling through a stack I left on the counter one day. When I confronted her, she said she was looking for ads. After that, I began taking the mail to my room whenever I pick it up. The letter that came yesterday was from the DMV, and it was addressed to Xena Yeager."

"Who names their kid Xena?" Tuper mumbled.

"Someone into Greek history," Lana offered. "Or a fan of *Xena: Warrior Princess*. Lots of people named their girls Xena when that TV show first came on in 1995. Is Sloopy in her early twenties?"

"She says she's twenty-three. I don't know for sure."

"There you go. Her mother was probably a fan," Lana said. "Does she have a car?"

"A red Ford Focus. I don't know what year, but it's an older one."

"You don't happen to know the license plate number, do you?" Lana sounded eager.

"No. Sorry."

Hawk suddenly stood. "I'll take care of Sloopy right now."

"I'm going with you," Tuper said.

CHAPTER 30

Friday morning

On the way, Lana texted Ron and told him the plan, so he was already at the house when she and Tuper arrived. Hawk, Tuper, and Willa went inside, but Lana stayed in the car and continued searching the internet for Xena.

Ron walked up to her window, and Lana gave him the update. "Sloopy/Xena drives a red Ford Focus. It must be up the street because we didn't pass it coming in. Can you get the license number?"

"Sure." Ron hustled off.

Lana kept searching and soon discovered Xena's tragic childhood. Ron returned with the plate number, then added, "It's parked three cars away. You can't see it because of that SUV."

"That girl has had a horrible life," Lana said, "but she didn't lie about her age. She is twenty-three. At eight years old, she was placed in foster care after her father beat her mother to death right in front of her. I'll read the newspaper articles later when I have more time. Oh, and she was born in Grand Forks, North Dakota."

Lana went back to her search for a few minutes. When she looked up to tell Ron what she'd found, he wasn't at her window. He opened the driver's door of the Mazda and got in. She pivoted toward him. "The car is in Xena's name with this address listed, but it was recently changed from Billings. I can check that location to see what she's been up to."

"What do you mean?" Ron asked.

Lana didn't answer. She was already searching. Finally, she said, "Xena has a juvenile record, a drunk driving charge she got in Missoula. But the real action was in Billings. A few months ago, she was charged with trespassing, grand theft, and receiving stolen property, all in conjunction with a guy who got similar charges." She skimmed ahead in the police report. "The fact sheet indicates she moved into a house with someone, then wouldn't leave when they evicted her. When she finally did go, she wiped them out. Sound familiar?" Before Ron could answer, Lana added, "Willa is lucky Xena didn't steal everything already. But she was probably waiting for her car registration, so she had to lie low. If she knows it arrived, she might be tearing up the house now. Maybe Willa should just give her the registration. Xena won't want to stay long because she has warrants."

"What warrants?"

"She was awaiting trial and took off." Lana closed her laptop. "I'd better tell Tuper." She dug through the console and found a small pad of paper. She jotted down a note, climbed out, and took off toward the house.

~

When they walked in, Sloopy appeared to have just woken up. She was wearing sweats and holding a coffee mug. Her shoulder-length brown hair was disheveled, and her mascara smeared.

"I'm sorry, but you have to leave," Willa said. They were all standing in the living room.

"Good morning to you too," Sloopy said.

"I mean it. You can't stay any longer."

"I know. I can be out by Monday night. How's that?"

"No," Hawk said. "You have to leave right now."

"Who are you?" She gave him a look. "Willa and Gillian said I could stay."

"For a day or two," Willa cut in. "That's long past. You're breaking too many rules, and other residents need the room."

"I haven't broken any rules, and I always offer to sleep on the sofa. No one lets me do that, but that's not my fault."

"You need to pack up right now and get out." Hawk's voice boomed. "I own this house, and you're trespassing."

Xena put her hand on her hip and glared. "I don't think you can make me do that."

"I know I can."

"So, take me to court. That'll buy me another six months. I know the law."

Someone knocked on the door, and Willa hurried over. Lana stepped in and handed her a note.

"I probably know the law a little better than you do," Hawk said. "I'm a retired cop."

Tuper knew he was blowing smoke about that, but Hawk did have his share of connections in the force.

"You got the *tired* part right, old man," Xena snapped, her face flushed. "I'm not going anywhere until I'm ready." She walked into a bedroom and slammed the door.

"Grandpa," Willa said, "I just got a note from Lana. Xena has warrants."

"She doesn't have a gun in there, does she?" Tuper asked.

"Not that I know of, but I suppose she could."

"Willa, you get out of here." When she hesitated, Hawk raised his voice. "Go! And call Bill." His granddaughter hurried toward the door.

Tuper and Hawk positioned themselves on either side of the bedroom door, weapons drawn.

"Xena Yeager!" Hawk shouted. "Come out now or you'll see cops swarming this place. They'll take you in on your warrants."

"All right," she yelled back.

"Come out slowly so we can see your hands."

She opened the door, showed her palms, and walked out. "I don't want any trouble. Those warrants are all a misunderstanding."

"They always are," Hawk said.

"You can put your guns away. I'm not carrying." She lifted her shirt, emptied her pockets, and ran her hands down her pant legs.

They lowered their weapons. "Tell us what you know about Kingston Wylde," Tuper said.

"Apparently not as much as you do. I didn't even know his last name. But it suits him. He's definitely wild."

"Do you have something going with him?"

"You mean, like a relationship? Heck no. He was just a hookup."

"I mean something illegal." Tuper put his weapon back in its holster.

"We're both consenting adults."

"I don't mean that," Tuper said. "Do you know anything about missing girls from around this area?"

"Look, man, I'm not involved with anything like that. I've been known to pull a con or two, but I wouldn't get into any kind of kidnapping thing."

"How well do you know Kingston?"

"I met him a few days ago at a gas station. He's a funny guy. That's it."

Hawk pointed at the bedroom. "Start packing. You have ten minutes. I'll watch."

Xena reluctantly turned around, and Tuper and Hawk followed. Tuper sensed Hawk was stalling.

In the messy room, she started tossing her belongings into a suitcase. When she picked up a replica of a Fabergé egg, Hawk said, "Not that."

"It's mine."

"No. That belonged to Willa's grandmother."

Xena put it back on the dresser.

"Leave anything else that isn't yours. I'll have Willa search your stuff before you leave."

Xena filled another suitcase and set both on the dining table. Then she brought out hanging clothes and placed them on top.

"You got everything?" Hawk asked.

"Yes."

"Good. We're escorting you out."

"You'd better get her key," Tuper said.

"Don't need to. I'm changing the locks before I leave."

"How are you going to do that?"

"I can feel my way through most of it, but Willa will help me when I need it. She's used to being my eyes."

~

Lana got an uneasy feeling about Willa, as if she were waiting for someone. Hawk's granddaughter had come out ten minutes earlier and had been leaning against Xena's car since. A minute later, a dark sedan pulled up and parked in front of the Ford. A man got out and walked over to Willa. They talked for a bit, and he went back to his car. Another sedan drove up and parked across the street. That guy remained in the driver's seat.

Lana slumped down, trying not to be conspicuous about it, but she was sure Ron noticed. "They're cops," she said.

"Are you sure?"

"I'd bet on it."

"Is that a bad thing for you?"

"I'm just never sure what side they're on." She looked at Ron and added, "I assume they're here to pick up Xena."

A few more minutes passed, then Tuper, Hawk, and Xena exited the house and went directly to her car. Xena opened the trunk. As she put a suitcase inside, the first cop arrested her, and the second charged across the street. Tuper and Hawk put the rest of her things in the trunk and walked back to where Lana and Ron waited.

Hawk patted Tuper's shoulder. "I don't want Kingston going near Willa again. I'll explain everything to my friend, Bill, and he'll check on her."

"I welcome the help keeping an eye on Kingston, but please don't tell them what I suspect yet. They have enough reason to keep him away from here. If I learn anything else, I'll let you know."

"Your phone is ringing," Hawk said.

It was on the fourth ring before Tuper finally got it out of

his pocket and opened it. "Hello." As he listened, his face tightened, then he snapped the phone closed.

Lana flinched as Tuper spun toward the car. Then he
slammed his fist against the hood, and shouted, "Dang!
Another girl is missing."

CHAPTER 31

Friday morning

Tuper and Ron stood outside the Mazda, still parked in front of Willa's house. Hawk came out of the garage carrying a set of locks.

"I offered to help him change those," Ron said. "But he declined, saying it gave him something to do."

"I did the same," Tuper said.

Lana had stayed in the passenger seat. "What do we know about the missing girl?" she asked.

"She disappeared last night from Pronghorn Colony. It's northwest of Great Falls, not far from Diamond Valley. Her name is Inger, and she turned eighteen last week."

"That means Kingston didn't do it," Ron said.

"Not the actual kidnapping," Lana countered. "But obviously, he's not acting alone. If he's part of an organized ring, they may have several people snatching the girls. He could be just one. Or he could have some other role. Or maybe Kingston had nothing to do with the missing girls. The way he followed those women last night makes him seem like a whole different kind of creep. But what else have we got? We—"

"Agony." Tuper cut her off. "We don't have much, but sitting around jawin' about it ain't gonna cut it. Let's do something, even if it's wrong."

"I think that's what we've been doing, because, so far, we haven't found anything that leads us to those girls," Lana muttered. "Should we go to Pronghorn and see what we can find out? I've got nothing else."

"We have Finn," Tuper said.

"I don't know." Lana shook her head. "That kid comes across as such a good guy. And I think he's smitten with Rita. He seemed genuinely concerned about her."

"Which is exactly what I would do if I was tryin' to hide something."

"I've done a lot of background work on Finn," Lana argued. "There's nothing in his life to suggest he's involved with anything like this. He does well in school, stays out of trouble, and has a relatively normal family life. His parents are divorced, but the kid has a relationship with both. He's shy, but not psycho shy. He just seems so ... *normal*."

"So did Ted Bundy," Ron said.

"I'll keep looking." Lana glanced down at her laptop.

"I'm heading to Smith's to see what else I can find out," Tuper said. "Why don't you and Ron go to Pronghorn and ask questions? I'll call ahead and let them know you're coming."

She tipped her head. "Do you also know someone at that colony?"

"I know a guy or two."

Lana packed up her laptop, got in Ron's car, and they drove off.

~

At Smith's Supermarket, Tuper was glad to find Rhonda. He bought her a cup of free coffee at the deli counter.

"You're so generous, Toop." Rhonda teased. "You know employees don't pay for coffee, right?"

"I know." He gave her his charming smile. "What else can you tell me about Finn?"

"Nothing really. He's a good worker, always on time, never causes any trouble."

"Does he talk to a lot of the Hutterite girls?"

"He's always quick to help them. He seems particularly eager to be involved when they show up from Little Boulder, the other colonies not so much. Still, he's always helpful."

"Does he just talk to the girls or the guys too?"

"Both. I heard him asking about one of the girls. I forgot her name."

"Was it Rita?"

"Yes. That's it." She sipped her coffee. "Oh, that's right. You said she was Jacob's granddaughter and that she was missing. Do you think Finn did something wrong? Because he sure doesn't seem like the type."

"Maybe."

"If anything, it seems like he would protect her rather than hurt her."

"Maybe he's protecting her from the awful lifestyle he thinks she's living." Tuper shrugged, not sure about any of it. "Finn's young and may not understand that it's her choice."

"Is it really though? Her choice, I mean. She grew up with the indoctrination. Maybe she doesn't feel like it's a choice."

"They won't make her stay if she wants to leave. That's not the way it works. When their young people turn eighteen, they do have a choice." Tuper paused. "Other girls are missing from other colonies."

"Oh my. I didn't know that."

"Please keep it quiet. If word gets out, it'll be harder to find the culprit."

"That changes things up." Rhonda shook her head. "But I still don't think it's Finn. He doesn't seem to be interested in anyone except Rita."

CHAPTER 32

Friday midday

The drive to Pronghorn Colony took half an hour. The *Haushalter* welcomed Lana and Ron and was very helpful. Lana had come to expect nothing less from them. Like at the other colonies, the men had searched for Inger for several hours after she left, even though it had been nearly nine o'clock and already bedtime. Inger had gone to the bathroom and hadn't returned.

Lana talked to several of Inger's close friends and heard the same information from each. The only person they knew she'd talked to at Smith's was Prince Dreamy. Only one other girl had seen him, and the description was consistent—tall, blond hair, and blue eyes. The girl didn't know his real name.

"But he worked at Smith's?"

"He said he did, and he was wearing the same kind of shirt."

"Did he have a nametag?"

"No."

An hour later, they were headed back to Great Falls. Lana opened her phone and looked at the image she'd taken of the letter from Rita.

"Do you think you missed something?" Ron asked.

"Maybe. But I sure can't figure out what. I need to see the other letter, the one from Gertrude. Maybe we could stop by Green Valley Colony and take a photo of it. Or maybe Peter can take a picture and send it to me. That's not very likely, is it? He doesn't seem too handy with his phone. Maybe I could walk him through it."

"That might work. Call him."

"I need to call Tuper and get Peter's number."

"I have it in my phone; just use it."

Lana reached for Ron's phone, but hers rang, so she grabbed it instead and turned on the speaker. "What's up, Pops?"

"I just got a call from Benjamin. Tiffany sent a letter, and it sounds like the other two."

"We're not far from Diamond Valley. We'll swing by and take a picture of it."

Lana hung up and keyed the colony name into Google Maps. "We need to turn around and backtrack for a mile. It's ten miles shorter if we cut across."

Ron braked and made a U-turn.

A mile later, Lana pointed. "Take the next right. That will lead to the colony. I'll call Peter and see if he can send a picture of the letter. It's even more important now. Maybe we'll see some subtle differences. Or even if they are exactly the same, that should tell us something, don't you think? Maybe it just means they're all together. Or they were together at one time. Who knows where they are now?"

Lana ignored Ron's smirk and called Peter. She struggled

to explain the steps to take the photo. It had been a long time since she'd used a flip phone, and she couldn't remember where the option and media buttons were located. She smacked her forehead. "Of course." She googled *flip phone* and finally got Peter through the process. A minute later, the text and image arrived. "Got it. Thanks, Peter."

Lana looked up as they pulled into Diamond Valley Colony. "Are we here already?"

"Yeah, that process took you a while." Ron sounded amused.

"They should be expecting us," Lana said, hopping out of the car. "Tuper said he would call."

Ron caught up to her as she reached the *Haushalter's* door. Benjamin opened it and let them in. "Thanks for coming by." Without any other formalities, he handed Ron the letter. Ron skimmed it and gave it to Lana. She read it through.

Dear Katrina,

I'm finally on my dreamy adventure. It's not quite what I would expect, but exciting just the same. I know the Lord meant for me to do this.

Please don't tell anyone about this letter. I'll write more later when I have time and tell you all about it.

May the Lord, the prince, bless you.

Your best friend,

Tiff

It was almost identical to the others. "You're sure Tiffany wrote this?" Lana asked.

"I am certain, and her parents believe the same."

"Is there anything odd to you about the letter?"

Benjamin hesitated. "The way she signed it is unusual."

"How so?"

"No one calls her *Tiff*. Her name is already a source of irritation to some of the elders, so it was agreed that shortened versions would not be tolerated."

"May I speak to Katrina?"

"Of course. I'll get her."

"Do you mind if we talk alone? Young girls are often more forthcoming one to one. They're especially reluctant to talk in front of authoritarian figures. I mean no disrespect, but I pose no threat to them. Not that you do, but young girls may not see it quite that way. They go through a lot of stuff in their head. I know, I was one not that long ago."

"It's quite all right," Benjamin said. "We welcome the help, and Tuper vouches for you."

When he left, Lana turned to Ron. "Shortened names not tolerated? Do you think the teenage girls follow that rule? Maybe Benjamin just doesn't know what they call her when they're alone."

Ron nodded. "What I've noticed with the young people in the colonies is that they often break the rules, but as long as they're discreet and the infraction is minor, it goes *unnoticed*— if you will."

Lana set Tiffany's letter on the table, and they both took photos. They discussed the letter until Benjamin came back with Katrina and made introductions.

"Let's step outside," Lana suggested to Katrina. "It's a nice day to take a walk."

As they strolled around the compound, Lana talked about the weather first, then delved in. "Did you read Tiffany's letter?"

"Yes. It was given to me first. I read it and immediately took it to the *Haushalter*."

"You recognized her handwriting?"

"Oh, yes. Tiffany's hand is very distinct and quite beautiful."

"I noticed she signed the letter *Tiff*. Benjamin said she doesn't go by that. But I know when I was a teenager, we had all kinds of nicknames for our friends. Is that what you call her? You're not in any trouble here. I just want to know if that signature is an anomaly."

"I would never call her Tiff. No one does, not even Mary E."

"Who's Mary E.?"

"Benjamin's daughter and Tiffany's best friend."

"But she addressed the letter to you and called you her best friend. Why would she do that?"

"I don't know. It seems so strange."

"Do you think she was afraid Mary E. might nark on her?"

Katrina glanced over, puzzled.

"I mean concerned that Mary might tell on her?"

"No. Mary E. is good at keeping secrets and would never *nark* on her best friend. I'm the one who would be most likely to tell. I'm a stickler for rules, and everyone knows that. I'm not ashamed of it. I think it's important."

"Is it possible she wrote the letter to you to make sure it was reported?"

"Mary E. and I both believe that."

"Could you get her for me?"

"Sure."

"Thank you, Katrina," Lana said. "By the way, you might want to drop the word *nark* from your vocabulary. It's not a bad word, but it's probably not appropriate either."

Out of respect for their customs, Lana went inside and told Benjamin that she'd summoned Mary E. He didn't seem the least bit concerned, so she went back out to wait.

Mary E. appeared quickly and gave the same information: no one called her Tiff, not even her BFF, and Tiffany must have wanted the letter shared.

"Would you have told your father about the letter if you had received it?"

The girl paused for several seconds. "Probably not, but I'm not sure. If I thought she was in danger, then I would have. It's hard to know what to do. We all have secrets we don't tell. I know she wouldn't betray mine."

Lana knew the girl was holding back. "Mary, I know it's important to be able to trust someone with your private thoughts and actions, but I believe Tiffany is in grave danger and that something you know might save her." Lana stopped walking and turned to face Mary, who stopped as well. "I assure you that I won't tell anyone at the colonies what you share with me. I will only use your information to find Tiffany. And we will only bring her home if she wants to come. If we discover she is with the *Welt Leut* of her own free will, then that's the way it will stay."

After a troubled moment, the girl pressed her hands to her face and dropped her chin. Then she took a deep breath and began to speak. "Tiffany always talked about going out on her own. She was even making a plan to do so, but it included how she would tell her parents. And she promised she would tell me." Seeming nervous, Mary started walking again. "Tiffany would go to town whenever she could and talk to strangers. She wanted to learn everything she could before she left us. The plan was still a ways off because she didn't have all the information she needed. But she knew she had to do it before she got married. She couldn't count on a husband wanting to leave."

"But she is engaged, right?"

"Yes. And I think that pushed the timeline up for her."

"So, you believe she left on her own?"

"At first I did, but after she sent that letter, I don't anymore."

"Do you know the names of anyone she talked to in town?"

Mary E. shook her head.

"There's a tall, blond guy at Smith's. Did she ever mention him?"

"You mean Prince Dreamy?"

"That's the one."

"She talked to him a lot."

"You don't know his real name?"

She shook her head again. "Tiffany asked him once, and he just said, 'The girls all call me Prince Dreamy.' I thought it was kind of arrogant, but Tiffany said he was really charming."

"You never met him?"

"No. I don't go to town much. It scares me out there."

"Right now, that's probably very smart."

CHAPTER 33

Friday afternoon

Lana and Ron pulled into the lot at the Double Barrel Coffee House. Tuper was waiting in his Mazda, and they all got out and went inside. It was past the lunch rush, so the café wasn't crowded. Lana headed for a table near an outlet so she could plug in her laptop.

"Why don't you two sit at the next table? I need to concentrate."

"Humpf," Tuper grunted. But he and Ron sat down a few feet away.

Lana pivoted to them. "Don't you think it's odd that Rita and Trudi used their formal names on their letters, and Tiffany used a nickname that no one ever called her?"

"Thought you were trying to concentrate?" Tuper said.

"I am. I will. But doesn't that seem strange? Maybe they had a little leeway in what they wrote, and they did what they could to send a message."

"What message?"

"That they were in trouble. That someone was holding them hostage. Or maybe their names mean something."

"Or maybe they mean nothin'."

"It just doesn't sit well with me. I keep reading the letters, and something is bugging me, but I don't know what it is."

Lana studied the menu. The only thing she saw that was vegetarian was a salad, which she wasn't in the mood for. When the waiter arrived, she said, "I'll have a grilled cheese-burger, hold the meat."

"So, you want a grilled cheese?" the waiter asked.

"That'll work." She smiled, and pointed toward Tuper and Ron. "Put my lunch on their bill."

She hacked into the local police department's database again. A few minutes later, she said, "Kingston is still in jail. Just wanted you to know."

Her next project was Finn Nelson. She searched his social media again, looking for references to Prince Dreamy. He had seemed sincere, but if he was telling women his name was Prince Dreamy, that shed a whole different light on him.

"What are you working on?" Ron asked.

Lana looked up from her laptop. "Finn Nelson. But nothing I find paints him as a predator, or even a womanizer. He seemed so believable when we talked to him."

"If he could fool you," Tuper said, "he sure could fool those unworldly Hutterite girls."

"What do you mean?" Lana gave him a look.

"Come on. You don't trust nobody, and you fell for his line."

"I'm still not sure."

"That's 'cause you don't want to admit you might be wrong."

When Tuper's chicken strips were served, he put one in a

napkin and set it aside. Ron smiled at the gesture, and Tuper shrugged. "I thought Dually might want one. I always shared with Ringo."

"I'm sure he'll love it."

In an obvious attempt to change the subject, Tuper said, "When this is all over, we'll take that horseback ride you came all the way to Montana for."

"I'd like that. I bet Dually will too."

The waiter set Lana's food down, but she ignored it. She was deep into the dark web. She had checked Frinkers again, and it had led to more messages involving Steller. This time with King Midas. From what she'd read, Steller seemed too smart to give much away, but his customers might not be. In the private messages, she followed a conversation that read:

King Midas—*I can't wait much longer. Any chance for tonight?*
Steller—*Saturday*
King Midas—*Time?*
Steller—*10:05 p.m.*
King Midas—*My cabin?*
Steller—*OK*
King Midas—*How many?*
Steller—*3*
King Midas—*They better be well behaved. And no skinny dogs.*

Shuffling noises made her look up. Tuper and Ron were on their feet.

"We're done," Tuper said. "And you haven't eaten."

"I'll take it to the car." She signaled for the waiter. "Some kind of trade is going down Saturday night at five minutes after ten. That's pretty precise. It sounds like Steller is delivering some girls." Lana read the exchange out loud.

"He could be selling puppies," Tuper commented. "The

customer did refer to them as dogs. Or maybe it's about cattle."

"At ten o'clock at night? Yeah, I don't think so." She closed her laptop. "We have to do something."

"What do you propose?" Tuper asked.

"Maybe I can go undercover."

"No," Ron and Tuper said in unison.

"I still have my Hutterite stuff. One of you can deliver me. Ron's younger and faster, but you have a gun, Pops, so I think I should go with you."

"No one is doing anything of the sort." Tuper crossed his arms.

"What if the trade involves the girls we're looking for?"

"What if it don't? You have no idea what you might be steppin' into."

"But—"

"But nothin'." Tuper's tone softened. "Do you know where this trade is goin' down?"

"No. But I plan to find out."

Ron cut into the conversation. "Can you really do that?"

"I have a hunch. Based on other things I've discovered; I think the exchange might be in Ulm. That's not far from here. I googled it yesterday when Ulm was mentioned in one of the conversations I read. I don't know exactly where though, so that will take a little work, but I'll find it." She was eager to get started but hadn't worked through it yet. "I'm not certain it's the same guy, but I'll figure that out too. I do know that the drop is at King Midas' cabin, wherever that is. So, all I have to do is figure out who King Midas is and then find his cabin. Shouldn't be too hard. The rest will be easy. It all depends on how smart King Midas is."

The waiter brought a to-go box and handed it to her.

Tuper shook his head. "Let me know if you find out where that—whatever it is—is goin' down."

Lana grabbed her grilled cheese, stuffed it into the container, and followed them out. "Where to, Pops?"

"You and Ron need to trail Finn when he leaves Smith's. He gets off work at three and drives a yellow Jeep Wrangler."

"I know that, but how do you?"

"That contraption isn't the only source of information. I talked to Rhonda earlier."

"But Finn? Really?"

"That's what I said."

"Why? Do you really think he's involved? He's awfully young, but I suppose he could be. I doubt he's leading the pack though. There has to be someone else. Maybe he's the lure."

"Do you have a better idea?"

"Not really. I can keep searching online for information about Finn. Maybe something will come to me." They were at Tuper's car before Lana realized it. "Where are you going?"

"To see a guy."

CHAPTER 34

Friday afternoon

Lana and Ron waited in the Smith's parking lot until Finn came out. The kid got in his Jeep and drove across the lot to McDonald's. They watched as he went through the drive-up window. From there, he headed east, and they tailed him to Great Falls College.

"Looks like he's going to class," Lana said.

"I'll follow him inside. Why don't you wait here and text me if he comes back out without me?" Ron handed Lana the keys. "If I get in a jam, I'll let you know."

While he was gone, Lana hacked into the college database and brought up Finn's schedule. He had a class at three o'clock. Four minutes to spare. She sent a text to Ron.

Lana—*English 101, 3-4:30, room 201*

Ron—*Got it*

Lana went back to searching Frinkers for the Saturday night exchange. She tried again to follow Steller's digital footprint but couldn't get far. She decided to zero in on King

Midas. If she could just find out who he was, she could probably figure out the drop location. But she hit one dead end after another.

Ron startled her when he opened the car door. "You need to keep the doors locked when you're on surveillance."

"I don't think this kid is dangerous."

"If he's in the sex-trafficking business, he may be more dangerous than you think. Besides, if you're watching someone, you need to assume someone is watching you. That was one of the first lessons I learned when I started working for JP."

"Did something happen to you?"

"Let's just say it didn't end well." Ron smiled. "Did you discover anything while I was gone?"

"This is Finn's only class today. I assume he attended?"

"Yes. He went right in. I didn't see any reason to stick around. I'll go back before the class lets out in case he decides to meet up with some friends or something."

~

Tuper drove out of town, heading south on I-15. About five miles past the airport, he turned right. He stopped at a farmhouse that sat by itself on several acres of unfarmed land. He parked in front and walked up to the door. An older, bald man came outside to greet him.

"You're a far piece from home," the man said.

"Hi, Pat." Tuper shook his hand. "Last time we talked, you was in the hospital."

"I'm a lot better now. Probably not any smarter but just as ornery."

"Good to know. Are you back to work?"

"Yes. I'm back at Cascade County Sheriff's Department," Pat said. "I'm not doing much undercover anymore—getting too old for that—but they require my services occasionally when they need an old guy. Otherwise, I'm an ordinary detective, which suits me fine. But you didn't come all the way out here to talk about my health. What's up?" Pat took a seat on the porch.

Tuper joined him. "I've got something you might be interested in. I just don't know if I have enough information."

"Let's hear it."

"Some merchandise is changing hands tomorrow night near here, and it looks like a sex-trafficking ring. And it may be related to a case I'm working."

"You got my attention."

"They may be selling puppies for all I know, but it sure doesn't look like it." Tuper told him about the online conversation without mentioning how or where he got it.

"What do you know for certain?"

"The exchange is at five minutes after ten tomorrow night at a cabin."

"Do you have an address?"

"No. But it belongs to someone who uses the handle King Midas."

Pat's eyes widened. "Now we're getting somewhere."

"You know him?"

"We've never formally met, but we know who he is, and we've long suspected him of being on the buying end of the deal. Do you know who the seller is?"

"He uses the name Steller."

"That doesn't mean anything to me, but it might help with the search. How are you involved in this?"

"I'm looking for some missing girls."

"You haven't gone to the police?"

"It's a favor for a friend, someone I've known since childhood, and he asked me not to."

"Hutterites?"

"Yes."

"That explains it. But if these girls have been kidnapped, you need help."

"We don't know that for sure. They may have left on their own. They're all of age."

"Are they chubby?" Pat asked.

Tuper jerked his head, startled. "Are they what?"

"Overweight. Rumor has it King Midas likes fat girls. Although, I've heard he sometimes shares with others. If his acquaintances don't have the same preference, maybe he needs another type. I don't remember seeing too many overweight girls in the colonies."

"Most are pretty fit."

"King Midas is wealthy and well known in Ulm. We haven't been able to stop him because we haven't seen money change hands. But we've never actually witnessed a delivery either. This could be a big break for us."

"Do you know where his cabin is?"

"He has two, but we'll stake out both." Pat grinned. "I'm sure curious as to how you came about this information. Are you sure it's reliable?"

"No doubt in my military mind."

Lana watched Ron come out of the college ahead of Finn. Ron picked up his pace and quickly got back into their car. Finn didn't seem to be in a hurry and chatted with people right outside the building before sauntering to his Jeep.

They followed him out of the parking lot to another fast-food place, then Finn got back on the highway heading north. "Does he live out this way?" Ron asked.

"Not according to his payroll and driver's license," Lana said. "But maybe he moved and still uses his parents' address. Or maybe he's going to meet a girlfriend. Or maybe he'll lead us to Rita and the other girls. Although, I really don't think he's our guy. But who knows? I've been fooled by men before." Lana stopped, wishing she hadn't said that.

They drove in silence for several miles, then Finn turned off the highway. Lana and Ron exchanged looks of astonishment.

"This road leads to Little Boulder," Ron said. "You don't suppose he's there to snatch another girl, do you?"

"In broad daylight?" Lana didn't know what to think. "You'd better drop back, or he's going to see us." Her mind raced. "Maybe we'll catch him in the act. Do you think he has a gun? What am I saying? Doesn't everyone in Montana have a gun? Maybe not everyone, but there sure are a lot of them here. It's very different than"—she paused— "other places I've been."

Lana reached into her backpack and pulled out binoculars. "You carry binoculars?"

"We're on surveillance. Drop back more. I'll be able to keep him in sight with these."

"The road has curves ahead. I don't want to lose him."

"You can't let him see us."

Ron dropped back more. "Can you still spot him?"

"I will once we're around this curve and head downhill a

bit." After a minute, she pointed ahead. "He stopped right across from the entrance to the colony."

Ron pulled over.

"Finn just got out," Lana said. "What's the plan?"

"We'll wait and see what he does. If he tries to take another girl, we'll stop him."

With the binoculars, Lana watched Finn as he stood by his car. Suddenly he climbed back in. "Uh oh!"

"What happened?"

"Let's go. He's taking off and moving fast. I think he got spooked."

Ron sped up and tried to catch him, but the car didn't handle the curvy road well. Lana managed to keep Finn in sight until he went off-road across a field and disappeared in the twilight.

CHAPTER 35

Friday night

They came to a stop and watched the yellow Jeep disappear. "Dang!" Lana yelled. "I liked that kid. I was so hoping he wasn't involved."

"Me too. I'd rather think it was Kingston."

"This doesn't mean they're not working together, even though they're an unlikely pair. Although, I would guess Finn to be the lure and Kingston the kidnapper. Maybe that's the way it worked before, and now with Kingston locked up, Finn would have to do his job." Lana opened her laptop.

"What are you looking for?"

"I want to check if either Finn or Kingston could be Steller, the dealmaker. I doubt it's Kingston. He doesn't strike me as a guy who sits in front of a computer. But you never know. Nah, he's not smart enough. Besides, he's in jail, so there's a good chance he doesn't have access." Lana loaded the Frinkers website. "I know sometimes those guys have really good connections in jail, but I don't believe Kingston is one of them. Besides, he's in a holding cell. How many people could he know there? And he's a two-time loser. Steller, on the other hand, really knows his way around a computer. There could be three people involved, with Steller as the salesman. I'll check for a connection between Steller and Finn."

Ron turned the car around and started back toward Little Boulder. Lana was surprised when they passed the colony's exit. "Where are we going?"

"I'm hungry, and I don't want to impose on Jacob again. I thought we'd get something to eat if you're okay with that."

"Sounds good." Lana's stomach fluttered, and she took a deep breath. *I hope he doesn't think this is a date.* "Nothing fancy though. I don't do fancy."

"Okay." Ron used the car's wireless system to call Tuper and update him. Then he invited Tuper to join them.

So, it wasn't a date. Lana went back to her search. After a while, she noticed that Ron kept glancing her way. She felt her face flush. *Was he looking at her or just fascinated by what she could accomplish on the internet?* She pushed the thought aside and refocused on her task.

But her search wasn't helpful. "Neither Finn nor Kingston appear to have an account on Frinkers," Lana said, breaking the silence. "They wouldn't use their real names, but I tried following their digital footprints. If either of them has an account, they're using a different computer for it, or their phones, which isn't likely. Kingston's probably not sophisticated online. And if Finn is Steller, he would be using a totally different device, and he would scramble it as well."

"So, then you couldn't trace it?"

"With the right information, it can still be traced, but it

takes more time than we have. Based on his social media posts, Finn doesn't appear to be a star either. Although, that could be a façade, and he might be really good at hiding his tech abilities. Based on what I've seen so far, he doesn't appear to be a hacker, but the best ones don't."

"Like you?"

"I don't know what you're talking about." Lana grinned. "But we don't really know that much about Finn. If he's good enough and has the time, he could find anything or anyone."

"How does someone keep from being found?"

"The trick is to keep moving."

"On the internet or in the real world?"

"Both."

Ron pulled into the parking lot at Roadhouse Diner.

"This is definitely not fancy." Lana closed her laptop and slid it into her backpack. At the door, she hesitated when she saw the flying pig logo, but went inside.

"I heard this place has the best burgers in town."

"Yum," Lana said with a twinge of sarcasm. She glanced around at the signs. The skull and crossbones with the words *Death by Bacon* were particularly unsettling.

They had just sat down when Tuper walked in and joined them.

"I'm glad you could make it, Pops."

"Best burgers in town. I wouldn't miss it. Besides, Ron's buyin.'"

"I can pay for my own," Lana said.

"Don't be silly," Ron said. "I'm on an expense account. And my Aunt Goldie would be proud of what we're doing. Thanks for helping us with that case."

"It was fun," Lana said. "Did everything work out?"

"Yes, but it's a long story. Maybe I'll tell you about it on a stakeout—when you get real bored and want to hear it."

The waiter approached and asked for their orders.

"The Winchester," Tuper said.

"I'll have the Sin City," Ron ordered.

"The Black Bean Burger, please," Lana said.

Ron gave Lana a quizzical look, and Tuper said, "She don't eat no meat."

"I can't eat living creatures."

"They ain't livin' when you eat them." Tuper grinned.

"I apologize," Ron said. "I brought you to a restaurant that is known for their meat."

"It's not like it's a date or anything." Lana felt her face flush and wished she hadn't said anything. To change the subject, she looked at Tuper. "Where have you been, Pops?"

"I went to see Pat Cox."

"That cop friend of yours?" Lana asked.

"Yep. And I know where the transaction is taking place tomorrow night. Sort of."

"What do you mean?"

"Pat knows a lot about King Midas; his real name and everything."

"What's his name?"

"*I* don't know. I said *Pat* knows."

"Did you ask him?"

"I did. He didn't choose to share that information. The point is King Midas has two cabins. I got the addresses for both, but I don't know which one he'll be at." Tuper reached in his pocket, pulled out a slip of paper, and handed it to Lana. "See if you can narrow it down, will ya?"

"Addresses. Cool. I'll see what I can do. But one thing's for sure. With this, I'll be able to figure out who King Midas is."

"I expect you can."

"Are we doing a stakeout there tomorrow night?" Ron asked.

"We'll have to split up," Tuper said. "After how Finn acted, I think we need to keep an eye on him too."

"Maybe we'll all end up at the cabin." Lana worked through the logistics. "If Finn is Steller, then he might be the one delivering the girls to King Midas. But how would he pull that off? It's not like he can make them stay in his Jeep. I guess he could if he has a gun and threatens them. They probably scare easy. If it were me, I'd bolt before I let him give me to some creep." She looked at the guys to see if they were listening. Tuper was shaking his head. Ron was smiling. Lana didn't let it slow her down. "Finn could have access to a van. That way, he could lock them inside and haul them anywhere. I wonder where he's keeping them."

The waiter brought their food. Lana started to offer another theory, but Tuper interrupted her. "Agony! Can we just eat in peace?"

After dinner, they walked out to Tuper's car, and he fed Dually scraps from his meal. "I'm going back to the colony. Are you two coming?"

Ron shook his head. "I think we should go by Finn's house and see if he's home." Ron glanced at Lana. "If he is, maybe we'll hang out for a while and see if he goes anywhere."

"Don't stay too long if you don't see any movement. We may be out late again tomorrow night."

"I checked his schedule at Smith's. Finn works eight to five tomorrow," Lana said. "It's Saturday, so lots of Hutterites will be at the store. I think we should check out who he talks to. It might save the next victim."

"Good idea." Tuper climbed behind the wheel. "I'll see you back at the Little Boulder barn."

CHAPTER 36

Friday night

Lana pointed to the street sign, and Ron made the turn. The neighborhood got slummier the further they drove. They pulled up almost directly in front of Finn's address and stopped the car. The house needed paint, but the yard was mowed and well-kept. The yellow Jeep was parked in the driveway, and lights were on in several rooms on both levels. A male figure walked past the window upstairs. Lana took out her binoculars to get a better look.

"That looks like Finn, and he's not wearing a shirt. That kid works out."

Ron extended his arm, palm up. "Let me see."

She gave him the binoculars. "I didn't know you'd be interested in a buff man with no shirt, but whatever."

"First of all, I'm not. Second, he's a kid. And third, Tuper's right. You can be a pain."

Ron watched their target, while Lana dug into the county property records.

"The house belongs to a corporation in Billings. Finn's mother rents it."

Lana did a little more research on the family. "Finn has an older brother. His parents are divorced. His father is in the picture, but he recently remarried and moved to Idaho. Mother works for Walmart, but she's been on sick leave for two months, which might explain why Finn needs another source of income." Lana sighed. "But I still don't think he's our guy."

"If he has to support his mother, and maybe his brother, while he goes to school, it sure gives him motive."

"Maybe, but I need more." Lana uploaded the Hutterite letters from her phone to her laptop, then enlarged the images and looked at them side by side.

"That's Finn all right." Ron put down the binoculars. "What are you looking at now?"

"The letters. Something is off."

"Let me see."

Lana turned her laptop toward Ron and leaned in, so they could share the screen.

"They refer to *the Lord* twice. That seems excessive for a short note. Is that what's bothering you?"

"No. They're religious, so it's not a surprise."

"When I'm trying to figure this sort of thing out, I look at every word individually, and then again as a whole." Ron sat back.

Lana jerked the laptop over and looked closer. "That's it."

"The Lord passages?"

"No. Yes. This isn't right. Either that or all these girls need to go back to school, or to church, or something."

"Why?"

"In all the letters they refer to the Lord as *the prince*."

"Yes," he said, drawing it out. "But that's acceptable, right? I don't know much about the Bible, but I remember passages that refer to *the Prince of Peace*."

"Yes, but these girls didn't capitalize the word *prince*. If they were referring to the Lord, they would have capitalized it. No way these educated, religious girls didn't give the Lord His due. They must be trying to signal something." A thought hit her. "That's it!"

"What?"

"Look." She stuck the computer in Ron's face again, her hand accidentally brushing against his. For a second, she held still, then let him take her laptop.

"The word *dream*."

"That's right. The only thing different in all these letters is their description of the adventure. And they all use the word *dream*. They're trying to call attention to that word in case we missed the lowercase *prince*."

"Prince Dreamy," Ron said.

They both looked up at the second-floor bedroom, and a moment later, the lights went out in that room. They waited another half hour to make sure Finn wasn't leaving. When all the lights went dark in the house, they left and drove back to the colony.

Lana couldn't sleep, so she sat up in her makeshift bed and opened her laptop. In the quiet barn, she could hear Ron's steady breathing, an occasional snort from Tuper, and the sweet sound of an owl. It was the perfect work atmosphere.

She used Google Maps to locate King Midas' cabins and studied the aerial views. Before she went further, curiosity overwhelmed her, and she searched for the owner. Both belonged to the same man. Further research gave her a good synopsis of his life. King Midas was married, with two teenage daughters, educated at Stanford, a successful businessman, and a school board member. *What was wrong with people?* A few more clicks brought up a family photo: a tall, lanky man in his late forties, with a stunning wife and two beautiful children. *They looked so normal.*

Lana took a deep breath, closed the site she was on, and moved into the dark web. She created a temporary account that resembled one for Steller. She had to be quick. Get in, get out. The best she could tell, he was not online. But if he were, and he was savvy, he could discover her. She stopped, thinking it was too risky. She could blow the whole operation and scare them away. That could ruin their chance of ever finding the girls. She had to check another source. She emailed her hacker friend.

Cricket—*Ravic?*

Ravic—*Yes, little one.*

Cricket—*Have you learned anything more about Steller?*

Ravic—*Ah, the sex broker.*

Cricket—*That's the one.*

Ravic—*Small-town Joe in our world. A loser in his. Thinks he knows far more than he does. I've been poking him, just for fun. He has no idea where it comes from. What else do you need to know?*

Cricket—*That's it. Thanks.*

Lana waited for King Midas to come online, then sent a message from her fake Steller account.

Fake Steller—*All set for tonight?*

She deleted the question mark, remembering that Steller used no punctuation, and sent the message. King Midas promptly responded.

King Midas—*Absolutely.*

Fake Steller—*Be outside waiting*

King Midas—*I will.*

Fake Steller—*Where exactly?*

Once again, she had to backspace over the question mark. Putting in punctuation was automatic for her, but she had to seem as authentic as possible and hope they had no further conversations. She also had to keep responding quickly now that they had started the conversation, or he might get suspicious.

King Midas—*Close to rosebushes. Park in front of birdbath.*

Before she could answer, a second message came in.

King Midas—*What time did you say?*

Was he testing her?

Fake Steller—*10:05*

King Midas—*See you there. Virgin queens, right?*

Dang! What did he mean by that? Was it another test? Lana took a deep breath and decided she was being paranoid.

Fake Steller—*Of course*

Lana signed off, closed her laptop, and lay back down. Thoughts of those poor girls ran rampant through her mind. It had been six days since Rita disappeared. Hannah from the Sandy Colony had been gone almost two weeks, and no one had heard from her at all. Lana didn't want to think about what suffering they'd already endured or whether they were even still alive. Up until now, she'd hoped they'd left on their own. She had been projecting her own attitude on them. She knew if she were living in that situation, she would feel trapped and would most certainly run. But the more she learned about the Hutterites, the more she realized they chose to be there. Albeit, their indoctrination led them to that choice. But that was true of everyone. *We all carry the hand we're dealt.* She was a prime example.

CHAPTER 37

Saturday morning

Just before five, Lana woke up to the sound of Tuper shuffling around.

"Hey, Pops," Lana said softly, so as not to wake Ron. "I think I should go to Smith's with Tobias this morning."

"Why on earth would you do that?"

"So I can keep an eye on Finn, AKA Prince Dreamy, maybe even get some information out of him."

"But he'll recognize you."

"He thinks I'm Helen, Rita's best friend. I never told him any different. I know he saw me in street clothes, but I don't think that really registered. Maybe he'll try to convince me to run away as well."

"I dunno. It don't sound like a smart move."

"What could it hurt? If tonight's bust doesn't pan out, with Kingston in jail, all we have is Prince Dreamy."

Tuper twisted his mustache. "I'll talk to Jacob," he mumbled and walked away.

Lana took her backpack and hurried to the showers. No one was there, so she took a quick shower and donned her Hutterite clothes. If Jacob didn't want her to go with Tobias, she would persuade Ron to take her. She had to get Finn's attention.

Ron was awake when she returned to the barn.

"That outfit becomes you," Ron teased.

"Right. Wearing these prairie clothes is the hardest part. I feel so strange. Although, I do kind of like the scarf. I've always liked polka dots."

"Really? I haven't seen you wear anything like that."

"Yeah," Lana said. "I don't have any." She told him about her pending plan.

"I'm heading to Smith's right after breakfast to keep an eye on Finn," Ron said. "There's no need to go any earlier because the Hutterite shoppers won't be there. If Tuper and Tobias don't like your idea, you can go with me."

That was easy. Lana thanked him, and they walked over to the dining hall to get some food.

Two hours later, Lana sat in the passenger side of Tobias' truck as it pulled into the parking lot at Smith's. The store was already busy. Tobias wasn't comfortable with the deceit, but that was quickly overridden by his concern for his daughter.

"Just remember, my name is Helen," Lana said. "That's all anyone needs to know."

Tobias went about his business, and Lana wandered through the store. She saw two Hutterite girls talking to a short, dark-haired teenage boy. Lana looked around for Finn but didn't see him. The two girls walked on and stopped near a tall, blond man in the deli section. Lana reached the girls just as they were walking away, giggling. The man said hello, and Lana nodded but didn't speak. The girls seemed to be on a mission to speak to every attractive boy or man in the store. She followed the girls into the produce section, where they must have spotted Finn. Lana stood back while they approached him. She heard him say, "Sorry, I have to go." Finn dashed off into the backroom.

Lana waited several minutes, looking around and watching the girls flit from one shelf to another, until they disappeared into another aisle.

A few minutes later, Finn came back carrying a box of apples. She caught his eye, and he came right over to her.

"Hi, Helen," he said.

"Hi, Finn."

"Has Rita come home?"

"No, but I got a letter from her."

Finn's eyes lit up. "Really? Is she okay?"

"She says she is, but I'm still not sure. Did she ever tell you anything about where she wanted to go? Maybe something special she wanted to do? I'm just sick with worry, and I really miss her."

"I miss her too. I'm just so afraid something bad has happened to her. I can't believe she left the colony of her own free will and hasn't contacted me. She just wouldn't do that."

Dang. You're good. "Think about it, and see if you can remember any place or thing she mentioned that might help. I'm here with her father this morning, and I'll be around until he's ready. Let me know if you come up with something."

Finn looked solemn, but he gave a half smile, nodded, and walked away.

You're going to slip up, Prince Dreamy, and we will be there.

Lana saw Ron enter the canned vegetable aisle. She walked around the other end and met him in the middle.

"I didn't really get anything out of Finn," Lana said, "but I'll talk to him again before Tobias leaves. I don't want to go back to the colony. Is it okay if I stay here with you?"

"Of course." He beamed with pleasure. "I welcome the company."

"I'll help Tobias load the truck, then come to your car. Where is it parked?"

"Near Finn's at the far end of the lot, toward Petco. It's easy to spot that yellow Jeep."

Lana found Tobias up front, getting ready to take his supplies out. The clerk called for Finn, and he hustled up, pushing a flat cart with large bags of flour and sugar.

When they reached the truck, Tobias left them to load while he went back into the store.

Lana tried again. "Finn, I know you don't believe Rita would leave the colony and not be with you, but did you think of anywhere she might go?" Lana wasn't sure what she hoped to gain from her questioning because he certainly wasn't going to tell her where Rita was, but maybe he would give something away, something she could research.

"She talked about going to college, but it's mid-semester, so she couldn't do that." A pained expression crossed Finn's face. "Rita dreamed of seeing the world, traveling to foreign countries, and about flying."

He sounded so sincere. It was easy to see how he had lured those girls into his web.

CHAPTER 38

Saturday afternoon

Lana and Ron followed Finn when he left work. He went straight home, and they parked across the street again. After an hour, Lana said, "Well, this is boring."

"Why don't you take a nap? You must be tired."

"A little. I went to sleep late, then Tuper woke me up, and I couldn't get back to sleep. I guess there's nothing else I can research to help us out. I think I will nap."

Lana laid her head against the door and tried to sleep, but without success. Finally, she said, "This isn't working. I can watch if you want to nap."

"I'm not that tired."

Lana twisted and turned in her seat, trying to get comfortable.

"I've been thinking," Ron said. "This kid is young and doesn't seem that sophisticated."

"Part of his act, I would say."

"But do you think he could pull this off by himself? Or is he part of some ring?"

"I don't think he's doing it alone. If he is, he's a real psycho. Kingston doesn't seem to be part of it. Although, I guess he still could be. Naw, that's not very likely. But someone is leading this operation, and it's not Finn, so there's at least one other person involved. Maybe that's Steller. I hope we find out tonight. Wouldn't it be great if we rescued all the Hutterite girls?" Lana realized that was unrealistic. "But that doesn't seem likely either. We have five or six missing girls, and Steller said he had three for King Midas. So, not all of them will be there. But if the cops do catch Steller, hopefully, it will lead to the other girls. There could be even more we don't know about, not just Hutterites but others. It's hard to say how big this thing is." A big smile on Ron's face made her stop. "I'm jibber-jabbering, like Tuper says, aren't I?"

"I enjoy your jibber-jabber. It's fascinating to hear you think out loud."

"Thanks. Most people find me irritating."

"Since we have time to kill, why don't you tell me about your family?"

"Not much to tell." Lana fidgeted in her seat. "What about you? I know a little from what Tuper and Clarice have said. Most of it came from Clarice. As you know, Tuper doesn't say much. Clarice said you have a sister named Sabre, right?"

"Yes. She's a few years younger than me, and we're very close. Our father passed away some years ago, but our mom is still living. Sabre has a great boyfriend, JP, who she lives with. They're raising JP's brother's two children because both of their parents are in prison." Ron paused. "Your turn. Siblings? Parents? Where are you from?"

Lana reached for the door handle. "I'm going for a quick run. I'm getting antsy just sitting here."

"What if he comes out and we have to follow?"

Lana was already out of the car. "I'll just run up and down this block. Call me if he comes out, and I'll come right back."

"Be careful. This isn't the best neighborhood."

Lana heard him but didn't respond. She started to run. That had been worse than a date. That kind of getting-to-know-you conversation was exactly what she wanted to avoid. She jogged to the end of the block and turned around. She'd created a whole scenario for a past life, but she didn't feel right using it on Ron. Tuper liked him. *She* liked him, and she halfway trusted him. That was more than she usually gave. She ran past Ron's car to the other end of the block. She hated the short route, but it was better than sitting in the car and avoiding that conversation.

The third time she approached Ron's car, she saw a dark-haired kid about Finn's age pull up to the curb and park. Lana jumped in Ron's car. "Sorry," she said. "I hope he didn't see me."

"Actually, it's a good cover."

The young man went into the house. Less than five minutes later, he and Finn both came out and walked toward the Jeep.

Ron waited a moment, then followed them down the street. A few blocks passed before Ron spoke. "Look, Lana, I didn't mean to pry."

"It's fine. I wonder where he's going. Maybe he'll lead us to Steller. That would be great. But if he does, that means the other kid is also involved. I feel so bad for those girls. I hate to think what they're going through. And Steller might not even be the leader. He might just be the computer guy."

A few miles later, Ron said, "He's taking the off-ramp for Smith's. I wonder if he's going back to the store."

"Maybe he's getting his paycheck. Why else would a teenager go to his workplace during his off hours?"

Finn drove into the lot at Smith's but continued past it and parked in front of the AMC theater.

"It looks like we're going to the movies," Ron said.

Lana grinned. "We?"

"This could be a meet-up with his boss. We should follow him inside, get a ticket, and sit close enough that we can see what happens. Besides, I need to use the restroom, and I'm hungry. Let's go."

"I don't know."

"It will pass the time quicker. And it's on me."

"Popcorn does sound good."

Lana grabbed her backpack, and they followed the boys inside. They took turns watching them as the other used the restroom. The boys bought sodas, then Lana followed them into the theater. She snagged two seats a couple rows behind them. When Ron entered, she stood and waved, then sat back down. He brought two sodas, a bucket of popcorn, and an empty box so he could share with her.

They sat through the entire show—an action flick she mostly enjoyed—without anyone approaching the teenagers. Nor did the boys speak to anyone on their way out. They drove back to Finn's house, the other kid left, and Finn went inside. About twenty minutes later, his upstairs light went out.

"I think he's done for the night," Ron said.

"Looks that way. Do you want to join Tuper?"

CHAPTER 39

Saturday night

Tuper parked far enough away from the cabin so he couldn't be seen by anyone. He retrieved binoculars from his glove compartment and checked his watch. He still had twenty-two minutes, assuming the exchange occurred at the exact time Steller had indicated. He couldn't see any activity around the cabin, although the lights were on and the yard was well lit. Between that and the full moon, he had a good visual, except for the trees in front of him. He spotted the birdbath and the rosebushes Lana had told him to look for, but no sign of Pat or any other law enforcement. He hoped they were just good at hiding and not at King Midas' other cabin. Lana didn't miss many, but she could've misread the clues. *There was nothing to do now but wait.*

Tuper climbed out of his car and eased through the brush and the trees to a spot that gave him a better view. With the binoculars, he could see all around one side of the cabin. He thought he noticed movement about twenty feet from the front door. He hoped it was the good guys. Tuper scanned slowly from one side of the cabin to the other, then leaned against a tree and tried to get comfortable. His phone rang, startling him, and he struggled to pull it from his pocket. *Lana!*

"Why the heck are you callin' me?" Tuper whispered. "I'm on a stakeout."

"Then shut off your phone, Pops," Lana said. "We're on our way."

"You don't need to come here."

"We're already here. We just need to know where you are. Or we can find another spot to watch from."

"I'm not sure there is one without you getting in the way. It took me a while to find this one."

"Where are you?"

Tuper explained it the best he could. Before Lana hung up, she said, "Shut off your volume, but keep the phone in your hand so you can feel it, in case I need to call. I'd tell you to put it on vibrate, but I'm sure you don't know how to do that."

"Don't know how to turn the volume down either."

"Never mind. Just turn it off. We're approaching your car. We don't have our lights on, so don't panic and have a heart attack."

Tuper heard their engine, turned, and saw them park next to his car. When they stepped out, he called to them in a low voice, then made his way to Ron's car.

"You have a good view from up here," Ron said in a hushed tone.

"Yep." Tuper nodded. "But won't be able to hear anything."

"I guess we'll leave that to the cops," Ron said. "We just need to watch for the Hutterite girls."

"In one way, I hope they're here," Lana said. "But if they

are, that means they're being trafficked, and who knows where they've already been for a week. So, what I really hope is that they're not here, and we find them safe and sound somewhere else. Although, I know that's—"

"Agony! It's a stakeout. Be quiet."

"So, Pops," Lana said, "if we can't hear them, how can they hear us?"

"They can't. I was just hopin' to shut you up. Besides, there could be others close by on lookout, or cops we don't know about."

"It's cold out here." Lana pulled her cap down over her ears.

"Feel free to wait in the car." Tuper turned to Ron. "Why aren't you with Finn?" When Lana started to explain, Tuper interrupted. "Didn't ask *you*. I need the Reader's Digest version."

"He went to the movies with a friend, then to bed," Ron said. "He's probably good until morning."

"See how that's done, Agony? I don't need to know what he was wearing, whether he ate popcorn, or if his boots weren't shined."

"But, Pops, sometimes the details are the most important part, and—"

"Not this time," Tuper said. "Do you both have binoculars?"

"I do, but Ron doesn't."

"I have another pair in the glove compartment," Tuper said. "Will you get them for him?"

"I can," Ron walked toward the Mazda.

Lana watched him go. "Where's Dually?"

"I left him with Jacob."

"Smart move."

"Where do you want us?" Ron asked when he returned.

"Maybe over that way." He pointed to the trees on his left. "That gives you a view of the road so you can see them comin'. This spot has a better shot at the cabin."

"It's too dark to give you a signal, unless we flash a light," Ron said. "But that's probably not smart."

"No. That won't do."

"I've got it." Lana turned to him. "I'll stay here with you, Pops, and Ron can text me if he sees anything."

"Good idea," Ron said.

"Humpf. Good for you, maybe."

Lana ignored him and carried on. "That way, Ron can tell us exactly how many cars arrive, or if he sees police activity. We'll get more information that way. I already have the volume off so my phone can't ring. And I turned the brightness down, so Ron's texts won't flash."

"I'll do the same," Ron said. "I'd better find my spot. We only have seven minutes before the big event."

As soon as Ron left, Tuper walked back to the tree he'd established as his best view. Lana followed. Every time she started to speak, he hushed her. A few minutes later, her phone gave a dim flash.

"It's Ron," Lana said. "He says a van stopped about a hundred yards back. Maybe Steller is waiting for the clock to run out. He has three minutes before his scheduled time. That's pretty weird if he has to be exactly on time, but I imagine a guy who sells women has to be pretty weird. At least pretty sick."

"I got the point."

Lana's phone lit up again. "They're moving."

At exactly five minutes after ten, a man walked out of the cabin and stood by the birdbath.

"That's King Midas," Lana said.

"How do you know?"

"Because I checked out who owns the cabins."

The van stopped near the man, and he walked around to the rear doors. The driver climbed out.

Lana's phone blinked.

"Ron says three more cars are approaching."

"The cavalry, I hope," Tuper said.

The driver and King Midas exchanged what looked like cash. Lana tried to take a picture, but it was too dark, and she couldn't zoom in enough. "I wish I could get a photo of the driver, so I could figure out who he is."

The driver opened the van's back door, and his cargo stepped out. Lana exclaimed, "Oh my God! Now I know what he meant by *virgin queens*. Those poor girls."

All of a sudden, spotlights came on and illuminated the area like a bright summer day. Cops swarmed the place and quickly handcuffed King Midas and the driver.

"I guess we're done here," Tuper said.

CHAPTER 40

Sunday morning

Tuper quietly gathered up his bedding, laid it in a corner, and left the barn without disturbing Ron or Lana. He had a cup of tea with Jacob, then drove to see his friend, Pat Cox, who welcomed him inside.

"I see you made your bust last night," Tuper said.

"Were you there?" Pat asked.

"Yep."

"I figured you would be. You did a good job of staying out of sight. Did you find what you were looking for?"

"Nope. Wrong girls."

"I figured as much, or you would have come to me sooner. I sure appreciate your help. You saved those girls and probably others. We would've eventually narrowed it down, but you gave us a time and place." Pat met his eyes. "Want to share how you knew that?"

"Nope."

"Thanks anyway, Toop."

"Did those girls get back home?"

"Two did, and the other will soon. They were all underage and easily conned into what they thought would be an exciting, luxurious life. Even though they went with the trafficker willingly, they had been duped and would've soon lost their free will."

"Did you get Steller?"

"No, but we're getting closer," Pat said. "If you get any more information about him, I'd appreciate hearing it. Steller is getting bolder and more dangerous. So far, he's working locally, but if the money is right, he'll be spreading out soon."

"Will do."

"And if there's anything I can do to help you without losing my job, let me know."

"Just contact me if you hear anything about Hutterite women."

"What do we do now?" Lana rolled up her bedding to take to the loft. "Steller is off the grid. Kingston's in jail, and Finn seems to be a boy scout—except for his little diversion where he plays Prince Dreamy and abducts young women. Everything else he does is like a normal kid his age. He goes to work and to college. He plays video games with his friends and occasionally takes in a movie. If it weren't for those references to Prince Dreamy, we wouldn't even suspect him."

"What about his trip to the colony the other night?" Ron reminded her.

"Yeah, there is that."

"So, I guess we concentrate on Finn, keep an eye on Kingston, and hope something turns up."

"There has to be more we can do." Lana's frustration mounted. "Rita has been gone a week, and Hannah for two weeks now. I have no idea where else to look online. I'm keeping feelers out for anything Hutterite, but not much has turned up."

"I know Jacob doesn't like the idea." Ron grabbed his bedroll and started up the steps to the loft. "But isn't it time to get law enforcement involved?"

Just then Tuper entered the barn. He and Lana both said, "No."

"Do either of you have a better idea?"

"I do," Lana said. "I need to find a way to get kidnapped. I can—"

This time Tuper and Ron both said, "No."

"Hand me your bedding," Ron said. Lana gave it to him, and Ron put it away. "Tuper?"

"Mine's fine right there." Tuper pointed to the corner.

Ron came down the steps.

"So, what do we do?" Lana asked again.

"Jacob is making arrangements for Helen to go to Smith's. She knows Rita best, and we hope she can get through to Finn."

"That's a good idea, Pops. Maybe Finn genuinely cares for Rita. If he does, and he's working with someone, he might just want to save her. But then, why wouldn't he have done that already? The control is probably out of his hands once he passes the girls on. But maybe Helen can reach his heart. Can I go with her? I'm going. When can we leave?"

"Shortly."

"Right now?"

"Didn't you say Finn is workin' today?"

"Yes. But it's the Sabbath. Is Jacob okay with that?"

"He knows it can't wait."

Lana got dressed in her Hutterite outfit, put on her polka-dot headscarf, and rode to town with Helen and Tuper in Jacob's truck. Tuper had borrowed a hat and jacket from Jacob, and he'd left his car keys, in case they had an emergency.

Lana looked at what Tuper was wearing. "I don't think those jeans will pass muster."

"I don't plan to get out of the truck unless you do somethin' stupid that makes me come to your rescue."

"I'll try to be the best Hutterite I can be, Pops."

Tuper parked in the side lot, and Ron, who'd followed them, parked a short distance away.

"There's Finn." Lana pointed to the big bins behind the store.

Finn was cutting up boxes and throwing them in the recycling bin. Lana and Helen got out and walked over to him.

"Hi, Finn. I'm Helen."

Finn jerked another box from the pile. "I thought *you* were Helen," he said to Lana, appearing irritated.

"I'm Helen R.," Lana said. "This is Helen J., Rita's best friend."

Finn studied Helen's face, and his attitude softened. "I do remember Rita saying you had freckles. Have you heard from her?"

"I got a letter a few days ago, but I think someone made her write it."

"Just the one letter?"

"Yes," Helen said. "Finn, I need your help to find her. She

could be in big trouble, and if she's not, we need to know that too."

"I wish I could help, but I have no idea where she is."

"She wouldn't leave of her own accord without you," Helen pleaded. "Rita is crazy about you."

"That's why I'm so worried. I don't believe she would either."

"You swear she's not with you."

He threw down a box and shouted, "I told you people, I don't know anything. I'm as upset as you are." He stormed off.

"I guess Prince Dreamy isn't always such a prince."

Helen tipped her head and stared at Lana. "That's not Prince Dreamy."

"What? I thought all the girls called Finn Prince Dreamy."

"No. That's someone else. Rita talked about him too, but he's not Finn. She didn't like Prince Dreamy. She thought he was an arrogant jerk. He was always saying sweet things to the girls, but he bragged about himself too often. He was definitely not of any interest to Rita."

"So, who's Prince Dreamy?"

"I don't know. I have never seen either of them until now, but I know it's not Finn."

CHAPTER 41

Monday morning

After breakfast in the Hutterite dining hall, Lana, Tuper, and Ron went back to the barn to regroup. Lana and Ron sat down on a bench, but Tuper remained standing. Dually scratched around Tuper's bedding, making it fit his need, then lay down.

"So, what do we know now?" Lana shook her head. "Finn is probably just an innocent kid who fell head-over-heels for Rita. Prince Dreamy is our best suspect, but we have no idea who he is, except that he's an attractive blond who hangs out at Smith's but probably doesn't work there." Lana stood and paced as she talked. "Kingston, who just happened to talk to Rita the day before she disappeared, also happens to *look* like a bad guy." She made air quotes around *look*. "So, we assumed he was, but he may not have any connection to Rita and the other girls. We were following him when Tiffany was kidnapped. Although, after he was arrested, the kidnappings stopped. But that's probably a coincidence. I guess we'll see if they start up again when he gets out."

Lana sat down again, so Tuper started pacing. She continued. "Steller is a long shot. I haven't been able to find anything more about him that connects him to these missing girls. He doesn't post online about acquiring girls, so he has to get them from somewhere on his own. Or he has a connection with someone who does."

"Are you done jabberin'?" Tuper cut in.

"Basically, we have nothing, and nowhere to go from here," Lana said. "Now, I'm done."

"We still need to see what Kingston does when he gets out," Tuper said. "Isn't his arraignment today?"

"This afternoon," Lana said.

"Should we go to the police department and see if he's released?" Ron asked.

"No need to yet," Tuper said. "There'll be plenty of time after his arraignment. After what he did, the judge will require bail, and it'll take some time to process."

"Pops is right. They'll make it as hard as they can for him to get out. They won't be able to control what the judge does, but the prosecutor will likely back the cops and ask for as much as they can."

"And you'll be able to tell in real time?" Ron looked at Lana.

"Not as it happens, but as soon as it's entered in the computer. The clerk often does it right from the courtroom. It could be different here, but there's still no need to leave until the hearing."

"What's your plan, Tuper?" Ron asked.

"I'm stayin' here with Jacob. If anything comes up, let me know." He turned toward the dog. "Come on, Dually. Yer stayin' with me." Tuper headed out, still talking to the dog. "No need for you to go on a boring stakeout, buddy."

Lana and Ron sat in the parking lot of the Great Falls Police Department, waiting to see if Kingston got released. Lana kept checking the court records, alternating with a search of Smith's employment accounts.

"You seem engrossed," Ron said. "What are you looking at?"

"If Finn isn't Prince Dreamy, then we need to find out who is. I've checked every Smith employee under thirty. Quite a few young men work there, but their social media photos indicate they're either too short, too heavy, or not blond."

"Maybe he's a customer."

"Must be." Lana clicked back to the court records. "Kingston has bail set for seven hundred fifty dollars. Let's see if anyone helps him out. This part could take a while. I saw a Dairy Queen not far from here. Why don't we get some food? We can bring it back here and wait. Trust me, we have plenty of time. You must be hungry too. We haven't eaten since early—"

"Lana," Ron interrupted. "You had me at Dairy Queen."

They drove to the restaurant, picked up lunch, and returned within fifteen minutes. Then they waited. Ron devoured his hamburger and fries, while Lana picked at her salad and watched her laptop.

The court records finally updated. "Someone posted bail."

"Can you see who?"

"Not yet." A few minutes later, she said, "I guess this is no surprise."

"Who?"

"His brother, the preacher. He's probably the only one who has any compassion for Kingston. I'll bet his mother gave up on him long ago, and she probably doesn't have the money anyway. Although, I wouldn't think Owen has that much either. I was hoping some stranger would do it, someone who would lead us to the criminal ringleader. But maybe Kingston isn't even involved."

Ron smiled at her.

"What?"

"Nothing." He pointed toward the front of the building. "There they are. And Owen doesn't look too happy."

"Of course not. He just had to spend his hard-earned money on his loser brother. I'd be mad too." Lana pointed this time. "They're coming this way, and boy is Owen mad."

They could hear their voices, but only occasional words, like "idiot" and "stupid," were audible from Owen. Kingston's language was more colorful. As they got closer, their conversation became more perceptible. They stopped at Owen's car, parked in the next row over.

"Don't you ever think about anyone but yourself?" Owen asked.

"We can't all be as holy as you pretend to be, brother," Kingston retorted.

Owen stepped forward and got in Kingston's face. "You have no right to question *my* morality. Look at you. And what's Mom going to think when she hears this? She'll be devastated."

"Then don't tell her." Kingston got in the car. Owen walked around to the driver's side, climbed in, and they drove away.

Ron followed.

CHAPTER 42

Monday afternoon

Owen drove directly to the parking lot where Kingston had been arrested and left the Cutlass. The car was still there.

"Things are so different here than they are in California," Ron said. "That car wouldn't still be in a public lot back home. If for some strange reason it was, thieves would have stripped it."

"It's a different world here, like someone set the clock back thirty years. Some things I like about it, others I don't. They have an old-school approach that doesn't always reach into my technology world. That makes things more difficult for me, but from Tuper's perspective, it's easier. He's always complaining about how things have gotten so out of hand, not like the 'good ol' days.' I like the quiet here though. And the solitude."

"Me too. Have you been to Tuper's cabin?"

"That was an experience. The cabin isn't much, but it sure is in a beautiful area. So tranquil."

Kingston stepped out of Owen's car and walked toward the Cutlass. Owen drove away.

"I guess he doesn't care if the car starts," Ron noted.

"I don't blame him." Lana heard the engine roar, and a moment later, the Cutlass backed out. "Kingston's moving."

They followed him out of the parking lot and straight to the Flying Monkey, where he'd been the night he got busted.

"Kind of early to be drinking," Lana said. "Maybe he's meeting someone."

"It's almost four o'clock. Want to bet that's not too early for Kingston?"

"I'm not taking that bet."

Kingston hustled inside, and they followed him into the nearly empty bar. Beer in hand, Kingston sat in the same area he had last time. Lana and Ron sat at a nearby table with a good view. For the next two hours, Lana sipped a soda, and Ron had beer, taking only an occasional drink, then ordering another when it got warm.

People straggled in, and by six the bar was fairly crowded for a Monday night. The happy hour specials seemed to be the attraction, and they continued until seven. Ron placed an order, making sure none of the appetizers had meat.

"Thanks," Lana said. "I'm hungry."

"Of course, you are. You seem to be hungry a lot."

"I like to eat."

When their food was delivered ten minutes later, Lana asked for a couple of to-go boxes.

"Why don't you just eat it here?"

"I will. But if we have to exit in a hurry, we won't have to leave the food behind. Who knows when we'll get another chance to eat?"

Kingston downed beer after beer and hit on several

women, who blew him off. By his fifth drink, he was more aggressive. Not a female could pass by him that he didn't approach in some manner. A few stopped and talked, then moved on. A woman sitting alone at the bar got his attention. He walked over and started chatting, standing next to her for quite a while. When she got up and went to the restroom, he waited. A few minutes later, she took a different seat, and Kingston followed her. She was obviously trying to ditch him, yet she remained polite.

"She has more patience than I would," Lana said. "I hate men like that. They're so obnoxious. And this guy is especially bad. He doesn't know when to quit."

Finally, the woman got up and mingled with a crowd. Kingston looked defeated but kept an eye on her. When she left the bar, he started to move in that direction.

Lana stood. "I'll hurry out ahead of him. Grab our food and follow if he leaves."

"Be careful," Ron called after her as she fled.

Outside, Lana caught up to the woman Kingston had hit on. "Are you okay?"

"Sure. Why?"

"I saw that guy bothering you, and I think he's coming out. Is your car close by?"

"My ride's right there." She pointed to a vehicle that was running and had its lights on.

"Goodnight." Lana turned when she heard the bar door open and saw Kingston step out. The other woman drove away, and Lana kept walking toward Ron's car.

Kingston called, "Hey, girl."

She glanced back and saw him ten feet behind her. Ron was about fifteen steps behind Kingston. Lana kept moving, listening to his footsteps. He was getting closer. She picked up her pace and so did he. Lana slowed down. He kept coming, calling out again. She was almost to Ron's car when he tapped her on the shoulder. Lana swung around and kneed him in the groin. Kingston fell to the ground, moaning.

"You pig!" Lana shouted. "Leave women alone!"

Kingston struggled to his feet, glanced at Ron who had just arrived, then stumbled toward his own car.

"I bet he won't sleep it off," Lana said. "He'll drive drunk again. I'm sure the cops would love to hear about that."

"You'll make the call?"

"I was hoping you would."

"It'd be my pleasure."

They climbed in the car. Ten minutes passed, and Kingston hadn't left.

Ron finally said, "We still have Prince Dreamy. Now that we know who he *isn't*, we just have to find out who he *is*."

Lana pivoted toward Ron. "That's it. You're a genius."

"I know," he joked. "But why?"

"Other Hutterite girls have seen Prince Dreamy. We just need one to identify him." Lana's phone rang. She put it on speaker for Ron.

"There's another girl missin'," Tuper said.

"When?" Lana's pulse raced. "From where? Did it just happen? Because if that's the case, it sure isn't Kingston."

"Saturday night from a remote colony called Antelope Creek, about a hundred miles north of here. Her name is Susanna."

"Why are we just now hearing about it? I thought the colonies were tuned into what's happening. How many other girls are missing that we don't know about?"

"Antelope Creek doesn't get good cell reception, so they

didn't know what was goin' on. Paul, their leader, drove to town and called Jacob a little while ago."

"Thanks, Pops."

"How are things with Kingston?"

"He's been drinking in a bar since this afternoon, but he's in his car now. We're just waiting for him to drive out of the parking lot, so the cops can give him another room for the night. He may not be our suspect, but he sure is a menace to society."

"He started his car," Ron said.

"We're taking off, Pops. We'll head back to Little Boulder after we see this through."

Kingston finally got moving and left the lot. Ron made a call to the local police, then followed him. Within minutes, lights flashed behind them. They pulled over and let the patrol cars pass, then got back on the road. It took another mile, plus sirens, before Kingston pulled over.

CHAPTER 43

Monday night

"Are you ready to go back to the colony?" Ron asked.

"I have another idea," Lana said.

"Let me guess, you're hungry."

"I am, but we should do something else first."

"Let's hear it."

"I think we should go by Diamond Valley. It's not far, and I'm sure Benjamin will let me talk to Judith. She's Tiffany's best friend, remember? Judith told me she had seen Prince Dreamy."

"So? What good will that do?"

"We need Judith to go with me to Smith's. Helen said Finn wasn't Prince Dreamy, but she's only going on what Rita told her. Judith could confirm that or have a different opinion since she's actually seen him. I checked Finn's schedule, and he's working tomorrow. If she says Finn is Prince Dreamy, then we can get back on his tail. If she says he isn't, then maybe Prince Dreamy is another employee or customer she can identify. Although, that seems rather unlikely after my extensive search of Smith's employees. What do you think?"

"We're almost there," Ron said.

"Good. Because we have to find these girls. Every single day they could be going through hell." She took a deep breath and blew it out.

"What are you thinking?"

"Nothing." She sighed.

A few minutes later, they pulled up to Benjamin's house and knocked on his door. It took him a long time to answer. When he did, he looked around. "Is Tuper with you?"

"No. He's at Little Boulder," Ron said.

"What can I do for you?" The *Haushalter* took a step back. "Come in. Come in."

Lana told him about the letters and the Prince Dreamy theory.

"How can I help?"

"Judith has seen Prince Dreamy. We're hoping she can go with us to the store tomorrow and identify him or eliminate another suspect."

"I'm sure she'll be more than willing to go. She's in bed now, but I'll talk to her first thing in the morning. Then I'll call Tuper."

"Thanks," Ron said. "We appreciate this."

"I'm very worried about Tiffany." Benjamin looked solemn. "I don't believe she went on her own. She needs our help, so anything we can do, we will."

On the drive back, Lana opened her laptop and started a google search. When they neared Great Falls, Ron asked, "Want to stop and eat?"

"You know I do."

"Is that what you're looking for? Because I'd be more than happy to take you to a vegetarian restaurant if you can find one."

"I googled *top ten vegetarian restaurants* in Great Falls. However, when you click on the top link it says *top ten vegan friendly restaurants.* Most have the word *steakhouse* in their description." She kept searching while Ron drove. "How about the MacKenzie River Pizza Company? It appears to have the largest vegan menu. I prefer small mom-and-pop restaurants, but it's not easy to find anything here that serves what I'm willing to eat. And this one does have a view of the river, so that might be nice. What do you think?"

"Sounds great. How do I get there?"

"Good choice," Ron said after they finished their meals. "Would you like an after-dinner drink?"

Lana hesitated, then said, "I would."

When the waitress came back to their table, Ron ordered a beer. Lana said, "I'd like an Affogato Martini."

The server wrote it down without hesitation.

"Do you know what it is?"

"Not a clue, but our bartender can make anything. If he isn't familiar with it, he'll come ask you."

Lana was surprised, but pleased. She wasn't much of a drinker, but when she indulged, she wanted something she really liked.

She and Ron were chatting when the bartender approached. "Are you the one who wants the Affogato Martini?"

"Yes. Can you make it?"

"Only with your help. I'd look it up, but drinks are often made differently in other parts of the country. Where have you had one before?"

Lana didn't want to disclose that information. She avoided any mention of California, still not totally trusting Ron. "You put two ounces of vanilla vodka, half an ounce of crème de cocoa, and one ounce of Kahlúa into a shaker. Drop in a couple of ice cubes and shake it until it's chilled. Then pour the mixture into a martini glass and drop in a hefty scoop of vanilla ice cream."

The bartender thanked her and walked away.

"That was impressive," Ron said. "Where did you learn that?"

"I was with someone years ago who ordered one, and it looked yummy. Later, I experimented with the drink until I got it right. I make myself one occasionally, but I have to bring my own ice cream to the bar because Nickel's doesn't stock it."

They stayed at the restaurant for another hour chatting and enjoying the view of the river. It was the most relaxed and pleasant evening Lana had spent in a long time. There were even a few moments when she didn't stress about the missing girls.

CHAPTER 44

Tuesday morning

"Where were you last night?" Lana asked Tuper when he came into the barn around eight. "You never showed up. Did you find yourself a lady friend? Who was it? Did she give you breakfast? You know Louise doesn't like other women feeding you breakfast. She may put up with you sleeping with other women but giving you breakfast is her thing. You'd better be careful."

"Maybe I came in after you went to sleep."

"You didn't. So, what do you have to say for yourself?"

"I say it's none of yer business."

Ron climbed down from the loft where he'd taken the bedding. "Hi, Toop. Where've you been?"

"It ain't your business either."

Ron laughed. "I see Lana has been interrogating you."

"You goin' to Smith's this morning?"

"Yes," Ron answered. "Finn doesn't start work until ten today. We're leaving shortly to pick up Judith at Diamond

Valley. Then we'll drive to Smith's and hopefully find Prince Dreamy." He paused. "What's on your schedule? Or shouldn't I ask?"

"Humpf." Tuper walked toward the barn door.

"Can you watch Dually?" Ron called out.

"There ain't no place I'm goin' that he can't go."

"I think he's getting attached to my dog," Ron said. "Maybe that's a good thing."

Lana shook her head. "It will be hard on him when you two leave."

"What about you?"

"I'll miss Dually too."

Ron smiled. "You ready?"

Judith sat in silence on the ride to Great Falls.

"Are you nervous?" Lana asked. "Because there's no need to be. Nothing is going to happen. We'll just walk around the store and look at people."

"I'm a little nervous. But I like being in town. It's funny to see how some of the *Welt Leut* dress and how they wear their hair."

"Like me?" Lana smiled.

"Right now, you look like one of us."

Lana looked down at her Hutterite clothing. "True, but I dress differently than many women my age, and my hair is different too."

"Your hair isn't so bad."

"It would be if I weren't trying to pass as one of you. Does that bother you? That I'm wearing Hutterite clothing and trying to blend in?"

"Not at all. I think it's smart. Anything that will help bring Tiffany home is a good idea." She was quiet for a few seconds. "Do you think she's okay? I hope no one is hurting her."

"We hope that too," Lana said. "We'll find her no matter what it takes."

Ron pulled into the parking lot at Smith's. "How do you want to handle this?"

"It's best if you aren't seen," Lana said. "Wait where you want, but this could take a while."

"I'll just wait in or near the car. If you learn anything or need me, just text."

Lana and Judith went into the store. A clerk stared as they walked by.

"The way that woman looked at us, you'd think she never saw a Hutterite before."

"I'm used to that. But I guess I do it too. I find myself staring when I see a *Welt Leut* with blue hair or really short shorts or a low-cut blouse. But that's not why they look at us."

"What do you mean?"

"Some clerks watch us because they think we're going to steal stuff."

"Why would they think that?"

"Because we have big skirts, and they think we have big, deep pockets that we hide stuff in."

"Do you have big, deep pockets?"

She pulled out the pockets on each side of her skirt and left them hanging. They looked like big ears. "I do this when someone stares at me that way. It usually embarrasses them, and they leave me alone."

"You're pretty clever," Lana said.

They walked around the store for ten minutes before Lana spotted Finn heading into the cereal section. They hurried down the next aisle so they could approach him from the opposite direction. Lana wanted Judith to get a good look at his face.

Finn was about fifteen feet away when they turned the corner.

"Is that Prince Dreamy?" Lana whispered.

"No. That's Finn. All the girls know who he is."

Lana grabbed Judith's elbow, and they spun back around before Finn spotted them.

"They look kind of alike, but Finn's not as tall as Prince Dreamy," Judith added. "And I've heard Finn likes a girl from Little Boulder Colony."

They cruised the store, checking out employees. None were Prince Dreamy. After an hour, they finally gave up. As they approached the front doors to leave, Judith nudged her. "That's him." She nodded at a man coming into the store. He wore the same color shirt as the Smith employees, but it had no logo or nametag.

Lana spun them back around.

CHAPTER 45

Tuesday afternoon

"Watch where he goes," Lana told Judith, then ducked behind a free-standing display and texted Ron. *We found Prince Dreamy.*

They followed the man to the deli section and watched as he bought a cup of coffee and sat down. Lana texted Ron with their location.

"Wait here by the magazines," she told Judith. "I'll go talk to him. Ron will be in shortly." Lana glanced toward the front. "There he is now. Don't go near Ron. We don't want the Prince to know he's with us."

"Okay." She sounded disappointed.

Lana walked to a table near the man. When he looked over and said, "Hello," she remembered seeing him during an earlier trip to Smith's.

"You're looking very pretty today," the man said.

She pretended shyness by avoiding his eyes. "Thank you."

"Have a seat." He motioned to a chair.

"I'd better not."

"Suit yourself, but I promise I don't bite."

She faked a smile and cautiously sat down.

"What colony are you from?"

She should have been ready for that question. "A small colony north of here, but I'm visiting my cousin at Little Boulder. It's so much nicer in town. I never get to see anyone except Hutterites."

"It's a shame to keep a pretty girl like you all cooped up."

Lana looked away, then turned her eyes toward the floor, looking up occasionally as he spoke.

"You shouldn't be embarrassed by compliments. God gave you that beauty. You should wear it proudly."

"We are taught to not be proud or vain." She wished she knew a scripture to quote like Tuper had. *Where had he learned those anyway?*

"Do you ever wonder what the rest of the world is like?" He had a faraway look in his eyes. "What it's like to fly in an airplane or taste exotic foods? Have you ever seen the ocean or climbed to the top of a mountain? I live for these things, for the adventures life has to offer. There are so many places and things God wants me to experience. Why else would he put them here? And why would he give me an adventurous spirit?" The man tilted his head and locked eyes with Lana. "You have that too, don't you? I see it in your eyes, and I heard it in your voice. If you think Great Falls is an adventure, wait until you see the rest of the world."

"I'm afraid this is the most I'll see. My family would never allow anything else."

"You look old enough to make your own decisions."

"I am, but I can't disappoint them. They would be devastated."

"You'll never know what you're missing."

Lana looked down again and pretended to contemplate what he'd said.

He gave her a moment, then continued his pitch. "What happens if you leave the colony, then want to go back?"

"I could probably return, but few people do."

"Do you know why?"

"I'm not sure."

"Because they like it in our world. We can do whatever we want. This is America, and we're free. Once someone has a taste of freedom, it's hard to go back." He paused again. *This guy was good.* "The other thing I love about freedom is the opportunity to be alone, away from the crowd. I love to walk on a quiet beach or hike a mountain trail and just think and enjoy the air."

Lana acted enthralled with every word, but she didn't respond.

"Do you ever get any alone time?"

"Not much."

"What is your daily schedule like?"

Was this the setup? Did he find out when the girls were alone, then snatch them, or did he convince them to go willingly? She would play along.

Lana gave him a breakdown of a typical day for an unmarried Hutterite woman, then added, "After evening church service, I like to watch the sunset. That's my quiet, alone time. Pretty soon, the sun will be setting during supper, and I'll miss it."

"Maybe someday you'll get to experience a sunset on the beach. It's the most gorgeous thing you'll ever see."

"It sounds very exciting." Lana sighed. "But going out on my own would take money, and I don't have any. And I don't know any *Welt Leuts.*" She stopped. "Sorry, that's the word we use for people outside the colony."

"You know *this Welt Leut.*" He smiled and winked.

Lana looked away.

"I've embarrassed you again. I'm sorry. I just want you to know I would be glad to help you."

"Really?"

"All I ask is that you not mention me to anyone. I want to assist you anonymously." He checked the time and stood. "I need to go. If you change your mind while you're still in Great Falls, let me know."

"How would I reach you?"

"You could call me, but I don't suppose you have a phone."

"No." She giggled.

"I come in here almost every day. How long will you be staying at Little Boulder? It was Little Boulder, correct?"

"That's right. We leave the day after tomorrow."

"Keep an eye out for me. Maybe I'll sweep in and take you away on a magic carpet ride."

"Thanks. You've been very kind."

After he walked away, Lana dashed around the deli counter and sent Ron a text:

Lana—*Watch him. If he goes to a car, get his license plate number and follow him.*

Ron—*What about you and Judith?*

Lana—*We'll be fine.*

CHAPTER 46

Tuesday late afternoon

Prince Dreamy walked to a blue Volkswagen van. Ron passed behind the vehicle and committed the license plate to memory. He said it over and over as he hurried across the lot to his car. The van pulled out of its parking spot and headed in his direction. Ron had his car started when the blond man passed him and kept going east. Ron grabbed a pen and jotted down the license number on a fast-food bag. Then he called Lana.

"He's headed for the drive-up at McDonald's. It's a long line, so I have time to circle back and pick you up."

"We're out the door and walking in your direction."

"I see you. Wait there."

Ron pulled up, and Lana and Judith climbed inside.

"Did you get the license plate number?"

"It's on that bag. A Montana plate."

"I'm glad you came back. I left my laptop in the car."

Ron stopped near the McDonald's parking lot where they

had a good view of the cars leaving the drive-up window. He left his engine running. He hadn't seen the blue van come around the corner, and he hoped it hadn't pulled out of the line. Then he spotted the vehicle. It was still three cars from being in a position where Prince Dreamy would be trapped until passing the pickup window. Ron kept watch while Lana fired up her laptop.

"He's stuck in the line now," Ron said. "He still has five cars ahead of him."

"What are we going to do now?" Judith asked, her voice shaking.

"For starters," Lana said, "we need a way to get you home."

"I'd like that."

"Are you scared?" Lana asked.

"A little, maybe."

"You don't need to be. Nothing will happen. We'll just follow him for a little while to see where he goes. I promise we won't put you in any danger." She turned to Ron. "Any ideas?"

"Why don't you call Tuper?"

Lana called, but he didn't answer.

"He's only one car away from the exit," Ron said. "Come on, Tuper. Call back."

"I'll check the DMV," Lana said. "But if the van doesn't belong to him, the name on the registration might not help us." Lana got quiet as she clicked around the internet. "Dang it!"

"What's wrong?"

"I lost my internet connection."

"He's leaving," Ron said. "What do you want to do?"

"Follow him."

Lana's phone rang as they pulled away from McDonald's.

She put the phone on speaker and told Tuper what was going on.

"Where are you now?"

"We're following him on Market Place."

"Can you tell where's he going?"

"Not yet. Oh wait. He's turning into Home Depot."

"Ron should follow him inside. You and Judith wait in the car. I would come get Judith and take her home, but who knows where you'll be by the time I get there."

Ron got out and followed their suspect into the store.

"What now, boss?" Lana asked Tuper.

"Find out who he is on that contraption of yours, then when Ron comes out, take Judith home." Tuper hung up.

Lana tried again to search for the license plate but couldn't keep a connection. Frustrated, she thought, *WWTD? What would Tuper do?*

"Wait here." Lana jumped out of the car and jogged to Prince Dreamy's vehicle. She opened the passenger door, reached inside the glove compartment, and pulled out the registration. *Doesn't anyone in Montana lock their doors?* She took photos of the paperwork, then snapped a few of the van's interior. The back was set up like a living space, bed and all. Several red shirts lay on the floor. She opened the sliding side door and took more photos. She would process the details later. She was about to climb inside and search, but she looked up and saw Ron leaving the store. *Had she missed Prince Dreamy's exit?* Lana closed the door and dashed back to their car.

She and Ron climbed in at the same time, and a few seconds later, their suspect exited the store.

"How did you manage to get out first?"

"He was checking out, so I left," Ron said.

"Tuper wants us to take Judith home."

Ron started the car and pulled away. They got a glimpse of Prince Dreamy in the back of his van, eating.

"Were you able to trace his license plate?"

"No. But I got a picture of his registration."

Ron looked at her, surprised. "How did you do that?"

"Tuper style." Lana grinned. "By the way, what did Prince Dreamy buy in Home Depot?"

"A roll of duct tape."

CHAPTER 47

Tuesday evening

As soon as they returned to Little Boulder, Lana set up her laptop in the loft. She uploaded the photos she'd taken to scrutinize them later on a bigger screen, plugged in her phone so it would be fully charged, then went to see Helen. She found her walking to her dorm with two other young women.

"Helen," Lana called.

The freckle-faced girl stopped and waited while the other girls moved on.

"Hi." She eyed Lana's clothes and grinned. "I love the way you dress. Don't get me wrong, I like my clothes, but sometimes it would be fun to wear whatever I wanted." She dropped her head. "I shouldn't be like that. That's the way Rita thought all the time. She always wanted to see what life was like in other places. And look what happened to her. She may be in really big trouble."

"We all think at times that others' lives are better than ours, but until you've walked in their shoes, you don't really know what their life is like." Lana gave the girl a quick hug. "We have to live the life we're given and do it the best we can. That doesn't mean you can't embrace change, just make sure the change is worth what you're giving up."

"I know. I pray about it every day. I like my life here. It's safe, and I'm surrounded by love. I just wish Rita was back home."

"I'm working on that, and you can help. I need a favor."

"What is it?"

"Can you sew an extra inside pocket into my skirt? And make it long enough that I can move it around and big enough to hold my phone?"

"When?"

"Right now."

"It's almost time for evening meal."

"I know, but this is important. It may be our only chance to find Rita." Lana handed her the skirt. "Can you bring it to the barn as soon as you're finished?"

Helen smiled. "I'll be right there."

Lana walked back and met Ron at the door. They stepped inside.

"Have you told Tuper your plan?" He looked worried.

"Not yet. I know he's not going to like it, but I think it's our best bet."

"Are you ready?"

"I have to be. The Prince only has tonight and tomorrow night to come find me."

"What are you talking about, woman?" Tuper asked as he approached them.

"I set up Prince Dreamy so he could find me," Lana said.

"Just what good is that gonna do?" Tuper raised his voice.

"I'm hoping it will lead us to the other girls. I realize it's risky, but we're running out of options."

"We could just follow him and see where he goes," Tuper suggested.

"I thought about that." Lana shook her head. "If he's the pick-up guy, he won't lead us to the girls until he nabs another one. I'm just moving up the timeline." She glanced at Ron. "I'll set up Ron's phone to track mine. I would set yours, but that goofy flip phone couldn't track a mouse already caught in a trap. You and Ron can be right behind me all the time. As long as my phone stays charged, I'll be good."

"Or until he finds your phone and confiscates it."

"That could be a problem. All the more reason to stick close to me."

"I don't like it one bit." Tuper slapped his hand against the wall in frustration.

"You got a better idea, Pops?"

Tuper turned to face Ron. "You're going along with her scheme? I thought you had more sense than that."

"I told her it was crazy, but she doesn't listen to me any more than she does you."

"If the guy's coming tonight," Lana said, "I don't have a lot of time. So, either help me or get out of my way because I'm doing this." She reached her hand out to Ron. "Give me your phone so I can set up the tracker."

He looked at Tuper, shrugged, then handed his phone to Lana.

CHAPTER 48

Tuesday at sunset

After a meal in the dining hall, Lana went out by herself to watch the sunset from a bench in the commons. Ron and Tuper were positioned nearby but out of sight of anyone entering the colony. Jacob, Tobias, and a few others were on standby around the complex as well. She felt a little nervous, but soon realized it was more a sense of unpreparedness. She needed more time to get everything into place. She hadn't had a chance to find a name and an address for Prince Dreamy in Great Falls. The car was registered to David Johnston in Bozeman. She wasn't certain if that was a previous owner or if Johnston was the guy. If it was him, it was possible he still lived there, but more likely that he just hadn't updated his information. Either way, if something went wrong, it would be better if Tuper knew who to look for and where.

Lana moved to the side of the building facing west and gazed at the newly planted wheat fields that seemed to go on until they reached the mountains jutting up in bluish magnificence. She looked up at the vast sky that was just starting to darken and, for the first time, understood why Montana was called the Big Sky State. It seemed to have no end.

As the sun dropped below the horizon, Lana saw movement about thirty feet away. She shifted her eyes but didn't move her head. Lana sighed. It was Dually coming toward her. *Dang.* Prince Dreamy wouldn't approach with a big dog at her side.

"Dually," she heard Tuper call softly. The dog turned and made a beeline across the yard.

Good, Lana thought, *Tuper has a visual on me.*

She waited and watched as the sun sank into the distant mountains. A small part of her was grateful he didn't show, but she was determined to try again tomorrow night. When the sun was completely gone and the light started to fade, she headed toward the barn. Ron, Tuper, and Dually trailed her inside.

"Maybe he was here and got spooked," Lana said.

"He wasn't here," Tuper countered.

"How do you know?"

"Because Tobias was hidden by the only entrance. No one came."

"How would Tobias even let you know? Would he yell out to you? That wouldn't be very smart. If Prince Dreamy had shown up, you wouldn't know he was here until it was too late."

"He had Jacob's extra phone and would've called me."

She slapped him on the shoulder. "Way to go, Pops. I knew you'd take care of me. You would go crazy without me around to bug you, wouldn't you?"

"Going crazy *with* you around to bug me," he mumbled.

They were almost back to the barn when Jacob caught up with them. "I just got a call from Sandy Colony."

"Did Hannah send a letter?" Lana asked. "Or did they hear from her some other way? Is she back?"

"Agony, let Jacob tell us."

"Hannah is back. She went out on her own, and it did not take her long to know she did not want to be there."

"Does she know anything about—?"

"Agony." Tuper cut her off.

"She knows nothing about the other girls," Jacob said, sounding disappointed. "She did not plan anything with them and did not even know they were missing."

"Did Prince Dreamy or someone help her leave?" Lana asked.

"No one helped her. I asked about Prince Dreamy, about Finn, and about Kingston, but she knows nothing about any of them."

Lana moved her bedroll to the loft, then propped herself against the wall, laptop open. With a deep breath and determination, she resumed her search for information about Prince Dreamy. She started with David Johnston, the name on the registration. She hated when names were too common, making it so much harder to track down the right person. Step by step, she worked her way through the system she'd set up for herself. It took an hour to find a social media site with an account for who she thought was the right David. His profile picture was a blue Volkswagen van. She glanced through the photos on his page, and there he was.

After that, things got a little easier. She was able to find a more current address in Great Falls on 52nd Street, and soon discovered he was the oldest of three children, with one brother and one sister. His seventeen-year-old sister lived in Bozeman with their mother, and his twenty-two-year-old brother was in the Army and stationed in Colorado. Their father was in prison, serving the fifth year of a ten-year sentence. Lana rested her eyes for a moment, then her head dropped, waking her up. She decided to leave his work history for the morning.

CHAPTER 49

Wednesday morning

With Tuper as his passenger, Ron drove to the 52nd Street address Lana had given them for David Johnston.

"There's his VW van," Ron said. "This must be the right place."

"Good to know."

Ron parked nearby, and not long after, Tuper dozed off. Ron found himself wishing Lana had come along. He was used to having her around, and even though she could be pretty obstinate at times and could talk like no one he had ever met before, she was entertaining. He thought about texting her, but he didn't want to wake her, in case she'd gone back to sleep. He knew she'd been up most of the night.

At five minutes before noon, Johnston finally came out of his apartment, got in his van, and drove off. When Ron started the car, Tuper muttered, "Is he moving?"

"We're on the go again."

"Good. I was getting bored."

"How could you be bored? You were asleep."

"Just checking my eyelids for holes."

Soon they were parked at the same McDonald's, waiting for Prince Dreamy to get his morning nourishment. From there, he moved the van a few hundred yards and parked again.

"This guy doesn't go very far from his usual stomping grounds, does he?" Ron noted.

"Nope."

Ron's phone dinged, indicating a text. *Lana.* Hearing from her made his pulse jump, even if she was just checking in.

"What's that?" Tuper asked.

"Texts from Lana." He read them to Tuper as they came in, including his responses.

"That woman jabbers even when she's texting," Tuper said, and lay his head back against the window.

Lana slept until eleven thirty, took a shower, and then texted Ron. She was eager to get to work, but she was more hungry than anxious. She'd missed breakfast, but it was already time for lunch, so she walked over to the dining hall.

Lana hurried through her meal, then went back to her computer in the loft. Within half an hour, she'd determined that David Johnston had no criminal record, except for two speeding tickets that he'd taken care of without going to warrant. He'd graduated from high school but hadn't gone beyond that. Right out of high school, he'd gone to work for a small dude ranch just outside of Bozeman for a few years. Then he'd worked in Billings at a tractor supply company, only lasting a few months. After that, he'd moved back to his mom's house in Bozeman and got a job at Smith's. *That would explain why he felt so comfortable in the store.*

Lana took time perusing his work records at Smith's. He'd started out with good evaluations, but gradually became lax in his work ethic. His hours had been cut back until, eventually, he was fired after several warnings. That was three months ago, and as far as she could tell, he hadn't worked since.

Lana searched every social media site she knew of, looking for information about David Johnston. All she discovered was that he wasn't active online. The best she could tell, he only had a Facebook account, with fifteen friends and very few posts. His last post had been months before he left Bozeman.

Lana was still in the loft when Ron and Tuper returned. She saw them from the window and hurried down the steps to meet them. "Did you find out anything new? Where did he go? Did he meet up with anyone we can check out? I hope you got license plate numbers or at least photos if he did. Where is Prince Dreamy now?"

"If you'll stop jawin'," Tuper said, "we'll tell ya."

"We basically got nothing," Ron said. "The man ate every meal at McDonald's and hung out at Smith's for fifteen or twenty minutes. He drove to Albertsons, stayed there for about an hour, but never got out of his car. When he drove back home, we waited for thirty minutes, then left. We'll see if he shows up tonight."

"Why didn't you just stay and follow him here if he came?"

"We thought about that, but decided we would be better positioned here," Ron explained. "And if he drove up the road to the colony, we wouldn't be able to follow him without being seen."

"I bet he doesn't show," Lana said. "He likes to act all knight-in-shining-armor with the ladies, but he might smell a setup. I practically threw myself at him. Although, the girls get quite giddy when they talk about him, and he does have quite an ego. Maybe he just thinks he's so charming no one can resist and it's a chance to score again."

"Let's go eat," Tuper said.

"I wish I could take some food with me," Lana said.

"The way you like to eat, you might not do so well in captivity."

"*That* is my biggest concern."

Tuper shook his head. "Yeah, that's the thing to be most concerned about."

"Okay, maybe not my biggest concern, but what if he doesn't feed me? All he ever eats is McDonald's. What if the food he gives me isn't vegetarian? I hadn't thought about that. I could get real hungry real quick. You two better not leave me there too long. I could starve. You better find those girls fast and get us all out of there. I'll never forgive either of you if I starve to death."

"You can still change your mind," Tuper said.

"Nope. Let's eat and get into position."

CHAPTER 50

Wednesday evening

Lana once again took her spot on a bench by the side of the dorm away from the dining hall and church where members were milling around. Dually was in the barn across the compound. Everything was in place. The tracker on her phone was connected to Ron's, and her phone was in her hidden pocket. Her backpack with her laptop and extra clothes were in the trunk of Ron's car.

Lana looked around, hoping to spot the kidnapper before he got too close. Time was ticking along. The sun was dropping quickly from the beautiful, blue sky. She watched as the last bit of yellow disappeared. She felt her phone vibrate in her new pocket. She decided to check it, just in case Ron was warning her. She stood, stepped behind a tree, and glanced at the message—a notice of an email that could only be from Ravic. She checked her email. *Oh no! She had to let Tuper know.* She started to text Ron, but before she could finish, she heard footsteps and looked up. David Johnston was approaching. She hit send with a partial message: *He's working with M...*

"What are you doing here?" Lana asked, feigning surprise.

"I'm here to take you on a magic carpet ride," Johnston said. "You're about to have the adventure of a lifetime. Are you ready?"

"I'm not sure." She didn't want to appear too eager, and she wanted to see how much he would push. "Maybe I shouldn't go."

"Come on. You will love every minute of it. You've been wanting to do this for a long time. Don't chicken out now."

"I'm just not sure."

"We have to go." His voice was stern. "I can't get caught here. We can talk about it on the way." His voice softened. "If you change your mind, I'll bring you back."

"Okay," Lana said, and they hurried away.

Ron and Tuper ran back to the barn where the car was parked. Tuper had his phone to his ear.

"You better get Dually," Tuper said. "We may be gone a spell."

"Are you sure?" Ron was already opening the barn door and letting him out. Tuper opened the back door for Dually, then climbed in the front. Ron jumped in and eased the car forward.

"Take yer time. We don't want him to see us. They have to walk a ways to get to his car. Tobias is still watching them and said Johnston parked by the first curve."

Ron checked his phone and made sure Lana's icon was showing on the tracking map.

"We see 'em, Tobias. Thanks." Tuper hung up. "I don't like this one bit," Tuper said. "Why don't we stop him and take her back?"

"We could call the cops and have him arrested."

Tuper glared at him. "If we call the cops, they may move in too soon, and Johnston will go silent, and we won't find the girls. Or the cops might spook him, and he'll dump Lana and get away. Then we'll never find her or Rita. He's our last hope."

"I know. Besides that, Lana wouldn't want them involved. She has a terrible fear of cops. What is that about?"

"I don't know. She's never said, and I don't pry."

Ron stood his phone up on the dash so both he and Tuper could see it. "Look," Ron said, pointing at the blinking icon on the screen. "That's Lana."

"How did you do that?"

"Lana set it up. There isn't anything techie that woman can't do."

"I feel a little better having that to follow."

"He just turned onto the 87 toward Great Falls. When it gets a little darker, we'll tail closer. It shouldn't be too difficult to keep up with that VW."

"Maybe he's taking her to his apartment."

They continued to follow onto I-15 south.

"Nope," Ron said. "He passed that off-ramp. He's not going home."

"Stay close."

After several more miles, Ron said, "Before she left, Lana sent me a text, trying to tell me who Johnston was working with, but she got cut off."

"What did she say exactly?"

"It's on my phone; read it."

"I don't know how to work that fan-dangled thing."

"Just touch the screen and then swipe up." He hesitated. "That's right, I'm sorry. I forgot."

"What did you forget?"

"Nothing."

"Humpf."

"Hey, Siri," Ron said. "Read my last text."

The system vocalized, *"Your last message is from Lana. Lana said, 'He's working with M.' Would you like to reply?"*

"No." Ron turned to Tuper. "Who do we know whose name starts with M?"

"There's Margarete, but that doesn't make any sense. And how would Lana know that information before Johnston arrived?"

"Maybe he wasn't alone, and she saw someone else."

"He was alone. Tobias said so. And if he wasn't, the other person never got out of the car, so Lana couldn't have seen him."

They drove past Great Falls and the airport, continuing south on I-15 in silence. Finally, Ron said, "She's running from something, isn't she?"

"That much is obvious," Tuper said. "She ain't never said who or what."

"Is Lana even her name? And what is her last name?"

"Don't know. Never asked. I figure it's none of my business."

"I bet if you asked, she'd say Smith or Jones or some other common name. Anything that would be hard to track."

Tuper stared at Ron. "Why are you so interested?"

"Just curious."

"Curious will scare her away, you know?"

"It's not like that," Ron explained. "She's a good person,

and I don't want to see anything happen to her. And if something did, we don't even know how to find her family."

"I'm pretty sure that's the way she'd want it."

"But someone would eventually be looking for her."

"Someone is already lookin' for her. I thought we established that."

"I mean family or loved ones."

"Ron, she don't want to be found, and she don't want the police involved, so that's the way we do this."

CHAPTER 51

Wednesday night, twenty minutes earlier

Johnston led Lana through the fields to his VW, glancing behind as they went. When she complained about him going too fast, he told her to keep moving. He was abrupt, but not mean.

"If we get caught now, I'll be in a lot of trouble. They'd think I was kidnapping you. All I'm trying to do is help."

"You're right." Lana didn't move any faster. She wanted to make sure Tuper and Ron had time to get into their car.

When they reached the van, he opened the side door. Lana stood back a little. She didn't want to get into the back and wasn't sure what he was up to.

"Can't I sit up front?"

"Of course. I'm just getting some sodas from the refrigerator. Pepsi, Sprite, or Orange Crush?"

"Orange, please."

Johnston opened the front door, and she climbed in, relieved. He pulled sodas out of the back and opened them before he walked around to the driver's side. He got in and handed both to her. "Can you hold my Pepsi for a second?"

She nodded.

He started the van and drove off, turning left onto State Highway 87, then eventually picked up I-15 south.

"Where are we going?" Nervous, Lana took a drink of soda.

"You'll see. You'll like it there, and you'll meet others like you."

"What do you mean?" She was surprised he'd mentioned it.

"Other Hutterite girls who wanted to go on their own."

"I thought it would just be us." She tried to sound disappointed. "You said you would show me the world."

"And I will. But you need a safe place to stay until I can make travel arrangements. It wouldn't be proper for you to stay with me; besides, I don't have room in my tiny apartment. You'll be happy at the retreat until we can start our adventure."

Lana watched the terrain around her. She knew exactly where she was now, but she didn't want to miss anything, in case something went wrong. They passed Great Falls International Airport and the off-ramp to Ulm. So far, they were headed in the direction of Helena.

"I've never been on this road before. I've been north from Gilford to a couple of colonies, but never this way. I wish it was daylight so I could see the *Sehenswüridgkeiten*." Lana wanted to seem as authentic as she could. The German she spoke was a little different than Hutterisch, but she counted on Johnston not knowing the difference.

"The what?"

"I'm sorry. I got so excited, I slipped into my native language. I was wishing I could see the sights."

"There's not much here, but you'll get a chance to see a lot of things."

Lana yawned, suddenly feeling sleepy. She needed to keep talking so she could stay awake. "Tell me about yourself. I don't know much about you."

"Not much to tell," Johnston said.

"There has to be. You live in this big world"—she had trouble forming the words—"where the adventures are endless." Her head felt heavy, and her eyelids kept trying to close. *Oh no!* She looked at her orange soda. She tried to keep talking, but the words wouldn't come, only blackness.

CHAPTER 52

Wednesday night

As they neared Helena, Ron and Tuper still had a tracker signal as well as a good visual on the VW van.

"I hope this is as far as he's going," Ron said.

"Yep. Guess we'll see."

Johnston turned off on Ferry Canyon Road and into the Costco parking lot. It was nearly closing time, but the lot was still half full. He found a double parking place in the back and drove through, so the van faced the exit. Ron had to stop several rows over to get a good visual without parking directly behind him.

"Do you think he's going shopping?" Ron asked.

"Don't know."

Johnston sat for several minutes without moving.

"What do you suppose he's doing?"

"Don't know."

A few minutes later, the door on the driver's side opened. Johnston got out and started in the direction of the store.

"I'm gonna check on Lana," Tuper said, stepping out of the car.

Ron kept an eye on Johnston. When he reached the stall with the carts, he stopped. A car blocked his visual for a moment, but Ron assumed Johnston was getting a cart for his shopping. Instead, he turned around and headed straight back. When Tuper reached the van's passenger side, he pounded on the window, but Lana didn't respond. Shortly after, Johnston reached the driver's door. Tuper kept walking.

Ron started his engine, and Tuper circled around. Johnston pulled out and disappeared behind an oversized truck. Ron quickly backed out and drove to the end of the lane. He turned and headed toward Tuper, who was moving faster than Ron thought he could. He stopped, and Tuper hopped in.

"Where did he go?" Tuper asked.

Ron scanned the area. "I can't see him."

"At least we have the tracker." Tuper pointed at the phone screen. "Get that contraption going."

"It is."

"He must have stopped. The dot's not moving."

Fear squeezed Ron's heart. "He found her phone!"

"Go out that driveway and turn right."

"Do you see him?"

"I saw a van go west on Ferry Canyon Road. I can't say for sure it was him, but that's all I got."

Ron slammed out of the parking lot and sped down the road, passing cars and searching for the van—but to no avail.

"I think we lost him," Ron said. "He must have turned off somewhere."

"Dang! I knew this was a bad idea. Lana's in big trouble."

Tuper's use of her name instead of 'Agony' made Ron

realize how worried Tuper must be. "Did you see her in the van?"

"I think he drugged her. She was asleep with her head against the window. I knocked on it, and she didn't budge."

"Should we retrieve her phone?"

"Might as well. When we do find her, she'll be glad to have it."

Ron made a U-turn at the next cross street and drove back to Costco.

"It's still here according to the tracker," Ron said.

As they pulled up to the shopping cart stall, a scruffy young man who looked homeless was yanking the carts apart. He frantically pulled five carts out, letting them roll back, trying to get to the one on the end.

"Johnston must have dropped her phone in a cart." Ron jumped out, leaving the car running.

"The dot's moving," Tuper called after him.

Ron intercepted the man as he hurried away from the cart rack and the store. "Excuse me," Ron said.

The scruffy man spun around and growled, "What do you want?"

"You have my phone."

"I don't know what you're talking about."

"My phone. You just took it out of the cart."

"Come and get it."

"Just hand it back to me. I'll give you a finder's fee."

"How much?"

"Fifty bucks."

"For a thousand-dollar phone? I don't think so." The guy stepped up and got right in Ron's face. "I found this phone, and you ain't man enough to take it from me. Get lost."

"Give the man his dang phone!" Tuper's voice boomed as he rapidly approached.

The guy whipped around, looked at Tuper, and chuckled. "What are you gonna do about it, old man?"

Tuper slammed him in the jaw with a right punch, then landed another to his stomach. The man stumbled backward but regained his footing. He swung wildly at Tuper, who dodged and took the glancing hit to his left bicep. Tuper came up swinging and landed another blow square in the man's face. He fell backward against a parked car, his nose gushing blood.

"Does that answer your question?" Tuper held out his hand, palm up. "Now, give me that dad-burned phone."

Several customers had stopped to watch. A young man in a cowboy hat asked, "Can I help?"

"Thanks. But he can handle himself," Ron said.

The scruffy man stared silently at Tuper—until Tuper grabbed a handful of T-shirt and jerked him to a stand. The guy raised his hands in surrender. "Okay, okay."

Tuper let go but kept his stance. The man reached in his pocket and handed over the phone.

"Didn't your mama ever tell you not to take things that don't belong to you?" Tuper shook his head in disgust. "Git outta here."

As he scurried off, the crowd clapped. Tuper lowered his head and walked to the car, with Ron close behind.

"Lana will be glad to get her phone." Ron realized how trite it sounded.

"But how the heck are we gonna find her now?"

CHAPTER 53

Wednesday night

Lana woke in a fuzzy state but managed to sit up, and realized she was on a sofa. She tried to focus her eyes, but her surroundings blurred in and out. She blinked and tried to clear her head. She looked at the window. It was dark outside, and lights were on in the room. *What happened? Where was she?* She tried to stand but couldn't manage. She focused on her last memory. She'd been in the van with Prince Dreamy. And he had drugged her. She blinked again and took a deep breath. She stood, holding onto the edge of the sofa.

"Whoa there, young lady." Johnston came into the room, carrying a mug and a bottle of water. "Sit down until you get rid of your sea legs."

"Where am I?" Lana asked through a mouthful of cotton. She stayed on her feet, determined to shake off the fog.

"You're in a safe place."

"What happened?" she slurred.

"I had to give you a little something to help you sleep."

"Why?"

"I couldn't let you see where we were going. You'll understand in good time." He handed her the mug. "Here, drink this tea. It'll make you feel better."

She shook her head.

"There's nothing in it. I promise."

She waved her hand dismissively. "No."

"How about the water?" He stretched out his arm with the bottle. "You can see that the seal hasn't been broken."

She took the bottle and stared at it. She wanted to drink it, but she didn't trust him.

"Don't worry. I have no need to drug you now. I don't like doing that, but I had to get you to a safe place."

She checked the cap, which appeared sealed. She was so thirsty. She opened the bottle, sniffed the water, and took a sip. Then she downed half the liquid, wanting the water so badly, she didn't care.

Johnston reached for her arm. "Let me help you get your balance. You'll be okay shortly."

Lana's instinct was to yank her arm away and kick him in the groin, but instead she let the Hutterite Lana take over. She didn't have the wherewithal to land a decent blow, and she had to find the girls. She'd come this far. She needed to see it through. She relaxed and let him take her arm. He walked her around the room and back to the sofa. She sat down, picked up the water bottle, and drank the rest. She held up the empty bottle for him to see.

"I'll get you another in a minute," Johnston said. "You don't want too much at once."

Lana's mind felt less befuddled. Her eyes were able to focus. She glanced around at her surroundings. From her spot on the sofa in the small living room, she could see the kitchen off to her left and what looked like a hallway on the right. She wondered how many bedrooms there were and if this was where the other girls were. She thought about the evening's events. "What day is it?"

"Wednesday night. You were only out a few hours."

Lana remembered her phone and slid her hand down her skirt over the extra pocket.

"It's gone," he said. "Where did you get that phone anyway? I know you don't have those at the colony."

"I stole it." Lana was surprised by how quickly a response came to her. "A woman set it down in the produce aisle while she was picking out apples. She walked away, and I grabbed it."

"I didn't know you had it in you."

"I thought I might need it. I tried to use it, but I think it was locked. Do you have it?"

"No. I got rid of it." He smiled. "You won't need it."

He seemed … nice. So far, he hadn't actually forced her to do anything. She wondered if he'd done the same with the other girls. The girls all seemed to find him charming. Lana wasn't impressed with him at all. But except for the drugs, he hadn't hurt her. At least, as far as she knew, he hadn't. She squirmed. She didn't feel violated, but she was concerned and wanted to check.

"I need to use the restroom."

She managed to stand on her own, but he took her arm and led her down the hallway to the first door. He opened the door and let her go inside by herself.

Lana checked herself for any signs of abuse and found none. She felt relieved and hoped the other girls were still okay. But they'd been captive much longer.

Lana was about to walk out when she heard a man say, "David?"

"In here," Johnston said.

She heard a door open and close.

"Where is she?"

"In the bathroom."

"Everything okay?"

"No problems."

Lana stepped back into the room and saw the man give Johnston a stack of cash. His back was turned so she couldn't see his face. He praised Johnston for his work, then turned to Lana. "Welcome."

Ravic was right. It was him.

The man turned back to Johnston. "Have her write the letter, show her to her room, and be on your way. Drop the letter in a mailbox as soon as you get back to Great Falls. No need for them to look for her when she left on her own." He turned and left the room.

Johnston pointed to a small desk with a stack of paper. "Sit down and write a letter to someone at your colony, letting them know you're safe and you left on your own. Here's an example." He showed her a sample letter that read:

Dear _____,

I'm finally on my adventure, my dream. It's not quite what I would expect, but exciting just the same. I know the Lord, my prince, meant for me to do this.

Please don't tell anyone about this letter. I'll write more later when I have time and tell you all about it.

May the Lord bless you.

Lana thought the handwriting looked familiar, like one of the letters from the Hutterite girls. She couldn't remember which one, but she was certain one of them had written it.

"This is basically what you need to write," Johnston said. "You can change it up a little, but don't try to say anything about me or where we are."

"I don't know where we are or who you really are."

"That's a good thing. Now, write it so I can go."

She sat down, and he watched over her shoulder as she wrote: *Dear Ron,*

"Who's Ron?"

"My betrothed."

"Your what?"

"My fiancé. We were to be married in the spring. I'm sorry I wasn't totally truthful with you, but that's why I was at the Little Boulder Colony. To spend time with Ron. But I just can't marry him," she explained. "At least not until I've seen some of the world. I have to send the letter to *him* or it will make the others suspicious."

"Okay. Just finish it up."

Lana wrote the letter, making only minor changes from the sample, and hoped they were enough to send Ron the message.

Johnston looked over her shoulder and read it. "Address the envelope."

"What about a return address?" she asked.

"Just put your name."

After she sealed the letter, he picked it up using a paper towel and stuck it in his pocket. Lana checked the clock on the wall. It was just after midnight. Johnston walked her down the hallway past the bathroom and unlocked the door to a master bedroom.

"The first bunk on the bottom is empty," he said in a soft voice. "That will be your bed. Try not to wake the others. You can talk to them in the morning."

"What if I need to use the restroom in the night? Will the door be locked?"

"There's a bathroom in your room."

She heard the door lock behind her and footsteps leading away. There was a little bit of light coming from the window, but not enough to really get around. She gave her eyes a few minutes to adjust, then found her way to her bed, crawled in, and fell asleep.

CHAPTER 54

Thursday early morning

Lana woke to daylight and five pairs of eyes looking at her. Three girls sat on the bottom bunk of a bed only four feet away, and one peered over from the mattress above. Another girl stood at the end of the bunks.

"Good morning," one said.

Lana sat up. "Good morning." She studied their faces, remembering the descriptions she'd been given. "Are you Rita?" she asked the girl who'd greeted her.

"Yes. How did you know?"

"Do you know a man named Tuper?"

"*Mein GroBonkel?*" she said.

Her great uncle? So, Tuper was Jacob's brother. Lana hoped she'd get a chance to confront him about it.

"Do you know Ron Brown? He was at your colony a few years ago with his sister Sabre and their friend JP."

"Oh yes. I remember him. He is a very handsome man."

"I guess he's okay. The important thing is they're looking for you." Lana glanced around. "For all of you."

"Why?" A girl with brown curly hair squinted at Lana. "I don't know them."

"You must be Gertrude from Green Valley."

"Yes." She still looked stymied. "Who are you?"

"My name is Lana, and I'll explain everything. But before I do, I need to ask a few things." She looked at the other girls. The blonde sitting next to Gertrude was nearly a head taller than her and had a big, beautiful smile. Lana nodded at her. "Are you Tiffany?"

"Yes."

They all started chatting, surprised that Lana knew who they were. The only one who didn't participate was the thin girl standing at the end of the bed.

Lana met her eyes. "I'm guessing you're Sarah from Wild Grass. Is that right?"

She nodded.

Lana looked up to the girl on the top bunk. "That must make you Inger." She smiled in acknowledgment.

The third girl sitting on the bunk in front of her appeared to be waiting for Lana to address her. She smiled coyly at Lana.

"Susanna?"

"Yes," she grinned, apparently pleased that Lana knew who she was.

"Now, I need to know if you're *Weglaufens*?"

"No!" they said almost in unison.

"We did not run away," Tiffany added.

"Does that mean you want to go home?"

Again, she got an overwhelming response with everyone talking at once.

Lana put her hands in the air. "Please. One at a time."

"We don't want to be here," Rita said. "Can you help us?"

"I hope so."

"We've tried to find a way out." Rita glanced around. "But the door is always locked, and when we're allowed out a few at a time, we're always escorted to do chores."

"Do you know who Prince Dreamy is?"

"Yes." They all nodded or responded.

"He's the one who took us from our colonies," Rita said.

"Did he force you, or did you go voluntarily? Don't misunderstand me. I'm not judging you. It's just that each of you has talked about having an adventure and seeing the *Welt Leut* world. That may be the reason you were targeted."

"None of us came voluntarily." Rita seemed to speak for the group, but she was also eager to tell her own story. "He almost convinced me, but then I realized it wasn't what I wanted, and I didn't trust him completely. I knew he might come for me, so I took the trash out by myself so I could tell him I wasn't going. That's when he covered my mouth and dragged me away." Her voice shook, and she stopped to compose herself. "He told me he would kill me if I fought him, then come back and kill my family and friends. When we got to the van, he tied me up and drugged me. The next thing I knew, I was here."

"You have no idea where we are?"

"No."

"Any of you?"

They shook their heads and said no.

"The rest of the girls have similar stories, except for Sarah who was caught completely unaware and dragged away," Rita said. "We've all shared our experiences with each other. We were all drugged, and as far as we know, we were brought here the night we were captured."

Everyone sat in silence for a few seconds. Lana finally said, "I read your letters. That was clever the way you told us about Prince Dreamy. That was your intention, right?"

"That worked?" Rita smiled, and the other girls joined her. "That was Tiffany's idea."

Lana turned to Tiffany. "That was clever, but how did you manage to all put a hint in the letters? He had me write mine already."

"All of us except Inger were together when we wrote the letters," Tiffany explained. "And I suggested we all put in a distinct hint about Prince Dreamy. I never really expected it to work."

"But it did. And it outsmarted David Johnston, which is his real name. He won't be thinking he's that smart when he goes to prison for kidnapping." Lana tried to keep up a positive front for the girls, but she had no idea how she would get them free. How would Ron and Tuper figure out where they were?

"But what about the sample letter? You wrote that, right?"

"Yes, Prince Dreamy may be good-looking, but he's not that bright. I wrote that out for him, so he would have it for other girls. He used it for Inger, but she copied it word for word because he had her write it before we could talk to her. Just like he did with you."

All of a sudden, Rita's eyes widened. "Oh no!" She looked from one girl to another. They seemed to know what she was thinking.

"What?" Lana asked. "You all look scared."

"Because your being here is not good."

"Why?"

"Because you make six. We heard that when they have six, they plan to take us on a mission to Mexico."

"What kind of a mission?"

"We don't know. Whenever we get a chance, we listen, but most of the time they speak Spanish."

"Do you have any idea when they would go?"

"The first Sunday night after they have six girls."

"That gives us four days and three nights to find a way out."

CHAPTER 55

Thursday morning

Ron tried everything he knew to unlock Lana's phone and laptop but got nowhere. He finally pushed them both aside when Clarice handed him a plate of eggs, bacon, and toast. Tuper took a seat after a trip to the bathroom, and she gave him a similar plate.

"You gettin' anywhere?" Tuper asked.

"No. It's locked up tight. Or as JP would say, 'Tighter than last year's swimsuit.' I wish he were here right now to help us. I'm not that great at this detective stuff."

"Yer better'n you think. Yer pretty good at figurin' out puzzles. You helped Lana with the clues in that letter."

"But what do we do now?"

"We eat our breakfast, then we go see David Johnston."

"If he tries to take another girl, we can follow him, even though that didn't work out last time." Ron couldn't shake off his worry and guilt about Lana.

"I was thinkin' about somethin' a little more along the lines of friendly persuasion."

"You're getting a little old for that, aren't you, Toop?" Clarice said.

"That's why I'm takin' this young whippersnapper with me."

"We don't even know if Johnston's back home," Ron countered. "For all we know, he might still be in Helena, or even Colorado if he kept driving."

"You got a better idea?"

"No. I guess it's worth a try."

"Besides, I need to get my car." After following Johnston to Helena, they'd both stayed at Clarice's. But Tuper's car was still at the Little Boulder Colony.

"Clarice," Ron said, "do you mind if I leave Dually here?"

"He can come," Tuper said. "He won't be no trouble. He can keep me company on the ride home."

Once they reached Great Falls, Tuper suggested they check Johnston's apartment first. The blue van wasn't there, so Tuper got out and knocked on the door. No one answered. Their next stop was Smith's, but they saw no sign of the VW in the parking lot. Tuper went inside and found Rhonda.

"You're becoming a regular," Rhonda said. "Still looking for the Hutterite girls?"

"Yep."

"Sorry to hear that."

"You may be able to help."

"Anything."

"There's a guy who comes in here and sits in the deli

section. He's tall and blond and wears red T-shirts that look like Smith's."

"I know that guy. I've never talked to him and I don't know his name, but I know who you're talking about."

"The Hutterite girls call him Prince Dreamy."

"He *is* good looking. I'll give him that."

"Have you seen him today?"

"No. But I'll keep an eye out for him."

"You got my number?"

"Everyone has your number, Toop."

He walked back to the car and climbed in.

"Where to?" Ron asked.

"The colony. I'll get my car."

They weren't even out of the parking lot when Tuper's phone rang. "Stop, until I see who this is. It could be Rhonda." He answered the call.

"This is the *Haushalter* from Pronghorn Colony. We received a letter from Inger."

"Hold on a second," Tuper said. He handed the phone to Ron, who put it on speaker.

"Can you take a photo of the letter and send it to me?" Ron asked.

"My son can do that."

"Thanks." Ron gave him his phone number. "I'll let you know when I get it."

Ron hung up, then re-parked the car while they waited. Three minutes passed, then four. Ron was about to call back, but Tuper wanted to give him a little more time. Another minute, and Ron's phone dinged. He read the letter out loud. Tuper thought it sounded like all the others.

Ron pulled up the other letters on his cell and tried to compare them, but it was difficult on the small screen. He had to keep going back and forth. He stared at his phone for a while, then looked at Tuper.

"It's very similar to the others, almost identical. I don't think there's anything new, but I'll study it more later."

They drove back to the colony, met with Jacob, and explained what had happened.

"That is a shame about Lana," Jacob said. "Now they have one more innocent girl."

"We may have to call the police in on this," Tuper said.

"You do what you want for Lana. She is your friend. That is your decision."

"We'll try a couple more things first. I'll keep you posted."

When Jacob left the room for a minute, Ron asked, "What things?"

"I don't know yet."

"I'm headed back to Johnston's apartment to wait for a while," Ron said. "There's no need for you to come with me. I'll call if he shows up."

"Don't talk to him 'til I get there."

"I won't. I wouldn't want you to miss the fun."

CHAPTER 56

Thursday morning

The girls took turns getting cleaned up. They offered to let Lana go first, but she declined, even though she wanted to wash away Johnston's stench.

"We decided to make a schedule based on the order in which we arrived," Tiffany explained. "It seemed like as good a way as any."

"No need to change the schedule. I'll go last."

"Come, I'll show you where things are while you wait. Not that there's much to see." Tiffany pointed to the little night-stand by her bed. "They gave us each a toothbrush and tooth-paste, and there are clean towels in the bathroom. That dresser has an empty drawer if you want to use it."

Lana had nothing to put in it. "I noticed none of you are wearing Hutterite clothing. Where did you get the dresses?"

"They gave them to us. I'm sure they'll have one for you as well."

Lana walked over to the window, opened the curtain, and

discovered a metal grid on the outside. She opened the window and pushed on the grid.

"We tried that," Tiffany said. "It won't budge."

"So, we're locked in this room."

Rita walked up. "It's your turn for the shower, Tiffany."

"I'm hungry," Lana said. "Will they feed us?"

Rita nodded. "The food isn't bad. There's a woman named Maria who cooks it."

"Have you met her?"

"Yes. But she speaks only Spanish, so we haven't talked."

Lana walked over to her bunk and sat down. She motioned for Rita to sit across from her. They chatted for a while, with Rita asking a lot of questions about her Opa and Oma and about Helen and the other girls at Little Boulder.

"Tell me about Finn," Lana said.

Rita tried to stop a smile but couldn't. "You've met Finn?"

"Yes. At first, we thought he was involved in your disappearance."

"He would never do that. He always encouraged me to wait and do everything right. He said he would be there for me if things worked out for us."

"He's very worried about you." Lana hesitated. "Have you ever seen him talking to Prince Dreamy?"

"Prince of Darkness, you mean. We don't call him Dreamy anymore."

"That is a better name." Lana reached out and touched Rita's hand. "I need you to be very honest with me."

"I have been."

"I know, but I need to ask you some personal questions."

"Okay."

"Has anyone tried to hurt you or any of the girls? Or touch you in inappropriate ways?"

"No. We all keep wondering what's going to happen. So far, they've been good enough to us, but I don't like the way Big Man stares. He gives me the creeps, and we're afraid of what they might do. Especially now that there are six of us."

"What's a typical day like?" Lana hoped to recognize an opportunity for escape.

"Maria brings us our breakfast around nine. She's always accompanied by a really big guy. He's the one we call Big Man. Then just before lunch, one or two of us are taken to the kitchen. One helps with cooking and the other does the dishes. The same for dinner."

"But you eat all your meals in here?"

"Yes."

"Do you get outside at all?"

"I went out once to empty the trash, but Big Man went with me. I didn't want to take it out, but Maria wasn't in the kitchen, and he insisted. I was afraid, but then Maria came out and said she needed my help."

"What did you see when you were outside? Could you see any other houses? What was the terrain like?"

"I didn't see any other buildings, but I didn't see much at all except a lot of trees. I was too scared to look around much. I'm sorry."

Lana wanted to console her. "You did fine. The important thing is that he didn't hurt you." Lana was disappointed that she didn't get more information, but was also relieved that Maria had come out. She changed the subject. "Who decides who the meal helpers are?"

"We do. Most of us like to go just to get out of the room. Sarah never has because she doesn't want to. The rest of us take turns."

"I need you to let me take kitchen duty. I may be able to

see something or hear something that the others may not pick up on. I need to get you all out of here."

Rita stared at Lana for a second. "You're not Hutterite, are you?"

"No. I'm working with Tuper and your grandfather to find you. Your grandmother gave me the clothes, and I set myself up as bait for the kidnapper. Helen and some girls from other colonies gave me enough information to know what to do. When I told Johnston I wanted out of the colony, he couldn't resist. He came and got me. I left willingly, but he drugged me anyway, so I don't know where we are." Lana looked Rita in the eyes. "But I promise you, I will find a way to get us out of here or to make contact with Tuper."

Someone knocked on the door, then a key turned in the lock, and the door opened. Lana got her first glimpse of Big Man. He stood six feet tall and was sheer muscle, with dark hair and a dark complexion. When he opened the door, Lana stepped forward. He silently handed her a plain dress, similar to what the other girls wore.

"Thank you," Lana said.

"Por nada." He looked all the girls over, then nodded at Rita and raised two fingers. Then he left, locking the door behind him.

"They need two girls today."

"What time?"

"It's usually right around twelve. Big Man comes when they're ready for us."

Finally, it came time for Lana's shower. She felt dirty and wanted out of the clothes she was wearing, although the prospect of the new dress wasn't thrilling. She avoided washing her hair for fear she would wash out the brown color, but she hated leaving it unwashed. She lingered in the shower—knowing she was last—and the hot water ran out just as she got soaped up. She quickly rinsed off and got out. She put on the plain, modest dress, longing for a pair of jeans.

When she came out of the bathroom, she found the girls praying in a huddle. She kept to herself until they finished. Rita had apparently told them she was a *Welt Leut* because they asked dozens of questions about her life. They all seemed happy to have her there. No more was said about who would help with lunch until Big Man knocked on the door.

"Lana, you and I are taking kitchen duty," Rita announced.

CHAPTER 57

Thursday noon

Maria needed someone to peel potatoes, and Lana appointed Rita for that, taking dishwashing duty for herself, although she would've loved to get her hands on a sharp potato peeler. She had already noticed that there were no knives or forks in the dirty dish pile. Lana kept an eye on Maria as she maneuvered about the kitchen. Big Man was watching Rita carefully.

When Maria said, *"Pobrecitas,"* Lana knew she had some concern for them. Maria gave instructions to Big Man in Spanish, and he responded. Lana hadn't used her Spanish in a while and was thrilled when it came right back to her. She'd never felt totally fluent, but the truth was, she was almost as good at languages as she was on the internet. She worked hard at it, always striving for perfection. She had mastered Spanish, was nearly fluent in German, and had a basic knowledge of French and Russian. Russian was the hardest for her; she could read and write it better than speak it. She had noticed that the Hutterisch language the girls spoke was

271

mostly German, mixed with some Russian. She had already picked up a lot in the short time she'd spent at the colonies.

Lana gave no sign that she understood the conversations between Maria and Big Man. Most of what they talked about was making lunch, but every once in a while, Maria would voice her concern for the girls. When Big Man said they were safe and there was nothing to worry about, Maria said that was true for now, but there would be more to come. That was all Lana heard about their situation, but she did learn where Maria kept the kitchen knives, and she scoped out the layout of the kitchen. There was a back door that Big Man used once. She peered out when he exited and saw a white van parked outside. Other than that, all she saw were trees.

Back in the room, Lana shared everything she knew and had seen.

"You speak Spanish?" Inger asked.

"Where I'm from, it's a good language to know," Lana said.

"You need to go to the kitchen every time," Inger said. "Maybe they'll say something that will help us."

The girls all agreed. That evening, Lana went with Tiffany to help with dinner. This time Lana assisted Maria. She washed lettuce and tomatoes for salad and dished up the plates. And she listened to the conversation between Maria and Big Man, who apparently felt free to speak in their native tongue.

"He said to get things ready to leave on Sunday afternoon," Maria said.

"Then that's what we'll do," Big Man answered.

"But there's a snowstorm coming. We may not be able to get out of here."

"We'll be fine."

"Those girls need coats, mittens, and hats," Maria said. After a moment she added, "And boots."

"That's not our problem. Besides, they'll be in the car, and they won't need them where we're going. They'll be all right."

"You don't know what he has planned for them. Think about it. Why does he need six virgins?"

"You worry about them too much."

"At least get them coats. We don't want them sick."

When Lana returned to their room, she shared the conversation with the other girls. She considered leaving out the comment about the "virgins" but decided to be as open as she could. She didn't want the girls to become complacent because nothing had happened yet.

"Why would Maria call us virgins?" Rita asked. "Does she know they have something else planned for us?" The girl swallowed hard. "Something sexual?"

"It's very likely," Lana said. "I don't want to scare you, but we need to do everything we can to get away before Sunday afternoon. We don't know what they might have in store for us."

CHAPTER 58

Friday morning

Ron was asleep in the barn when Tuper came in and woke him.

"What time is it?" Ron asked.

"Almost eleven."

"I didn't get in until after six. Johnston never showed." He rubbed his eyes. "I need more sleep."

"You got a letter from Lana."

Ron sat upright. "Let me see." He looked at the envelope. "I haven't seen her write much, but that looks like her handwriting." He tore it open and read it to Tuper without reading it himself first.

Dear Ron,

I'm finally on my adventure, my dream come true. It's not quite what I would expect, but exciting just the same. I know the Lord, the prince, meant for me to do this. I Owe no one, but Him.

Please don't tell anyone about this letter. I'll write more later when I have time and tell you all about it.

May the Lord, the King, bless you and the brother.
Your betrothed,
Lana

"I know she's trying to tell us something." Ron stood. "This was probably her only shot at communicating."

"What is she trying to say?"

"I don't know, but I'll figure it out. She sent it to me because she must've thought I'd be able to decipher her code." He looked at the envelope again. "It's postmarked Great Falls."

"Someone brought the letter back here to mail it," Tuper said. "Why would she sign it *Your betrothed?* Does that mean something to you?"

"Nothing."

"What else is different from the other letters?"

"She wrote *I Owe no one, but Him.* I'm sure that means something, but I have no idea. She also changed the last *prince* to *King*, with a capital K, then added *and the brother.* I don't know." Ron showed Tuper the letter. "The prince's father, maybe?"

"Maybe Johnston's dad is the ringleader."

"I'm pretty sure Lana said his father was serving a ten-year sentence."

"Maybe he's out or calling the shots from the joint."

"She also said 'and the brother,' but his brother is in Colorado, in the army. It doesn't seem likely that he's in on it."

"Do you remember their names?"

"The brother is Elliot, and the father is…" Ron paused to think. "Something that starts with an I. Igor, Ian. No, it's Ivan. Ivan Johnston."

"Good. Call me if you find the prince."

"Where are you going?"

"To see a guy."

Tuper drove to see his friend who worked for the sheriff's department. Pat greeted him at the door. "Come in."

"I don't have a lot of time, and I need a favor."

"You know I'll do it if I can," Pat said, "but come inside. It's a little chilly out there."

In the house, Pat sat down at the kitchen table, but Tuper remained standing. "I can't tell you everything that's going on."

"Of course, you can't. Let's hear what you got."

"I have my eye on a guy named David Johnston. I know for a fact he's involved in the kidnappings, but I don't know where he is."

"And you want me to find him?"

"That would be nice, but I think his father and brother might also be involved. The father was in prison, might still be, and the brother is in the army in Colorado. Can you check on them to see if they are where they're supposed to be?"

"Is that it?"

"If you find out they're connected in some way to the kidnappings, that would be a good thing to know."

"Are you sure you don't want to make this official?"

"Not yet. But you'll be the first one I call if I do."

Ron drove around Smith's parking lot several times but saw no sign of Johnston's van. He went inside and walked around the store, passing through the deli twice. Johnston wasn't there. Ron drove around the lot again before heading to the kidnapper's apartment. Johnston's van wasn't there either, and no one answered when he knocked on the door. Ron hadn't intended to confront him, but instead just act as if he was at the wrong apartment. Now all he could do was sit in his car and watch for Johnston's return.

Ron studied Lana's letter, frustrated that he was failing to save her. He was deep in thought when Tuper suddenly opened the passenger door. Dually jumped in the back, nudging Ron until he petted him.

Tuper hadn't been there twenty minutes when he got a call. After listening briefly, he said, "Thanks," and hung up. "That was Pat Cox. He checked on Johnston's family for me."

"And?"

"His brother is in Afghanistan, and his father is dying of cancer in prison."

"So, that wasn't the message Lana was sending us."

Ron analyzed her letter again, trying to find another meaning in the unusual words. All of a sudden, it hit him. "Look!" He showed Tuper the letter, pointing to the line with the code. "It's right there."

Tuper tipped his head and raised his eyebrows.

"Sorry, wrong brother." Ron started the car. "Are you riding with me or driving yourself?"

CHAPTER 59

Friday noon

Maria asked for only one lunch assistant, so Lana went alone. She did the dishes and helped load the meals onto plates, noticing the bulge of Maria's cell phone in her pocket. The cook only took it out once. She glanced at it, shook her head, and returned it to her pocket. Lana wondered if she was checking for a connection. Perhaps her service came and went. Or maybe she was expecting a call. *If only she could get her hands on that phone.*

Lana tried to be friendly to Maria, always smiling. When Maria asked her in Spanish to get a certain dish from the cupboard, Lana had to stop herself from reacting. She showed her hands, shrugged her shoulders, and hoped it was the universal gesture for not understanding. Maria apologized and got the bowl herself.

Lana was putting rolls in a basket when she heard Maria say to Big Man, "I'm worried about the girls. What he's doing is not right."

Big Man shook his head. "It's none of our business."

"Unless he's committing a crime. He says the girls are on a retreat, but what kind of retreat keeps you locked in your room? They are prisoners."

"We are paid to cook, clean, and watch them, not to ask questions." He turned to Lana and made a gesture for her to follow.

Lana carried the tray to the room, and Big Man unlocked the door. As she stepped past him to go inside, she smelled alcohol on his breath. When he left, Lana summarized the conversation she'd heard. "Maria is concerned about us. You girls know her better than I do. Do you think she would help us if we asked her?"

"What could she do?" Tiffany asked.

"She could unlock our door and let us out," Inger said.

"She has never come to our room alone," Tiffany said. "She may not even have a key."

Rita joined in. "We'll never get through to Big Man, and I can't be certain Maria would do anything without him."

"Have you ever seen either of them use a cell phone? Do they ever set it down?" Lana asked. "If we could get our hands on a phone, we could get help."

"Yes," Rita said. "I saw Maria try to make a call one day, but she couldn't. She seemed upset. I don't know what she said, but I'm pretty sure it had something to do with the service not working here."

"So, even if we get access to a phone, we have to get away from here to get a connection." Lana was mostly thinking out loud. "Unless there's a signal in parts of the house and not others, or perhaps it's intermittent. Maybe if we hold it out the window, we can get one. I think if anyone gets a chance to grab her phone, we need to do it."

"You mean steal it?" Sarah asked.

Lana was surprised to hear her speak. She said little, but she was the most anxious to get home. "Borrow it," Lana corrected. "We'll give it back. It may take us a while, but we wouldn't be taking it to keep, only to use. I realize that's a thin line, but what they're doing isn't right either, and we have a right to protect ourselves." She looked around at the faces of the girls. "Do you think you can do it?"

They all nodded. "I know I can," Rita said. "I took a Holly-wood magazine from the doctor's office. I know I shouldn't have, but I did. Then I had to hide it from everyone but Helen. I always wanted to go to Hollywood." She paused. "But not as much now as I used to."

The other girls all mentioned things they had taken, mostly a piece of candy or other innocuous items.

"Okay. It's settled then," Lana said. "If anyone gets the opportunity, grab the phone and bring it to me as quickly as possible. Agreed?"

Nods and affirmations from the girls reassured Lana that they wouldn't miss the opportunity. But since Maria had yet to be seen setting her phone down anywhere, Lana had to come up with a backup plan. She had ruled out any possibility of getting past Big Man when he came to the door. That left either convincing Maria to help them or trying to escape during kitchen duty, then coming back with reinforcements. She discussed the alternate plans with the girls.

"Asking Maria to help is risky. If she turns us down, they'll be watching us even closer," Lana said. "And it means revealing that I speak Spanish, so they'll never talk in front of me again."

They discussed whether Maria could be counted on. Most of the girls thought she couldn't. Lana disagreed. She had heard the concern in Maria's voice, but maybe it was just wishful thinking.

The more Lana thought about it, the more she realized how hopeless their situation was. She had no idea where they were, except that they were surrounded by trees and somewhere cold. She assumed they were in the mountains, but that could be anywhere. From her experience and reports from the other girls, she estimated they were somewhere between two and five hours from Great Falls. They could be miles from another living soul. She didn't want the girls to give up, but she felt like she had to let them know the reality of the situation.

"Even if we get the phone, it could be locked and take me a while to break into. We can call nine-one-one, but only if we get a connection. Maria might be our only hope."

"We have to make our move tomorrow or early Sunday morning, or it may be too late," Sarah said. Everyone listened when Sarah spoke—because she did it so seldom.

CHAPTER 60

Friday late afternoon

Ron and Tuper drove their separate cars back to Clarice's house in Helena. Ron made a pot of coffee, and Clarice packed a cooler with sandwiches and fruit.

"Are you sure we're on the right track?" Tuper asked.

"Lana was telling us who it is, and I think she was obvious. She wrote his name right in the letter. Look, it says *Owen*." Ron glanced at Tuper's puzzled face. "Sorry, it's right here." He pointed to the line in the letter. "See how she didn't leave enough space between the word *Owe* and *no*, making it spell O-W-E-N. She even capitalized *Owe*."

"That was smart," Clarice said.

"And then she wrote *May the Lord, the King, bless you and the brother*," Ron said. "At first, I thought of King Midas, but then I realized it was Kingston, and *the brother* meant Owen. She knew exactly what she was doing and hoped I would figure it out."

"But what motive would they have?" Tuper asked.

"My guess is money. That's usually the motive, but who knows? Regardless, Lana must have found out before Johnston picked her up. When she sent the text, *He's working with M...*, she was probably writing *minister*, but got interrupted."

Tuper nodded. "That would also explain why Kingston was at Smith's the weekend Rita disappeared. He was probably helpin' deliver the girls to Owen."

"Or was backup muscle in case Johnston needed help. And it explains why Owen bailed Kingston out. He either needs his assistance or wants to keep him from talking."

"I just hope Owen leads us to Lana."

Clarice handed Tuper the cooler, and Ron picked up the thermoses he'd filled with coffee and hot tea. "Good luck," she said as they went out the door.

Ron and Tuper sat outside Altered Life Assembly Church waiting for Owen. It was nearly six o'clock when he finally got in his green Infiniti and left. Ron followed. They drove south into the mountains toward Park City. The first snow of the season was falling lightly, and the sky was dark with clouds. The higher they climbed into the mountains, the fewer cars they encountered, making it difficult to keep close and not be detected. When the Infiniti turned onto a side road, Ron slowed way down, hoping Owen wouldn't check his rearview mirror and see them make the turn. They followed him for another mile and a half before he turned onto a dirt road that curved out of sight.

"Stop here," Tuper said. "I'll walk up and take a look. If we get any closer, he may see or hear the car."

Ron stopped, let him out, then eased the car to the side of

the road. He kept the engine running as he waited. Binoculars in hand, Tuper walked ahead. About five minutes later, he returned.

"There's a small clearing just around that curve," he said, climbing inside. "It's getting cold out." Tuper shivered. "Pull up as far as the curve. Owen parked in front of a cabin not far beyond that. I expect it's where the girls are."

"What's your plan?"

"To get 'em out."

"I figured that, but how? Are we going to just barge in? And what if Lana or the others aren't there?"

"Then we beat it out of him."

"I guess that's a plan. Let's go."

They headed for the cabin, staying in the trees lining the road. They hid in a cluster of Douglas firs about twenty yards from the cabin's front door and tried to decide the best course of action.

"There's another vehicle, a white van," Ron said. "And we have no idea how many people are in there guarding the girls —if they're even here."

"I guess we'll find out pretty quick."

CHAPTER 61

Friday night

For the first time, Maria came to the door instead of Big Man. Lana's first reaction was to overpower her, but for all she knew, Big Man was waiting in the hall. Lana and Rita stepped out of the room and took the few short steps to the living room. A moment later, Big Man came in the front door and shouted at Maria for bringing them out without him. His words were slurred. Lana wondered if he had been drinking more since lunch.

"I need to get dinner started, and you were late getting back," Maria said in Spanish.

"Don't do it again!"

When they entered the kitchen, the smell of baked cookies made her stomach growl. Maria started the evening meal, while Rita helped with the prep. Lana washed the dishes that were left from lunch and from Maria's afternoon baking.

When the lock turned in the front door, Big Man dashed to the arched opening to see who it was. Owen walked in and came directly to the kitchen. Lana glanced up, but quickly turned back to the dishes. Rita was next to her, washing vegetables. Owen didn't acknowledge the girls but greeted Maria and Big Man in Spanish. His accent and sentence construction were both good. Lana suddenly wished she'd done more research on him. The more she knew, the easier it would be to anticipate his moves. But she'd never had a reason to suspect him.

"It's starting to snow, and a big storm is about to hit," Owen said in Spanish. "We can't wait until Sunday, or we'll be stuck. We have to move the girls out."

"When, señor?" Maria asked.

"Now. Forget dinner and make sandwiches for the road."

"But we're not ready," Maria pleaded. "We need more clothes and supplies."

"They can be bought later," Owen's tone was firm.

When Maria started to protest again, Big Man cut in. "No problem. We will get ready and leave as soon as you want us to."

"You'll have good cell reception when you get part way down the mountain. Call me as soon as you do." With that, he left the room.

Maria said something to Big Man, but Lana couldn't hear it. She leaned over to Rita and whispered, "They're taking us now. Follow my lead."

Maria grabbed a loaf of bread and a jar of peanut butter and set them on the table. Then she took a jar of jam out of the refrigerator, gave it to Rita, and motioned for her to start making sandwiches. Maria handed a box of plastic baggies to Lana, then started packing other food into a cooler Big Man had brought to her. Maria started shoving cookies into a bag, her motions a clear indication that she was not happy about the changes. Then she muttered, "I don't like what he has planned for these girls."

"You don't have to like it," Big Man said.

Owen walked into the kitchen. "It's time to leave. The storm is getting closer. Maria, have the girls get their stuff together."

"Now?"

"Right now."

Lana heard the front door burst open. She couldn't see who it was, but she decided it was a good time to make their break.

"Run, Rita!"

They darted toward the back door in the kitchen. Big Man reached out and grabbed Rita by the arm. Lana kept moving. She flung the door open and raced out. Her feet hit the icy concrete, and she fell face down. A moment later, Big Man's hands were on her. He grabbed her shoulders and jerked her up like a ragdoll. He reeked of alcohol.

Rita jumped on his back and pounded him with her fists. It didn't seem to faze him. He trudged toward the white van, dragging Lana and ignoring Rita. Several steps later, Big Man yanked the sliding door open and threw Lana inside. She hit her head against the wall as she fought back and was momentarily stunned. Big Man grabbed Rita and tossed her in beside Lana. They tried to keep the door from closing but didn't have the strength. Their captor jumped in the driver's seat and drove off.

Inside, Tuper confronted Owen. "Where are the girls?" he demanded.

"What girls?"

Tuper punched him in the face. Ron decided Tuper had Owen under control and ran to the kitchen. A woman in an apron stood frozen, staring at him. Through the open back door, Ron saw the van drive away toward the main road.

"Where are the girls?" Ron asked. "Lana, Rita, Tiffany?"

The woman pointed to the open back door and then to an interior door in the hall, but she couldn't seem to get any words out.

"Where's Lana?" Ron asked again.

She pointed outside and said in Spanish, "José has her."

Ron bolted out the door and sprinted back to his car, which was parked around the curve. He scrambled to get behind the wheel and sped down the hill, the only direction the van could go. When he reached the main road, he still hadn't seen any taillights. He turned toward Helena and headed down the mountain. He drove about two miles, but never saw the van. Anguished, he turned around and went back to the cabin.

Tuper was still in the living room, attempting to get information out of Owen—Tuper fashion. The cook sat on the kitchen floor, sobbing.

"I need your help," Ron pleaded.

She didn't seem to understand what he was saying. Her dark hair and eyes made him try his broken Spanish. *"¿Qué es tu nombre?"*

"Maria."

"Maria, necesito ayuda." He hoped that was the right word for help. *"Por favor."* He added please in a tone that showed his desperation.

She nodded and tried to compose herself.

"Where are the other girls?" Ron asked in broken Spanish.

Maria took a deep breath and stood. She removed a key from her pocket and quickly led Ron to a door down the hall. When she opened it, Ron looked in and saw four young girls, staring wide-eyed.

"Where's Lana?"

"She was helping in the kitchen," a tall girl said. "Who are you?"

"I'm a friend of Lana's. And a friend of Jacob's, from Little Boulder Colony. Is one of you Rita?"

"No, she's with Lana."

Maria started to explain, but she was talking too fast for Ron to understand. He made a motion for her to slow down and said, *"Más despacio, por favor."*

Maria spoke a little slower, and Ron picked up enough to confirm his suspicion that José had gotten away with Lana and Rita.

The girls followed Ron to the living room. Tuper had Owen against the wall with his hand on his throat. He let up when he saw the young women.

"Lana and Rita are gone. Their guard got away with them."

With Tuper's attention diverted, Owen ducked down and tried to escape. Tuper grabbed him by his shirt and threw him down onto the sofa. When Owen pushed himself back up, Tuper punched him in the face and shouted, "Where did they go?"

"I don't know."

Tuper hit him again. "I guess you didn't hear me."

"If you want me to tell you where they are, you'd better stop beating on me," Owen said with a mouthful of blood.

"If you want to live, you'd better start talkin'."

Maria said something in Spanish that Ron didn't catch, and Owen yelled at her in Spanish. She yelled back and walked over to Ron. Maria pointed at her chest, then put her hand up to her ear as if she were making a call. Her Spanish was too fast for Ron to understand.

"Shut up!" Owen yelled at her.

"Give me your keys," Tuper said. When Owen didn't move, Tuper hit him in the stomach. "You sure are hard of hearin'."

Owen reached in his pocket and handed his keys to Tuper, who tossed them to Ron. "Take Maria in the Infiniti. That way, the guard won't be suspicious when he sees the car. I'll take the girls in your car and follow."

Ron turned to Tiffany. "Gather up your stuff. Lana and Rita's as well."

"Un momento," Maria said. She went to the kitchen and retrieved bags for them to put their belongings in. When the girls hurried off, Maria took Ron to the kitchen to get the cooler and the bag of sandwiches. He loaded them in Owen's car and went back inside. The girls were wearing oversized jackets and ready to go. Maria carried two more coats but wasn't wearing one herself.

Ron handed his keys to Tuper. "Drive carefully. I don't want to have to make any repairs before I head home."

"Humpf."

"Are you ready?" Ron asked.

"Get everyone loaded. I'll be right out. I have to finish what I started here."

"Don't do anything stupid, Toop."

Ron walked out, and the five women followed. He instructed Inger and Susanna to get in the car Tuper was going to drive. The others squeezed into the Infiniti, moving quickly, anxious to get out of there.

"Are you taking us home?" Tiffany asked.

"Soon. But right now, we have to find Rita and Lana. We'll

call and let your folks know you're okay as soon as we get cell service."

Ron looked up and saw Tuper leaving the cabin. He stuck his head out the window. "I'll call you as soon as I know where we're going."

CHAPTER 62

Friday night

By the time Ron reached the main road, he had cell service. In awkward Spanish, he asked Maria to put her phone on speaker. When she looked puzzled, he reached his hand out for her phone. She gave it to him, and he pressed the icon.

She smiled. "*Sí, sí.*"

Maria punched in a number and José answered. Ron listened intently, understanding about half of it. He called Tuper to let him know they were headed back to Altered Life Assembly Church.

Tuper called Clarice. "We have four of the girls, but—"

"Is Lana one of them?" Clarice interrupted.

"No. But we know where she is. Can you meet me at Altered Life Assembly Church and take the girls home with you? Things may get messy here." He hoped to deliver *all* the girls to their colonies up north in the morning.

"Of course. I'll be right there."

"Don't rush. We'll be on the road a while. Be careful if you get there before we do. The man who has Lana and Rita is driving a white van. Don't go near it."

Tuper hung up and called Pat Cox. "There's some garbage that needs to be cleaned out of a cabin near Park City." He explained the best he could where the cabin was.

"What did you do, Toop?"

"Nothin'. I got a little lost, stumbled onto the cabin, and someone was beating up on the guy. I tried to catch him, but he got away."

"Sure. We'll go with that. I'll take care of it."

When Tuper pulled into the strip mall parking lot, Clarice and Ron were already there. The white van was not. Tuper parked near them, glad they were at the end where José wouldn't see them. It was late and dark, and no other cars were in the lot. Tuper quickly introduced the girls to Clarice, and they all piled into her car.

"Help them call their colonies," Tuper said. "If they don't know the phone numbers, get them from Jacob. I know it's late, but they'll be glad to hear the girls are okay. We'll get them home tomorrow."

Maria handed the food to Tiffany who was in Clarice's car. Maria kept saying, "I'm sorry. I'm so sorry."

The girls thanked Tuper repeatedly, then Clarice drove away.

Tuper moved Owen's car to the same area they'd seen it

before, then hustled back to Ron's car and got in to wait for the van.

"He should've been here before us," Ron said. "I don't think he's coming."

"I don't either," Tuper said. He glanced at the backseat. "Maria better call again."

～

Speaking Spanish and using hand signals, Ron told Maria to call José again and find out where he was.

This time Maria put the speaker on herself. When José answered, he sounded groggy.

"Where are you?" Maria asked in Spanish.

"I made a stop. Don't worry."

"Owen wants you here now. We have the other girls, and we need to get on the road."

"Let me talk to Owen."

Maria looked at Ron and shrugged.

"I'm driving," Ron said in Spanish, hoping his voice and accent would suffice.

"He's driving," Maria repeated. "Just tell us where you are, and we will meet you."

In the background, Lana yelled what sounded like, "Bear Gulch, Bear Gulch, Bear Gulch!"

"Shut up. I can't hear!" José yelled at her, then lowered his voice again. "Tell Owen I'm too tired to drive. I'll be there first thing in the morning."

"José," Maria said, but the phone went dead.

"That was Lana," Ron said to Tuper. "Do you know where Bear Gulch is?"

"Go back up the mountain. There's a road just a few miles up. She must have seen the sign."

Ron sped out of the parking lot. "I don't think José understood what Lana was saying, and he didn't seem to know I wasn't Owen."

"But Lana did."

"I didn't hear any road noise, so hopefully he's stopped."

"But why would he be stopped?"

"That part worries me too."

CHAPTER 63

Friday night

"It feels like we're in a cage with that metal screen between us and the front," Rita said.

"That's exactly what this is. We're in a cage, like animals."

Lana had to make a plan. She had tried several times to get out, but they were locked up tight. There was no handle on the inside of the sliding door, so they had to wait for Big Man to open it. If he did, she had to be ready. For now, all she could do was wait and hope that his erratic driving didn't cause a crash and kill them all.

Their abductor had tried several different roads before settling on this one. José was obviously not familiar with the area and didn't seem to understand that she'd given the name of the road to Ron. She'd been lucky enough to see a white post with the name when he'd made the turn. She could only hope it was enough to lead them in the right direction. Tuper knew every inch of every road around here, and it was all she had. They had passed Ron's car when they started down the hill. She didn't realize until then that Ron and Tuper had arrived at the cabin door or she would've run toward them instead of out the side door.

She was concerned—more for Rita than herself—that José had stopped. He seemed enamored with Rita's beauty and kept saying over and over how pretty she was. Lana didn't translate that for Rita, because she didn't want to upset the girl and didn't know how much English José understood. She wasn't ready to give up her secret weapon yet.

What was José up to? He'd been sleeping when Maria called and woke him, but Lana knew they were only a few miles from town. She'd prefer that he not sleep off his drunken state if he was going to attack them. They had a much better chance if he was impaired.

When he started snoring, Rita asked what the conversation with Maria was about. Lana told her in a whisper.

"Why is he just sitting here?" Rita asked.

"I don't know," Lana said, "but as long as he's asleep, we're safe."

"I don't like the way he looks at us. He's creepy."

"Rita, if he tries to hurt either one of us, we need to fight him with everything we have. Can you do that?"

"I don't know. We are taught not to fight."

"That's our only chance of survival. If you can't do it for yourself, then please do it for me."

"I will." Rita nodded, but her voice shook.

José shifted in his seat. Lana put her finger to her lips, making a shushing gesture. Rita got very still. When Big Man opened his door, Lana knew it was time. She positioned Rita away from the side door and sat down in front of her, facing the door.

"Brace me," Lana said.

Rita put both feet on Lana's back. When José opened the door and leaned inside, Lana kicked him in the face as hard as she could. It was like trying to move a mountain. He staggered back but was soon lunging at her. Lana tried kicking again, but he grabbed her feet and dragged her out of the vehicle. Her head hit the ground as she bounced across the rugged terrain.

"Run, Rita!"

The girl jumped out of the van, but instead of running she tried to reach for Lana.

"Run!" Lana yelled again.

José let go of Lana and stepped toward Rita. Lana grabbed his leg and held on. José dragged her along as he tried to get to Rita.

Rita grabbed a rock and hustled around behind him. She jumped on his back and pounded his head with the rock. He flinched but kept his balance. Rita kept swinging. Big Man reached up and grabbed Rita's arm, then slammed her to the ground.

On her knees now, Lana pushed hard against his leg, trying to knock him over. He stumbled but steadied himself within seconds. Lana glanced at Rita. She wasn't moving. Before she could get to Rita, Big Man locked his arm around Lana's neck and yanked her up. He tried kicking Rita, but Lana was flailing so much his kick didn't have any power behind it.

Just then, headlights lit up the area, and Lana heard a car engine. José dropped her and ran for the driver's side of the van. Lana got to her feet in time to see Tuper jump out of Ron's car, gun in hand. He pointed the weapon directly at José, who stopped when he saw it.

"I wouldn't git in that van if I were you," Tuper said. "It could be unhealthy."

Ron and Maria rushed over to check on her and Rita. "I'm fine," Lana said. "But Rita landed hard." Lana knelt and touched her face. "Talk to me, Rita."

Rita didn't respond. Enraged, Lana grabbed the rock from Rita's hand and rushed at Big Man. Before anyone could stop her, she leaped and smacked José on the back of his head. He staggered, then swung around, but Tuper grabbed his shoulder. When José spun back, Tuper punched him, again and again. Big Man finally collapsed to the ground, unconscious.

"Dang!" Tuper said, "I'm getting too old for this."

Lana rushed back to Rita, who had opened her eyes. "She's okay!" Lana cried out with joy.

Rita sat up and looked around. "Tuper? *Mein GroBonkel.*"

Ron and Lana helped Rita to her feet.

"I'm here, *Kleiner.* Everything is all right now." Tuper turned to Lana, his voice changing from sweet to angry. "Did he touch her?"

"No," Lana said. "He didn't get the chance."

"And you?"

"No, Pops. We're okay."

"I guess I don't have to shoot him then." Tuper gave him a kick to the ribs instead.

Lana went to the van, opened the driver's door, and took the keys. "Do you need these?" she asked Tuper.

"No, but I know who might." He turned to Ron. "Want to give me a hand?"

"Sure," Ron said.

Tuper grabbed José by one arm, and Ron grabbed the other. They tossed him in the van and locked it.

"Let's see how he likes his own cage," Tuper said, slapping his hands together as if he was finished with a dirty job.

"Can I have those keys now?" Lana asked.

Tuper handed them to her, and she threw them as far as she could into the brush.

They all got into Ron's car. Rita cried with relief for a minute, then leaned her head on Lana's shoulder.

They started back toward Helena.

"I'm hungry," Lana said. "Do you have anything to eat?"

Once they were on the road, Tuper called Pat Cox. "There's some garbage that needs to be picked up on Bear Gulch Road."

"What did you do now?"

"Nothin'. I got a little lost and stumbled onto some guy lying alongside the road. He looks like he's in pretty bad shape."

"Didn't we just have this conversation?"

"Different garbage."

"Tuper, you can't go wreaking havoc across the mountain."

"I'm done now, but you still have a little work to do. There's a guy named Kingston Wylde who is in custody right now for two DUIs within a week who is heavily involved. And that guy you checked on for me, David Johnston, is smack in the middle of it. You'll never get the Hutterite girls to testify, and I hope you can keep them out of it entirely. But Johnston and Wylde are both pretty weak links. I'm betting they'll squeal like stuck pigs and you can get a plea out of them all."

"Thanks. I'll take care of it."

CHAPTER 64

Friday nearly midnight

They were nearing Helena when Maria asked, "What will you do with me?" She spoke slowly for Ron to understand.

"Do you want to field this one, Lana?" Ron asked.

"Where would you like to go?" Lana looked at Tuper, who nodded. Lana patted Maria's shoulder and spoke in Spanish. "We'll take you there. I know you didn't want us hurt, and for whatever reason, got caught up in this mess."

"You speak very good Spanish. You knew what we were saying all along?"

"Yes."

"Why didn't you talk to me? Maybe I could have helped."

"I wanted to, but I wasn't sure I could trust you."

"I know I don't deserve your compassion, but I don't want to go to jail. My mother is very sick. Owen promised to take me to Mexico so I could see her. I know what I did was wrong, but I never knew what he had planned. He told me it was a retreat for girls who had lost their way and needed to find God again. I had heard of that before, and at first, I thought he was doing something good. But then I heard him tell José that they were virgins and would bring top dollar."

Lana translated for the others, then said to Maria, "We'll drop you wherever you want."

"There's a McDonald's at the edge of Helena. You can leave me there. I'll call my friend and have her pick me up."

Tuper called Jacob to let him know Rita was safe. "We have all the girls, unharmed. Mostly unharmed. Rita has a few bruises, but she's a real trooper. I'll bring them all back to their colonies tomorrow."

Within minutes, they had dropped off Maria, and they soon parked near the church to pick up Tuper's car.

"Are you staying at Clarice's?" Ron asked.

"She has a full house. I'll see you in the morning."

"Before or after breakfast, Pops?" Lana asked.

"After."

"Tell Louise hello for me."

"Humpf," Tuper said and walked away.

CHAPTER 65

Saturday morning

Clarice made breakfast with the help of the girls. They were all up early and anxious to get home. Ron and Lana sat at the table, drinking coffee. When they all finished eating, Tiffany chased Clarice out of the kitchen.

"We can do the cleanup," Tiffany said. "You've done enough."

Tuper walked in moments later.

"Want some breakfast?" Clarice asked.

"He doesn't," Lana said. "Louise fed him." She smiled. "Didn't she, Pops?"

"None of yer business." He poured himself a cup of tea. "Where's Rita?"

"She went for a little walk." Clarice looked out the window. "Oh, there she is. She's back and sitting on the porch."

Tuper went outside to join her. "You doin' okay, kid?"

"I feel bad about what happened last night. Attacking that man was a betrayal of our faith. *Opa* will be so disappointed in me. How do I ever regain my position in the family and the church?"

"You listen to me, *Kleiner*," Tuper said, using the German word for *little one*. "Your grandfather loves you very much. Even though he is a dedicated Hutterite, he is also a wise man, and he knows the way of the world. All he will expect of you is that you come home and be happy."

"You don't think he'll reject me?"

"Of course not. I've known Jacob all my life. Look how differently we live. He doesn't reject me, does he?"

"No."

"He has no reason to reject you."

"What if he asks me what happened?"

"He won't. He'll tell you to start your life anew and that this happened in the past and should stay there. Can you live with that?"

"I think so." She hugged him. "Thank you, *Mein GroBonkel*."

"You ready to go home?"

"I'm ready."

"Good. Let's get the other girls and head out."

Inside, Ron offered to drive the girls to Great Falls.

"I'd rather do it myself," Tuper said. "I'll feel better seein' them all home, especially Rita."

"Fair enough."

"That storm passed us. I know it's a little chilly, but when I get back, maybe we can take that horseback ride you came here for."

"That's a great idea."

～

Lana sat across from Ron at the table, thinking it was their last meal together. Clarice had invited Tuper as well, and they were all having a drink and talking.

"Thanks for the ride this afternoon, Toop," Ron said. "That was worth the trip."

"Anytime." Tuper grinned.

"I'm leaving in the morning," Ron added. "I'm headed to Glacier Park to spread Aunt Goldie's ashes, then I'll drive home from there. I know you aren't much for goodbyes, so I won't stop by and make a big deal of it. But I sure enjoyed seeing you again. It's always an adventure."

"I appreciate all your help. I couldn't have done this one without you."

"My pleasure," Ron said. "I still owe you big time."

Clarice stood. "I'm going to bed. I have to open the bar in the morning." Ron stood too and gave her a hug. Clarice's eyes watered. "You be safe and come back anytime."

After Clarice left, Ron shook Tuper's hand. "Guess I'll be going."

"Wait," Lana said. "We have something for you." She'd been lost in her mixed emotions all evening.

"We do?" Tuper asked.

"Yes, *we* do. It's from all of us." She walked over to the sofa, reached behind it, and came back with a dark brown cowboy hat. She handed it to Ron. "I know it's a little late, but you'll fit in better during the rest of your trip."

Ron put it on and strutted to the mirror in the front room. "Yeah. I like it. And JP will be jealous." He couldn't stop smiling. "Thank you, Lana. You too, Toop."

Tuper rolled his eyes.

Ron touched her shoulder. "Lana, will you walk me out?"

Once outside, Ron stopped on the porch, Dually by his side. "It's been fun hanging with you. I mean, in spite of all the chaos, I enjoyed your company."

"Thank you," Lana said. She was glad it was dark enough that Ron couldn't see her blush. "You're a bit of a pain, but you're better company than Pops."

"That's not a very high bar, but I'll take it," Ron said. "Hey, if you're ever in Southern California, I'd be glad to show you around." He paused, then added, "But that's where you're from, isn't it?"

"It doesn't matter where I'm from. Here's where I am for the moment, and it's not so bad."

"If I can ever help you find what you're looking for—or who you're hiding from—let me know. I know Sabre and JP would also be glad to help."

She looked up at him. Ron gently touched her cheek, looked her lovingly in the eyes, then bent down and kissed her lightly on the lips. She kissed him back, then pulled away.

"I'd better get going," Ron said. He knelt and hugged Dually, then stood back up.

Lana tipped her head at Ron. "That's your plan, isn't it? To leave Dually with Tuper. You came here just to bring Tuper a dog to replace Ringo. Not a bad idea. He sure loves Dually. In time, it'll make not having Ringo a little easier."

Ron smiled but was quiet for a moment.

"I'm right, aren't I?"

"I didn't come here just for that, but I was hoping they would be a good match. I'd love to keep Dually, but Tuper needs him more than I do. And right now, I'm living with my mother, whose allergies can't handle him. I'll be getting my own place soon, but it'll likely be an apartment. And I wouldn't want to keep him cooped up there. Do you think it'll work?"

"I think it would break his heart if you tried to take him back with you."

"Tuper's or Dually's?"

"Both. That dog has really gotten attached to him."

"I've noticed that."

"You're a good man, Ron Brown."

Ron told Dually to stay and walked toward his car. Tuper came out just as Ron climbed in.

"He didn't take Dually," Tuper said.

"He brought him for you."

Tuper scratched the dog's head. "You're gonna miss Ron, aren't you?"

Lana forced a smile. "What do we need him for?" She slapped Tuper on the shoulder. "I've got you, Pops, and you have Dually. What more could we possibly need?"

Dear Reader,

Would you like a free short story about one of my characters? If so, please go to www.teresaburrell.com and sign up for my mailing list. You will receive a code to retrieve the story.

What did you think of RECOVERING RITA? I would love to hear from you. Please email me at teresa@teresaburrell.com.

If you liked Tuper, you can find him in The Advocate's Felony, book #6 of Teresa Burrell's THE ADVOCATE SERIES.

Thank you,

Teresa

ABOUT THE AUTHOR

Teresa Burrell has dedicated her life to helping children and their families. Her first career was spent teaching elementary school in the San Bernardino City School District. As an attorney, Ms. Burrell has spent countless hours working pro bono in the family court system. For twelve years she practiced law in San Diego Superior Court, Juvenile Division. She continues to advocate children's issues and write novels, many of which are inspired by actual legal cases.

If you like this author's writing, the best ways to compliment her are by writing a review and telling your friends.

OTHER MYSTERIES BY TERESA BURRELL

THE TUPER MYSTERY SERIES

THE ADVOCATE'S FELONY

(Book 6 of The Advocate Series)

MASON'S MISSING (Book 1)

FINDING FRANKIE (Book 2)

RECOVERING RITA (Book 3)

THE ADVOCATE SERIES

THE ADVOCATE (Book 1)

THE ADVOCATE'S BETRAYAL (Book 2)

THE ADVOCATE'S CONVICTION (Book 3)

THE ADVOCATE'S DILEMMA (Book 4)

THE ADVOCATE'S EX PARTE (Book5)

THE ADVOCATE'S FELONY (Book 6)

THE ADVOCATE'S GEOCACHE (Book 7)

THE ADVOCATE'S HOMICIDES (Book 8)

THE ADVOCATE'S ILLUSION (Book 9)

THE ADVOCATE'S JUSTICE (Book 10)

THE ADVOCATE'S KILLER (Book 11)

THE ADVOCATE'S LABYRINTH (Book 12)

Made in the USA
Middletown, DE
26 January 2023

23166845R00191